ABSOLUTE VENGEANCE

The Alex Shepherd Story

C.W. LEMOINE

This book is a work of fiction. Names, characters, places, and incidents are either products of the author's imagination or used fictitiously. Any resemblance to actual events or locales or persons living or dead is entirely coincidental. The views in this book do not represent those of the St. Tammany Parish Sheriff's Office, United States Air Force Reserve or United States Navy Reserve. All units, descriptions, and details related to the military or law enforcement are used solely to enhance the realism and credibility of the story.

Cover artwork by Barclay Publicity Services.
www.barclaypublicity.com

This book is dedicated to the men and women of the St. Tammany Parish Sheriff's Office.

AUTHOR'S NOTE

ABSOLUTE VENGEANCE is the first book I've written outside of the *Spectre Series*. Although it is set in the same universe, it is a standalone book featuring a first person perspective of the story of Alex Shepherd.

With that said, I think it's important to point out that this book follows the same general plot as *STAND AGAINST EVIL (Spectre Series Book 6)*, and as such contains many of the same elements. If you're a fan of the Spectre Series, you'll see one chapter in particular that's the same from both books. I did that to help sync both books to the same storyline. Otherwise, the book tells the same story from the view of the man most affected by those events, and how he coped with it.

If you're a new reader, welcome! Thanks for picking up *ABSOLUTE VENGEANCE.* I hope you will enjoy it.

-CWL

"Before you embark on a journey of revenge, dig two graves."

— *Confucius*

PROLOGUE

"Chelsea, the bus is here!" she yelled as she saw the bright yellow school bus rounding the corner. Lindsey Shepherd finished filling her thermos with the coffee her husband had started for her three hours earlier before he left for work. It was something he always did for her, either before leaving when he worked day shift or right after getting home at 5 a.m. when working nights.

"I'm coming, Momma," little Chelsea Shepherd replied excitedly as she dragged her book bag into the kitchen. The five-year-old struggled to lift the bag onto the nearby chair as their Miniature Dachshund, Rex, shadowed her every move.

"Do you have everything?" Lindsey asked, as the sound of the diesel engine grew louder.

"Wait!" Chelsea cried. "Where's Buttons?"

The troubled five-year-old frantically searched the kitchen and then ran to the living room as she continued the search for her favorite stuffed dog.

"Where did you last see him?" Lindsey asked.

Chelsea paused for a moment. Her face crinkled as she tried to remember the last time she had seen Buttons. "In the bathroom!" she yelled as she started for the bathroom. Her blonde pigtails bobbed as she ran through the living room with Rex close on her heels.

"Don't run sweetheart," Lindsey warned as she looked out to see the bus pull to a stop in front of their modest three-bedroom home. Lindsey threw her own bag over her shoulder as she picked up her coffee and Chelsea's bag. It was the first day of the new school year. For Lindsey, it was only her third year as a teacher at Mandeville Elementary School teaching Third Grade. For Chelsea, it was her first day of Kindergarten. Lindsey had decided to ride the bus with Chelsea on her first day to make sure everything went well, one of the perks of teaching at her daughter's school.

Chelsea returned with her tattered stuffed dog, smiling ear to ear as she hugged Buttons. "Put him in here, sweetie," Lindsey said as she held Chelsea's backpack open. Chelsea carefully placed Buttons in the backpack with its head and floppy ears exposed just above the partially open zipper.

"He needs to be able to see," she said cheerfully as her mom grabbed her tiny hand and led her out the front door.

Lindsey and Chelsea hurried toward the waiting school bus. Its red lights flashed as the driver waited for the two ladies to make their way around the front and up the stairs. "Thanks for waiting, Mr. Miller," Lindsey said as she ushered Chelsea to a seat next to another little girl and then took her own seat at the front of the bus. The bus was nearly full of kids from age five to nine on their way to the suburban elementary school.

"How many times do I have to ask you to call me Aaron?" the older man asked with a warm smile as he closed the door and started toward the next stop in the neighborhood.

"Sorry, first day back," Lindsey said with a shy smile. "How was your summer, Aaron?"

"Not bad," Aaron responded. "Not much different than any other day. Semi-retired life will do that for you."

Lindsey smiled. Aaron Miller had once been the Principal of Mandeville Elementary, but in retirement, he just couldn't let it go, opting to pick up a part-time job driving school buses during the school year. He had retired just as Lindsey was finishing her first year of teaching. The kids all seemed to love him, and Lindsey enjoyed hearing his stories of the "Golden Years" of teaching as he called them – before No Child Left Behind and Common Core.

"How about yours?" Aaron asked.

"It was good. Alex has been working a lot of overtime since they cut a lot of the details in the department. And when I wasn't teaching summer school, I was working with Chel-Bell on reading," she replied as she looked back to see Chelsea quickly making friends with her seatmate.

"I noticed his police car wasn't in the driveway. I take it he's working today?" Aaron asked.

"Five to five on day shift," Lindsey said before taking a sip of her coffee. "Plus SWAT training from six to ten tonight."

"Burning the candle from both ends, huh?" Aaron asked, shaking his head. "That has to be hard on both of y'all."

"It is," Lindsey said. "But Alex loves his job, and although the pay isn't great, the benefits are great, and he'll be able to retire with a full pension after thirty years when he's fifty."

"So what's that? Twenty more years?" Aaron asked as he picked up the last of the children in Lindsey's neighborhood and started toward the subdivision's exit.

"Fifteen," Lindsey replied.

"I appreciate his service," Aaron said. "Not many people stick it out the full thirty these days. It's pretty political, especially during election years like this one."

"Oh, he loves the Sheriff," Lindsey said. "And he's running unopposed again this year. But anyway, enough about us. How's Mrs. Miller?"

"Same as always. Why do you think I started driving this bus?" Miller replied with a wry smile.

"Oh, stop," Lindsey said playfully. "She's wonderful."

"If you say so," Aaron said with a hearty laugh as they pulled out onto the narrow two-lane road toward the elementary school.

Mandeville was a mostly affluent suburb of New Orleans on the north shore of Lake Pontchartrain. Mandeville Elementary School had been built on the outskirts of town in a wooded rural area, accessible only by a narrow two-lane highway. Its isolation was something of a concern Alex had often discussed with Lindsey. With the recent threats of active shooters in elementary schools throughout the nation, it posed tactical problems for quickly getting rescue personnel into the area while evacuating others. Lindsey didn't understand most of it, but she knew Alex was passionate about it, so she promised that she would be vigilant with the students. *That was Alex.*

As she thought of Alex, Lindsey pulled her phone out of her pocket to text him. She typed "Good morning, Babe. First day of school! I love you. Have a great day," and hit send, only to be greeted by a warning that she was outside her coverage area and that it would be sent when she received signal again. *That was the real downside of the school's location,* Lindsey thought. The cell phone reception in the woods north of I-12 was terrible.

"Uh oh," she heard Aaron say as she felt the bus slow. She looked up to see a late model Toyota Camry in the middle of the road with its hazard lights flashing. The bus slowed to a stop behind the broken-down car. There was no other traffic at that time of the morning, but Aaron activated the bus's red lights as he came to a stop.

"Probably a parent trying to get to school," Aaron said. "Stay here and watch the children. I'm going to make sure they're OK."

"OK," Lindsey said as she looked down at the time on her phone. 7:20 a.m. She still had forty minutes to get Chelsea settled into her new classroom, and then get ready for her own classes. She watched as Aaron opened the doors and hobbled down the stairs. The car looked empty, causing Lindsey to wonder if they hadn't already found a ride and would send for a tow truck later.

As she looked back down at her phone to see if her message had gone through, she was startled by a loud crack outside. It didn't register at first, but as she looked back up, she watched Aaron stumble forward toward the Camry. *Gunfire?* She heard four more shots in rapid succession as several of the children started screaming.

Lindsey froze as she tried to process the scene. She saw Aaron face down next to the Camry and three masked men approaching with rifles pointed at her.

"Everyone get down!" she yelled.

"Stop there!" one of the men yelled as he approached the bus with his rifle up.

Lindsey leapt toward the door and pressed the button, closing it as she scrambled into the driver's seat. She had no idea how to drive the bus, but she knew she needed to get the children out of there.

"Mommy!" she heard Chelsea scream behind her. It took everything she had to not run to grab Chelsea and shield her.

As she tried to get the bus in gear, one of the men maneuvered to the front of the bus and started firing, peppering the windshield. Glass shards sprayed around her, and the kids were screaming. "Get down!" she yelled.

Lindsey found the parking brake and disengaged it. The bus rolled forward in neutral as she watched one of the men approach the door. He fired another volley of bullets, striking her in the hip. The pain was almost blinding as the bus rolled forward into the Camry. The man tried to break through the bus doors.

Realizing he was moments away from entering, Lindsey rolled onto the floor and tried to drag herself to Chelsea who ran toward her.

"Mommy!" Chelsea screamed.

"Run, honey," Lindsey groaned. The five-year-old fell to her knees and wrapped her arms around her bleeding mother. The masked man forced entry through the bus door and ran up the stairs, followed by two other armed men.

Lindsey grabbed Chelsea and pulled her close in a last attempt to protect her. "Allahu Akbar," she heard as she closed her eyes and felt the hot rifle barrel press against the back of her head.

CHAPTER ONE

Alex Shepherd is dead. He died with his family on a warm August morning in southeast Louisiana. There was no funeral, and if he would have had one, his obituary would have simply read, "Died of a broken heart."

He was a loving father and husband, a devout Christian whose god had seemingly abandoned him. His family was his entire world. His soul was taken as tragically and brutally as their precious lives. He left no one behind.

Although his soul departed, his body lived on – as an emissary of death, the embodiment of vengeance. It was merely the vehicle by which a personal crusade, a war against evil, had to be waged. There would be no honor or glory in its victory. Like a sheep dog standing against the growling wolf in the darkness of night, his was a thankless but necessary mission, one to be fought to the end.

My story is not one of redemption. There can be no happy ending. For me, there is no salvation. Instead, I leave this as a warning, a cautionary tale of a quest for vengeance and its path through the gates of hell.

*   *   *

It was almost a year ago. I kissed my wife Lindsey on the forehead as I crawled out of bed and got ready for work as quietly as I could at 3:45 in the morning. I was on day shift in District 3 with the St. Tammany Parish Sheriff's Office, which meant I had to be at shift change at 5 a.m. As the corporal on the shift, I had to be there twenty minutes early to get the pass-on and prepare the shift change briefing for my team.

Once dressed, I made my way to my daughter's room. She was so beautiful, sleeping peacefully with her stuffed dog Buttons tucked under her arm. I quietly walked up to her bed and gave her a kiss. She looked like a little angel as I watched her sleep.

After a minute or two, I turned back toward the door. "Daddy," her little voice called as I reached the door.

"Go back to sleep, Chel-Bell," I said as I turned to see her stirring in bed. "Daddy will see you this evening."

"I love you, Daddy," she said as she turned and curled up with Buttons.

"I love you too, baby girl," I said softly, as I walked out of her room and closed the door behind me.

I set up a pot of coffee for Lindsey before grabbing a protein bar and heading out the door. I unlocked my marked unit, a Chevy Tahoe, and started the engine before going to the back cargo area to make sure I had everything I would need for SWAT training that evening after my shift.

Aside from being the shift's corporal, I was also a sniper on the SWAT Team. It was one of the things I was most proud of in my time with the Sheriff's Office. I had never been in the military, and SWAT was the closest I would ever come. I had volunteered for every school they would send me to, and after five years on the team, I had a feeling I was being eyed for command.

I closed the hatch after confirming everything was there. All of my uniforms, my Remington 700 rifle, my SWAT M4 carbine, and body armor were exactly where they should have been. The Tahoe was much better equipped for my role on SWAT than the Crown Victorias had been. My last Crown Vic unit had needed special springs installed to support the weight of all my additional gear.

Shift change went uneventfully as my team broke up into its various zone assignments. It was opening day for most of the schools throughout the parish, so we planned on enforcing school zone speed limits and keeping an eye out for suspicious persons near the campuses. As the corporal, I was essentially a float unit, able to back up any of the units on calls. For the most part, it was a typical quiet Monday morning. The roads were empty as the western side of the parish started its week.

I was busy approving reports when the first call came in at 0630. It was a 62A. An audible alarm at someone's house was going off, and the alarm company had called us to check it out. Even in a sleepy town like Mandeville, those were fairly common. Usually they were false alarms – someone's dog tripping a motion sensor or a door blown open by wind – but we never took any call for granted. Since I was in the area, I decided to back-up the responding unit.

The responding deputy and I arrived nearly simultaneously, and we parked away from the house in question. After a short investigation and verifying that the house was secure, the responding deputy cleared the call. The Rottweiler barking from within the house was the likely culprit for the motion alarm.

After the call was cleared, I decided to head toward the nearby town of Madisonville to do a school walkthrough and check on our School Resource Officer on his first day back. As I was heading west on Highway 22, my radar unit lit up showing the approaching vehicle on the two-lane highway doing 67 mph.

Now, generally speaking, I'm not big into pulling people over on their way to work, especially for speeding, but twenty-two miles per hour over the posted forty-five mile per hour speed limit was a bit excessive, so I decided to make the traffic stop.

I called the stop in to Central Dispatch as the driver noticed my lights and pulled over to the shoulder. As I approached, I noticed the personalized license plate of the small SUV read, "Remember the Fallen," and had a Gold Star on it.

"Good morning, ma'am, Corporal Shepherd of the St. Tammany Parish Sheriff's Office," I said as I reached the window. The woman was wearing blue scrubs and didn't acknowledge me.

"The reason I pulled you over is that I had you doing sixty-seven in a forty-five zone," I said as she hunched her shoulders. "Where are you heading this morning?"

"Just got off work at the hospital," the woman mumbled.

"Do you have your license, registration, and insurance card, ma'am?" I asked.

The woman found the items and handed them to me with shaking hands. "I'm really sorry," she said softly. I could tell she was shaken up by the stop.

"I'll be right back with you," I said as I returned to my Tahoe.

I ran her information through my laptop and then did a quick Google search on my phone for what the plate represented. I had never seen a plate like that before. The first result told me everything I needed to know.

"You're a Gold Star family member?" I asked as I returned to her window.

"Yes, sir," she said meekly.

"Do you mind if I asked who was killed in action?" I asked.

"My son," she replied slowly. "He was killed by an IED in Afghanistan."

I handed her information back to her. "Ma'am, please slow down. These roads are pretty dangerous," I said solemnly. "Drive safely."

"Is that it?" she asked, confused as she shuffled through her insurance card, ID, and registration, seemingly looking for the ticket that wasn't there.

"Yes, ma'am," I said. "Thank you for your sacrifice for our country. Please be safe."

The woman's shoulders started to shake as she began to cry. I couldn't imagine the pain she had gone through losing her son. I thanked her again and returned to my unit. I cleared the call as she drove off.

As I pulled back onto the highway, one of my deputies called into dispatch that he was stopping for a disabled vehicle near Mandeville Elementary School off Highway 1088. A vehicle breakdown was not an unusual occurrence for a Monday, especially on the first day of school, but I decided to turn around and start heading that way anyway. I'm not sure why, but something in my gut told me that it was more than just a vehicle breakdown.

"Ninety-eight forty-four, Central, we've got a 30-S here!" the deputy yelled over the radio moments later.

I tried to push the accelerator through the firewall as I activated my lights and siren. A 30-S was a homicide by shooting. Someone had been murdered within miles of a school, and the murderer was still potentially on the loose.

"Ninety-eight forty-eight is responding," I said over the radio as I maneuvered around the few cars on the roadway. "Any units in the area, step it up." I wanted to let any other units responding know that they should run Code 3 with lights and siren.

I pulled out my cell phone and dialed the shift sergeant as I sped toward the area.

"I'm headed that way," Sgt. Taylor said. I could hear the siren in the background.

"We might want to roll SWAT," I said. "And get the bird in the air."

"It's a little early for that, Alex," Taylor responded.

"The shooter is on the loose and near a school," I shot back. "I've got a bad feeling about this. We need to lock the area down."

"I'll make the call," Taylor conceded before hanging up.

Just as I hung up with the sergeant, my phone started ringing. The caller ID showed Justin Hyatt. He was the deputy that had found the car.

"What did you find, Justin?" I asked.

"The car was partially off the roadway. It looked like it had been hit from behind," Hyatt replied. "There are 7.62 casings everywhere."

"Shit!" I hissed. Small caliber handgun rounds would lend credence to the idea that it was an isolated roadside robbery, but 7.62 rifle rounds on the first day of school meant bad things. My stomach turned.

"The body is pretty fresh," Hyatt said. "And I don't think this is his car."

"Why's that?" I asked.

"Mississippi plates," Hyatt replied. "And the victim is from here. You probably know him."

"Who is he?"

"Remember Mr. Miller, the retired principal?" Hyatt asked.

"You're fucking shitting me!" I yelled.

"I wish I were, but I remember him from when I was in school," Hyatt replied.

"Secure the scene, I'll be there in a few minutes," I said.

As I ended the call and started to dial Taylor, I nearly dropped the phone as the realization hit me. Miller had started driving school buses in his retirement. Lindsey had told me the day prior that she and Chelsea would be riding to school on his bus that morning.

For the first time in my adult life, I started to have a panic attack.

CHAPTER TWO

I tried calming myself by taking deep breaths as I turned onto Highway 1088 toward the school. I bypassed the newly created crime scene and went straight to the Elementary School, where the School Resource Officer had already initiated lockdown procedures as other units from Districts 2 and 4 arrived to assist. A potential active shooter scenario was an "all hands" event. Units from around the parish would be descending upon our location to prevent another massacre like the Newtown shooting in Connecticut in 2012, when a lone gunman shot twenty children and six adults at Sandy Hook Elementary School.

Principal Mary Jenkins was directing student traffic as I pulled up to the front of the school. She immediately recognized me and handed off her director duties to a nearby teacher as I exited my Tahoe and approached her.

"Alex, what's going on?" she asked as I hurried toward her. "They just said lock it down and didn't say why."

"There was a shooting on 1088 about two miles from here. Where is Lindsey?" I asked frantically. My intentions were purely selfish at that point. I cared about my family's safety above anything else.

Mary frowned. "She was supposed to be riding Mr. Miller's bus in today. All of the buses have been diverted to Mandeville Junior High per our policy for events like these that happen before school hours," she said flatly.

"What bus was Mr. Miller driving?" I asked as calmly as I could. I could feel another panic attack coming on as I realized how much harder it was going to be to find Lindsey's bus with several buses being diverted to another school.

"Thirty-two, I think," Mary replied. "Deputy Shepherd, what exactly is going on here?"

"There's a possible shooter in the area," I replied as I turned back to my unit. "We'll get back with you."

As I got back into my unit, I took a deep breath before picking up the radio mic. Regardless of what was going on with my wife and daughter, I told myself, the best way to ensure their safety was to do my job. I wouldn't let them down.

"Ninety-eight forty-eight, Central," I said, using my radio number to call Central Dispatch.

"10-71," the dispatcher replied, letting me know the net was clear to talk.

"Do you have a twenty on school bus number thirty-two?" I asked. All of the buses had GPS trackers in them for the parish to keep track. I hoped the dispatcher could give us a location to hopefully find Lindsey, Chelsea, and the other students.

"10-23," she said, telling me to standby. I put the Tahoe in gear and spun around on the drive in front of the school, ready to head in whatever direction she gave me.

"Sir, it's not actively pinging," she said finally. "Last known location was Highway 1088 two miles south of Mandeville Elementary."

"10-4," I said over the radio before throwing the mic and letting loose a flurry of obscenities. As I calmed down, I picked the mic back up and calmly told dispatch to issue a Be On Lookout (BOLO) notice for Bus 32, last seen on Highway 1088. Moments later, my phone rang.

"Shepherd," I answered without looking at the caller ID.

"Alex, I'm taking over on scene command. What do you have so far?" I immediately recognized the unmistakable voice of the Operations Division Head, Major Sean Hackett.

"We found Aaron Miller's body next to an abandoned car with multiple gunshot wounds," I said as calmly as I could. "His bus is missing, and the school is on lockdown."

"Is that the one you just put the BOLO out on?"

"Yes, sir," I said as I sat watching more units arrive at the school.

"Nice work," he said gruffly.

"Thanks."

"Are you OK, Shepherd?"

"My wife and daughter are on that bus, and its GPS tracker has been turned off, sir," I replied. "So no, I'm not OK."

"Holy shit, Alex," Hackett mumbled after a long pause.

"I'm going to find my family or die trying," I replied.

"I totally understand," Hackett replied. "Every resource of this agency is being devoted to finding them. Air One should be airborne in the next few minutes. You know those guys will find it. I need you to keep it together until then though. You're the best guy I have on the ground until we get the command center set up."

"I know," I said meekly. I hated being out of the fight, but I knew the guys in the Air Wing were the best in the state. The Air Wing had become a full-time aviation support unit shortly after the last election. It had been taken over by a military guy with experience doing surveillance and reconnaissance during the Iraq War. He had converted it from a part-time helicopter unit with limited callout capability, to a twenty-four-hour operation capable of being airborne within minutes and staying airborne for hours in the high-wing Cessna 210. The Sheriff had also purchased an advanced suite of sensors and infrared pods paid for with federal grant money to assist in drug interdiction.

Most of my experience with the Air Wing was during SWAT missions. Our commander had a laptop that could receive video from the aircraft's FLIR pod. It gave him real-time imagery of the objective we were hitting, allowing us to know exactly where each threat would be. It was a lifesaver.

But beyond the SWAT side, I had also seen them find fugitives and missing kids in a quarter of the time it had taken the helicopter. It was this search capability that I prayed would find my wife and daughter before whatever assholes had taken them could do more harm. For the time being, Air One was my best hope for getting my family back alive.

"Alex if you're not up for it, let me know," Hackett said. "I would sideline anyone else, but I think you can handle it."

"I can handle it," I said as I stared off into the woods across the highway.

"Good," Hackett replied. "I'll let you know when we have the command center set up down the road." The command center was a converted RV filled with advanced communications equipment and its own contingent of dispatchers specially trained to handle major events and relay information directly from the field to the brass sitting a few feet away. It was typically only used for command and control during major events like Mardi Gras parades and other holiday events, but it was also a crucial piece of emergency command during hurricanes and mass casualty events.

Once the deputies secured the scene at the school, I decided to suit up. I knew SWAT would be rolling soon and I wanted to be prepared. I removed my duty belt and quickly changed into my Kryptek camouflage ACUs, readied my body armor, and prepared my rifles. I prayed I wouldn't have to use them.

As I finished setting up my gear, I heard my radio crackle to life. "Air One has eyes on the objective headed east on Highway 190 heading into Lacombe," the tactical flight officer announced.

I sprinted to my Tahoe, jumped in, and threw it in gear as I activated my siren. The bus had a twenty-mile head start on me.

Nothing was going to stop me from getting to my family.

CHAPTER THREE

C ars veered out of the way as I sped east on Interstate 12 with lights and siren blaring. I nearly pushed several out of the way with my push bar as they panicked like deer in headlights, ignoring the law and trying to yield to the left or not at all. It was something that seemingly happened every time I ran code to a call, but this time it wasn't just an annoyance - they were standing between my family and me.

Four other patrol Tahoes followed me as I maneuvered around the morning rush hour traffic. Air One was still calling out the position of the bus as it drove east through the small village of Lacombe toward Slidell on Ronald Reagan Highway. Deputies in pursuit were keeping their distance. With a hostage situation –

especially with kids – it was best not to risk their lives further by attempting to block or stop the vehicle.

I was paralleling the bus's path using I-12E as Air One called out its speed and crossing streets. The hostage-takers were only doing forty-five miles per hour. My plan was to get ahead of the pursuit in Slidell. I didn't necessarily have a plan of action once I got there, but for me, policy was out the window at that point. I was no longer acting as a corporal with the Sheriff's Office. I was acting as Alex Shepherd, husband and father.

Driving on the shoulder of the off-ramp, I flew past cars as I turned south onto Northshore Boulevard near the shopping areas on the outskirts of Slidell. Cars parted as I continued south past Wal-Mart and the mall. By the time I reached the intersection of Northshore Blvd and Ronald Reagan Highway, I could see the bright yellow school bus passing with its convoy of police vehicles in trail. I caught a glimpse of two men standing in the bus as it sped by.

As the line of Tahoes and Crown Victorias passed with sirens howling, I fell in behind them. The bus made a sharp left turn into an empty movie theater parking lot and screeched to a stop near the edge of the theater. Police cars filed into the empty lot behind it and created a buffer zone.

I parked my unit at the edge of the wall created by the units in front of me and killed my siren. I was out of my vehicle with my M4 up and ready as soon as I stopped. I started running toward the bus as I watched one of the masked men walk toward the front of the bus.

When I reached the hood of one of the first Tahoes, I felt someone grab the carry handle on the back of my vest and jerk me aside. "Where the fuck are you going, Shepherd?" a voice boomed as I stumbled into him.

"To get my family," I said without turning to look.

"The fuck you are," he said as he spun me around. It was my shift lieutenant, Dan Jacobson. "Snap out of it, Alex."

I lowered my weapon as my chest heaved. I kept my eyes darting back and forth between Dan and the school bus. All of my training had gone out the window. I just wanted to go get them out of there.

"I have to save my family!" I yelled as I tried to wrestle free. Two other deputies came to restrain me as I fought against Dan's grip. At six foot five, he was a nearly a half foot taller than I was, but my adrenaline was pumping. I overpowered him before the other two grabbed me and pulled me back behind the line of vehicles near the SWAT Bobcat armored vehicle that had just arrived.

I felt like time was standing still. It was like a bad dream from which there was no escape. I could hear the sound of helicopters approaching from the distance. They weren't ours. Air One was orbiting high above. As the chopper sounds grew louder, the bus door opened. One of the masked men descended the stairs. He was holding something in each hand. I watched as the lead hostage negotiator, Detective Stevens, moved to the front of the blockade.

The man walked a few feet from the bus and stopped, holding an object in his left hand up high. There was a collective gasp. I was just over fifty yards away, but as my heart rate settled and the tunnel vision subsided, I recognized what he was holding. It was a human head. *Lindsey.*

I dropped to my knees, vomiting as the realization hit me. I would later learn that he was holding a deadman switch tied to his suicide vest, but at the time, all I saw was Lindsey's lifeless face being held up for the news helicopter orbiting above to see and film. It had been part of their plan all along. The entire chase had been buying time to get the most media exposure. They had calculated it almost to the minute.

I made it back to my feet as the man tossed her head onto the ground and returned to the bus. The horror I was feeling turned to complete terror as I realized Chelsea was still in there.

All of the deputies that had been restraining me had turned to see the horrific sight of my wife's severed head tossed like a beach ball in front of them.

I drew my Glock 17 from my drop leg holster as I started pushing forward. They were going to have to shoot me to keep me from getting to my daughter. As I reached the negotiator, three men emerged from the bus wielding AK-47s. The last turned, throwing something into the bus as they calmly walked out and raised their AK-47s.

The negotiator tried to stop me as I rounded the line of Tahoes out in the open. I could hear the screams of the children inside the bus as the man closed the door behind him. I was sure I could hear Chelsea yelling for me. I watched in horror as the interior of the bus became engulfed in flames.

I raised my Glock as I ran toward the bus. The men started firing toward the line of Tahoes. I fired twice at the closest man, hitting him center of mass and dropping him. Gunfire erupted all around me. I was running through the crossfire as the masked gunmen fired at the line of police and the officers returned fire.

I stumbled as a round hit me in the thigh, but I kept going. Another round hit me in the chest plate, but despite the wind being knocked out of me, I kept running. I could see the children trying to escape the burning bus. Their little hands pressed against the glass with nowhere to go, no way to escape.

As I shifted my aim to the last gunman, I saw him raise the detonator for his vest. I fired, hitting him in the throat. As I looked up at the bus windows, Chelsea's face was the last thing I saw before I felt an intense blast of heat and my world went black.

CHAPTER FOUR

I woke up to a nurse trying to calm me down. I had been in and out of consciousness for the last few hours. It was always the same dream, but this time I woke up trying to scream while thrashing against the wires and IVs hooked up to me.

"You're OK, sir," she said as she tried to keep me from pulling the tube out of my throat. "You were just dreaming." Several more people piled into the small room as I frantically looked around the small hospital room. Two other nurses tried to get me to calm down as my whole body tensed. My heart was racing, confirmed by the high-pitched beeping of the machine next to me. *It was just a dream.*

It was always the same dream. Chelsea is playing on a playground, carrying Buttons around as she makes her way up the stairs to the slide. Lindsey is sitting on a nearby park bench watching her. They're both smiling and laughing and having a good time.

But then a storm rolls in. Lindsey grabs Chelsea as thunder claps and lightning flashes in the distance. The rain starts to fall. Lindsey starts running to the car. I try to keep up, but my legs feel like blocks. As they get into Lindsey's car, lightning strikes it. The car burns and they can't get out. I feel like I'm running through quicksand as I try to get them. I can see Chelsea's little face against the window as she calls out for me. Lindsey sits in the driver's seat as the car burns. It suddenly explodes, and I wake up.

As I finally started to relax against the nurse gently pushing me back down, I realized it hadn't been just a dream. The images I saw weren't figments of my imagination. They had been burned into my brain. My baby girl had burned alive, and I had been powerless to save her. My wife had been beheaded. It wasn't just a dream. It was a living nightmare.

I thrashed again as the realization hit me, nearly throwing the nurse across the room as she tried to calm me. I couldn't scream. I felt like I was choking as I tried to pull the tube out of my throat, but my hands were wrapped and unusable. Moments later I saw darkness again as the other nurse managed to sedate me.

I don't know how long I was out. I didn't dream. I didn't drift in and out of sleep as before. When I woke up, the room was empty. The tube down my throat was gone, but my mouth was still dry and my throat sore. I tried to move, but my ribs hurt and my arms and face felt stiff.

I tried to assess my surroundings. I was still in a hospital room – maybe ICU. My hands were still wrapped, and this time I realized my face was too. I tried to speak, but all I could get out was a visceral groan. Moments later, a nurse appeared.

"Mr. Shepherd, try to relax," she said as she rushed to my side. She was an attractive woman — mid-thirties, dark brown hair, and blue eyes. Her eyes watered as she looked at me.

"Where am I?" I groaned as she prevented me from moving.

"You're in the Burn Unit at the Heart Hospital," she said softly. "You're going to be OK; you just need to try to relax."

She pressed the call button on the bed rail. A speaker beeped and she said, "Page Dr. Neilson, please."

I grunted as I gave up. The pain was intense. Whatever they had been giving me had obviously worn off. The nurse picked up a button and pressed it. After a beep, whatever painkiller they were giving me intravenously started to kick in. It dulled the physical pain, but the longer I stayed awake, the more I thought about my family and the more I wanted to die.

"Kill me," I said as I looked up at the nurse. She started to cry as she reached down and grabbed my bandaged hand.

"I'm so sorry, Mr. Shepherd," she said as she wiped away the tears. "I'm so very sorry."

"Just let me die," I said as I closed my eyes.

But every time I closed my eyes, Chelsea and Lindsey were there staring back at me, begging me to save them. I had failed them in the worst possible way. Surviving was the worst punishment imaginable. I wanted to be with them, not in some hospital room with nurses pitying me.

"Good to see you're awake, Alex," a male voice said near the doorway. I opened my eyes and saw a man in green scrubs with a white lab coat approach. He was older, with salt and pepper hair and a graying mustache. "How is he?" he asked the nurse.

"His vitals are good," she said. "Still in pain, so I gave him a dose from his PCA."

He walked over and stood next to the bedside. "Considering his injuries, I'm not surprised," he said before turning to me. "You're lucky to be alive."

"Fuck you," I grumbled. I felt anything but lucky. Luck would have been saving my girls. Luck would have been dying with them. Luck had nothing to do with surviving without them. It was torture.

"I'm so sorry," he said as he held his hands up apologetically. "My God, I am so sorry, Alex. I didn't mean it like that."

I closed my eyes again. I longed for a well-placed 9MM round in my brainpan. Anything to make the pain go away.

"What I meant to say is that you're an incredibly strong man, Alex," Dr. Neilson offered. "We removed a piece of shrapnel just two inches from your heart. Any closer and it would have killed you. Your right lung was partially collapsed with three broken ribs, not to mention the three through-and-through bullet wounds in your legs. You sustained second- and third-degree burns on over sixty percent of your body. We kept you in a medically induced-coma for almost five weeks. It's amazing that you survived."

"Should've let me die," I said. "Asshole."

"Alex, I can't imagine what you're going through," the doctor said carefully. "If it were me, I would probably want the same thing. But you've been given a second chance in life that not many people get. It wasn't my call to make. God obviously has other plans for you."

"Go fuck yourself, Doc," I growled. "And take your god with you."

"I will be on call all evening if you need anything, Mr. Shepherd," Dr. Neilson said as he stepped back. "I will be back to check on you later."

"Bring a Glock next time," I said before he nodded and turned to walk out.

CHAPTER FIVE

I was staring at the ceiling, praying for death, when Lieutenant Jacobson, Sergeant Taylor, Deputy Hyatt, and Deputy Cindy Parker entered my room. I tilted my head to see them. They were all wearing civilian clothes. They looked tired and ragged. Jacobson was several inches taller than Taylor and Hyatt, and nearly a foot taller than Parker, but his posture was hunched – like a man that had accepted defeat. They all looked beaten and war-weary.

"Alex," Jacobson said as softly as he could with his booming southern drawl.

I said nothing as I returned to staring at the ceiling tiles. Aside from Lindsey and Chelsea, the people on my patrol team were the only family I had. My parents were dead, and Lindsey's parents had always hated me for being a cop. I didn't want my team to see me like this. I felt like I had let them down, along with my family.

"So you finally got that sex change you've always wanted, huh?" Hyatt asked, breaking the silence. There was a pause as the others exchanged looks. Like most in law enforcement, ours was a tight-knit brotherhood. In such a high-stress, high-risk profession, humor was often the best medicine. The reality of my situation, however, made it hard for me to go along with it. I watched as Cindy punched him in the shoulder and glared at him. Any other time, she would have been right there with him, but she knew this was beyond anything anyone in our small department had ever experienced. *Too soon.*

"Law enforcement discount," I mumbled, trying to throw Hyatt a bone. My face was still wrapped from the burns, making it difficult to speak more than a few words at a time. Regardless of the demons attacking my soul inside, they were still my team. I couldn't leave Hyatt hanging like that. "Your turn."

There was nervous laughter as the palpable tension in the room decreased. Jacobson walked to the right side of my bed, bending over as he leaned against the bed rail. Cindy took a seat in the corner of the room as Taylor and Hyatt kept a respectful distance.

"I'm so sorry," Jacobson said as he leaned in close. His eyes were bloodshot, and a tear rolled down his cheek as he said it. He had been my favorite lieutenant, a man who truly cared about his people. He shared my pain, and it showed. "I'm so goddamned sorry, Alex."

I closed my eyes again. Chelsea's sweet face was staring back at me. Although seeing my teammates again helped, there was nothing they could do or say to even put a dent into the glacier of pain I was feeling. I wanted death more than anything.

"Who did this?" I asked as I opened my eyes again.

"ISIS," Jacobson replied. "Or ISIL or whatever those goatfuckers are calling themselves now."

Jacobson was a combat veteran, having served in the early stages of Operation Enduring Freedom with the Army right after 9/11. He was very passionate about the fight against terrorism at home and abroad, using stories from the field to teach lessons in law enforcement and teamwork. It was part of the reason our team was so good under his leadership.

"How?" I asked. For a moment, the pain was replaced with anger, and it was slowly growing to rage. I could hear the heart rate monitor start to alarm as my heart rate and blood pressure spiked.

Jacobson frowned. "Three attacks, all smaller towns near major cities. Fredericksburg, Texas, Southaven, Mississippi, and here in Mandeville. Soft targets – a hospital, a mall, and…well, you know."

"How many did they kill?" I asked. The audible alarm was now making a higher pitched noise, prompting a nurse to come in to check on me.

"Are you in pain?" she asked as she scurried in and checked my IV. "You can press the button for more pain medicine if you're hurting."

"Leave me," I said, focusing on Jacobson as he stepped back to let the nurse work.

"I'm sorry," Jacobson said. "It's my fault. I shouldn't have brought it up."

"Tell me," I growled.

Jacobson shook his head in disgust. "None at the hospital. They were taken down before they could get anywhere," he replied.

"And here?" I asked as I watched Jacobson shift uncomfortably.

Jacobson hesitated, looking back at Taylor, who was leaning against the back wall of the small hospital room with his arms folded.

"How many?" I barked.

"Forty-seven," Cindy said, standing up from the chair in the corner and rushing to the foot of the bed. Tears were streaming down her face. "Forty-four kids, Mr. Miller, Deputy Fontenot, and-"

"Lindsey," I whispered as the images of her lifeless face in the hands of the masked man came rushing back.

"I'm so sorry," Cindy said between sobs. "Goddammit, I'm sorry."

"Where are they?" I asked.

"Who?" Jacobson asked as he stepped back to the bed rail.

"My girls," I said. My voice was trembling as the tears soaked the bandages on my face.

"Lindsey's parents buried them a month ago, Alex," Jacobson said.

"What?" Despite our rocky relationship, I couldn't believe Lindsey's parents would not give me the courtesy of saying goodbye to my family.

"They didn't know how long you were going to be in the coma, or if you'd even survive, Alex," Taylor interjected from the back. He was family friends with Lindsey's parents and had been the one to set us up in the first place. "I don't think they did it to spite you, man. They just wanted closure."

"Let me die," I said. "Please."

"Don't talk like that, Alex," Jacobson said, wiping away more tears as he grabbed my hand gently. "You're a fighter. Don't you dare give up. That's not who you are."

I pressed the pain button. It beeped and then I pressed it again and again and again, hoping to overdose as the machine beeped and denied me my release from the hell on earth.

"I should've died there," I said. "With them."

"Oh, Alex," Cindy yelped before walking out of the room, wiping the tears from her eyes. From the most gruesome murder scenes to the worst car accidents, I had never seen her walk away like that.

"Hang in there man," Hyatt said before rushing out to follow her, leaving our team leadership to deal with me.

Taylor walked up to the opposite bed rail from Jacobson. "I didn't let you quit in the academy, and I'm not going to let you quit now," he said calmly. "We're in this together, buddy. You won't have to get through this alone, I promise."

"Just leave," I said as I stared at the ceiling.

Taylor nodded at Jacobson and the two solemnly headed toward the door.

"There will be someone from this team here around the clock, Alex," Jacobson said as he stopped at the foot of my bed. "We've been here since we brought you to the ER, and we're not going to leave until you're ready to face life again."

CHAPTER SIX

M y recovery and discharge from the hospital took longer than it should have because I had lost the will to fight and live. The doctors pushed me, my criminal patrol teammates pushed me, and even my SWAT teammates pushed me. But no matter how hard they pushed, I just couldn't overcome the demons that were haunting me.

For their part, the department was as supportive as I could have expected. When I was finally moved from ICU to a regular room, I was greeted with flower baskets, cards, teddy bears, and other gestures. The Sheriff even stopped by with his family to tell me how sorry he was for what had happened and how proud he was of my courage under fire. It was the running narrative among the brass and even the news media, but it didn't bring my family back. Their words were hollow.

Every day, Jacobson would visit and try to get me back in the fight, and every day I would ask what the status of the investigation was. It was always the same answer – the FBI and Homeland Security had taken over. "These things take time," he'd offer.

But the weeks were ticking by, and no arrests had been made. The attacks had been linked to two separate cells claiming to be part of the Islamic State of Iraq and ash-Sham (ISIS). The cell responsible for the attempted attack in Fredericksburg was suspected to be a group operating out of El Paso, Texas. The cell responsible for the death of my family and the shootings at the mall in Southaven had been based out of Jackson, Mississippi.

The team that attempted the attack in Texas was said to be inexperienced. They had been young Americans that had been recruited through ISIS's extensive propaganda campaign using social media. They had been used by ISIS as force multipliers – expendable assets to carry out attacks at the same time as the Mississippi cell, designed to cause fear and panic across America. They chose small towns and soft targets to show average Americans that no one was safe in their daily lives, a departure from the average American's belief that only major cities were targets.

The cell in Mississippi was much different in both composition and tactics. It was composed of seven men, all of whom had seen direct combat in Iraq and Syria. They were battle-hardened terrorists. The man who had tossed my wife's severed head, Kamal Hamid Salman, had been part of the 2015 video showing the burning of a captured Jordanian pilot alive in a cage. *Fucking savages.*

The detectives in the major crimes unit had done their best. Detective Dan Abbott had taken the lead initially for our department. He was a good detective, and I trusted him as a skilled investigator, but as soon as the feds took over, our department was shut out. They got the information they needed from us and slammed the proverbial door in our faces. It was an active terror case that crossed state lines and therefore out of our jurisdiction. Even the Sheriff was powerless to intervene. I had watched child molesters walk on technicalities in my career. I knew there would be no justice for me.

It made the depression even worse. As I switched between feelings of intense sadness and pure rage, I knew there was nothing I could do about it. I could not bring my murdered family back, and there was no way to punish the people responsible because they were dead. Death had been part of their success criteria as martyrs. They won – we lost. It was that simple.

On the day of my discharge, I was greeted by at least ten patrol motorcycles from the traffic division and a motorcade of a dozen more units sitting in the parking lot with lights activated. The orderly wheeled me out to Jacobson's unmarked white Tahoe underneath the patient loading area and helped me into the passenger seat. I didn't even acknowledge the line of reporters and cameras as I was wheeled past them. The famed "thousand-yard stare" had become my default expression. I just didn't care anymore.

"Ready to go home, buddy?" Jacobson asked as he hopped into the driver's seat.

I stared blankly at him. The bandages were gone, and aside from a few new scars, my face was as ugly as before. There was nothing I could say. Home didn't exist anymore. I dreaded going back to that house.

"We're going to get through this," Jacobson said as he put his meaty hand on my shoulder. "You're a fighter."

I shrugged as I resumed my thousand-yard stare, trying futilely to not think of Lindsey and Chelsea, and how they always used to be excited to see me when I'd come home on day shift. I tried to think of anything else, but no matter how hard I tried, my mind just wouldn't comply.

Jacobson chirped the Tahoe's emergency horn, and the convoy of police vehicles started rolling. As we pulled out from beneath the covered loading area, I saw hundreds of people holding banners and waving American flags as we passed.

"You're a local hero," Jacobson said as he waved at the crowd.

"For what?" I asked. In the two months I had been in the hospital, I had avoided the news at all costs. I wasn't even sure the TV in my room worked as I had never turned it on, and I always refused the daily newspaper the nurses offered me. A world beyond the horrific events in the movie parking lot in Slidell simply didn't exist.

"This parish loves military and law enforcement," Jacobson explained. "And you took a couple of the terrorist fuckers down while putting it all on the line. They're just out here to show their support."

"I failed," I said flatly. "They should go home."

Our convoy passed what appeared to be hundreds of people lining the street before pulling out onto the highway toward the interstate. I made the mistake of looking out into the sea of cheering civilians. They were young and old. It was a Saturday, and people had brought their little kids out, probably just to see the procession of police cars, but I didn't see their faces. Every little girl was Chelsea. Every woman was Lindsey. I closed my eyes and tilted my head back against the headrest.

"We're going to get you help," Jacobson said. "What you've been through would scramble anyone. The department has great counselors that will help you."

"Can they bring back my girls?" I asked without opening my eyes.

I didn't wait for an answer as I turned my head and glared at Jacobson. "Can they erase the images of my baby girl burning alive? Or my wife's head rolling toward me like a basketball? Can they do that?" I asked angrily.

"I'm sorry," Jacobson said softly. "I really am, Alex."

I wasn't mad at Jacobson. He was a good man. It was the world that had wronged me, and I was riding a roller coaster of emotion that I just couldn't get off. "Me too," I said, my voice wavering. "Me too."

We sat in silence as we made the rest of the twenty-minute drive to my house. There were people lined up with signs at several street corners waving as before. I didn't even acknowledge them, but other units wailed their sirens briefly, and Jacobson's giant hand was big enough for both of us. I was too numb to really care about public perception anyway.

I felt sick as we turned into my subdivision. All of my neighbors were out to greet me. The motorcade kept going as Jacobson peeled off toward my house. There were two units already in the driveway, with Cindy and Hyatt standing in civilian clothes waiting for me.

"Someone will be staying with you for the foreseeable future," Jacobson said as he pulled up to the curb. Hyatt and Cindy rushed to my side of the truck and opened the door to help me out.

"I don't need babysitters," I said, looking at Jacobson as I ignored my two helpers.

"No one said you did," Jacobson replied. "But no man is an island, Alex. We're your family, and we're going to see you through this."

"Whether you like it or not," Cindy said as she reached across me and unbuckled my seatbelt.

"I don't want to go in there," I said as I slowly stepped out of the Tahoe.

Cindy hugged me and Hyatt squeezed my shoulder. In general, we weren't a very affectionate bunch. It was part of being a cop. Humor was often the best medicine, not hugging it out as a group. But I could tell they had all been affected by what happened that day, maybe not as badly as I was, but for the moment, cop humor had taken a backseat to genuine feelings.

"It's going to be OK," Cindy said, crying as she stepped back.

Tears streamed down my face as they walked me up the driveway past my parked pickup truck. I had a slight limp from the gunshot wounds, but the fear of entering my own house was what slowed me down.

I wiped away the tears as we reached the front door. I tried to control my breathing. I could feel a panic attack coming on. It was the same feeling I had gotten the day of the hijacking. My chest felt tight. I just wanted to run away.

I thought I had it under control as I walked in with Hyatt, Cindy, and Jacobson behind me. I made it two steps into the living room before Chelsea's stuffed giraffe caught my eye. I had won it for her at the state fair a year earlier. For a second, I thought I could hear her angelic giggle.

But soon after, the giggle was replaced with screams. I could hear her little voice painfully crying out, "Daddy! Daddy!" My chest tightened. I couldn't breathe. I collapsed to my knees, gasping as I started to sob.

"God, no," I sobbed as I curled into the fetal position on the carpeted floor. "Please let me die."

CHAPTER SEVEN

J ack Daniels became my new best friend. I hadn't been much of a drinker before the incident – I'd knock a few back maybe once or twice per month with my teammates. But in the days after getting home, I maintained a strict diet of Gentleman Jack, painkillers, and Tylenol PM.

I slept mostly, hoping to never wake up. Hoping to not dream about the girls. Hyatt stayed with me mostly, but he would switch out occasionally with Jacobson and Cindy to go home and see his family. They maintained this rotation for their off days and swapped out with guys from C and D team when they were back on patrol.

No one said anything about my drinking, although I hid the painkillers and Tylenol from them. They didn't remove my guns from the house, but they kept watch over the closet where I had my gun safe. No one seemed to blame me for being on the edge.

Jacobson was determined to get me counseling, but he didn't push the issue. We didn't talk much when I was sober and awake. There wasn't much to say. My life had ended that day in the movie theater parking lot. No amount of talking was ever going to change that.

I had lost track of the days when my SWAT commander and two other SWAT teammates showed up to visit. I knew it was a weekday, but I had no idea if it was early or late in the week. The days didn't seem to matter anymore.

Sgt. Neal Tompkins was a former Army Ranger. Like Jacobson, he had done his share of time overseas and was looking to make a difference in his community when he got out of the military. He wasn't that tall – maybe five-nine and a buck eighty, but his military haircut and no-bullshit demeanor easily added five inches to his stature. The man just had a presence about him.

Tompkins was accompanied by the SWAT team medic, Deputy Sean Claiborne, and fellow sniper, Deputy Paul Davis. They followed Tompkins into the living room after Cindy showed them into the house. I was sitting in my recliner, staring out the window in the painkiller-induced haze I'd come to depend on to escape my reality. Tompkins sat across from me on the couch as Claiborne and Davis took seats on the other couch next to me.

Tompkins exchanged a look with Claiborne as they waited for me to acknowledge them. I had probably lost ten pounds since the incident due to malnutrition and dehydration. My face was pale and unshaven, and I reeked of alcohol and sweat.

"You OK, buddy?" Tompkins asked softly. It was a tone I'd never heard from the gruff SWAT leader before. In training, in the field, or even during our trips to the local watering hole, Tompkins was a hard-nosed leader with a thunderous personality. I had no idea he could even lower his voice to such a non-threatening level. It was almost unsettling.

"Just a peach," I slurred as I stared out into the backyard at Chelsea's swing set.

Claiborne leaned forward to the edge of the seat. He was a big boy – six foot two, two-fifty. He was probably the slowest on the team, but no one ever gave him shit for it. He was the guy who saved our asses if we got shot and we loved him for it. I could see he was in medic mode as he leaned forward toward me.

"What did they give you for pain?" Claiborne asked as he leaned in close.

"Not enough," I mumbled.

"How many did you take?" he pressed.

"Not enough," I replied.

"Boss, he might need to take a ride," Claiborne said, using his trademark phrase for when he deemed a suspect or teammate needed to be transported to the emergency room after an op or during training.

Tompkins shook his head as he moved in closer. "You can't quit on us, Alex," Tompkins said, still masking his hard-edged persona. "You have to press forward."

"Would you?" I asked as I turned and looked him in the eyes. "Would any of you?"

There was a silence as the three men considered their own families. I could see it register with each of them. It was every husband and father's worst nightmare.

"I can't say I would, Alex," Tompkins said finally. "I don't know any man that could."

"Then just leave me," I said as I returned to my thousand-yard stare out into the backyard.

"But you're not just any man," Tompkins said. "And if anyone can get through this, you can."

"I can't see him like this," Davis said suddenly as he jumped up and shook his bald head. "I just can't."

"Dammit, Davis!" Tompkins roared as Davis turned to walk out. "Get your ass back here!"

Davis was still shaking his head as he walked back in the room and stood in front of me. "This is not Alex Shepherd," he said waving his finger in front of me. "The man I knew would never quit like this."

"Fuck you," I said. "You don't know what it's like!"

"You're right, I don't," Davis said, still staring me down. "But I do know that Alex Shepherd is not a quitter. I know that he wouldn't sit here and feel sorry for himself and drink himself to death. I know that much."

"What the fuck are you doing?" Tompkins said as he squared off with Davis. "This isn't the place for that shit."

"So we just sit here and watch him die?" Davis asked as he turned to face the much shorter SWAT commander. "We let him quit? What happened to never leaving a teammate behind?"

"He needs fluids," Claiborne interjected. "I've got a bag of saline in my unit; I'll be right back." Claiborne lumbered off, avoiding the tense situation between the commander and my SWAT partner.

"You need to lock it up, Davis," Tompkins growled. "This is not the time for that."

"He's right," I said as I turned my attention back to them. "I did quit."

"Goddammit, Alex," Davis said, taking a knee next me. "You and I have been through some shit together, you've saved my life more than once. I will do everything I can to help you, but you have to want to help yourself. You have to live on. You know they would have wanted you to." His voice was shaking. I could see him tearing up as the frustration mounted. He wanted desperately to pull me out of the depths of despair, but he didn't know how.

"This place only makes it worse," Davis added. "You've locked yourself up in here like a goddamned prisoner. Why don't we get you out of here? Anywhere you want. You can come stay at my house. Please."

"Fresh air might do you good, Alex," Tompkins added. "Exercise helps."

"Take me back there," I said as I looked at Davis. Claiborne returned with an IV and bag of saline as Davis tried to decipher my request.

"Where?" he asked.

"To the scene," I said. "Take me back to where it happened."

Davis frowned and looked at Tompkins. "You know that's probably not a good idea," Davis said.

"I have to," I said as my voice started to shake. "*Please.*"

"OK, but you have to take a shower first and get a fresh shave," Tompkins said. The softness was gone, replaced by the drill sergeant-like toughness we'd all grown to know and respect. "You smell like Claiborne's underwear after he trusted a fart."

"Hey!" Claiborne yelled as he worked the needle into my arm. "Usually you can just turn them inside out and keep going."

CHAPTER EIGHT

T here wasn't much to be said as we drove to the movie theater in Sgt. Tompkins's unmarked Tahoe. Davis and Claiborne followed in Claiborne's Crown Victoria as we made the twenty-minute drive from my house.

They had warned me that I wasn't ready for it. Claiborne insisted that I get help. The combination of alcohol, pain pills, dehydration, and malnourishment had me dangerously close to renal failure and a trip to the ICU. He argued that seeing the scene might trigger a physiological reaction that could be deadly. The bottle of water I sipped on the ride over was a direct result of his nagging. He was nothing if not persistent.

The parking lot was empty as Tompkins parked the Tahoe near the south side of the lot where we had faced off with the terrorists. Although the scene had been cleared, there were still police barricades around the area where it had all happened.

Before Tompkins could say anything, I was out of the vehicle and walking toward the barricades. I could see the charred concrete making a vague outline of the school bus as I got closer. I wanted to turn and run away, but I forced myself to keep walking toward it.

With every step I took, the despair and sorrow I felt multiplied. I started to feel numb. My mind was in overdrive as I relived the events. I kept walking, pushing aside a barricade as I entered the restricted area. I heard someone yell something behind me, but it didn't register. I was in a dreamlike state. I felt like I was at the bottom of a swimming pool looking up at the world.

I stopped at the blackened concrete. I stared at the bits of rubber and steel that had been burned into the ground. There were chunks of broken concrete where the explosion had cratered the surrounding area. I saw Chelsea's face.

I squatted down, rubbing my hand against the blackened and broken concrete. As I picked up and inspected the charred debris, I saw the man holding Lindsey's head. His eyes were black windows reflecting the depths of hell and pure evil. The numbness suddenly vanished.

I was suddenly filled with rage. I shot up, throwing the piece of concrete across the lot as I yelled out in anger. I felt a hand on my shoulder, spinning me around as I cursed the demons that had taken my family from me. As I came face to face with Tompkins, I pushed him away, nearly knocking him over a barricade as I clenched my fists and screamed.

It was a feeling unlike any I had ever experienced. It had a purity about it. It was raw and real. It consumed me, but it also felt as if I had been set free. It was invigorating.

Claiborne and Davis tried to calm me down. Claiborne dwarfed me, but I was operating on pure adrenaline as I wrestled away. I couldn't hear anything they were saying as they tried to tame me. As I turned back toward Tompkins, they were each able to grab one of my arms and steady me as I started to calm down.

My heart was still racing, and I was out of breath as Tompkins tried to comfort me. "I know, buddy," he said as he wrapped his arm around my neck and pulled me close. "It's going to be OK."

"They took everything from me!" I shouted breathlessly. My chest was heaving as I jerked away from Tompkins's embrace. "Everything!"

"We'll get you help," Tompkins said.

"I don't want help," I growled. "I want payback. I want justice!"

Tompkins frowned and shook his head. "I know you do. We all do. But that's the shitty part about this. The shitheads that did this are dead. It was part of their plan from the beginning."

"What about the people behind them?" I asked. It was like someone flipped a switch. I was suddenly calm, and for the first time since the incident, I was starting to think like a cop again.

"FBI says it was a lone wolf attack," Tompkins said as he nodded to Claiborne and Davis. The two eased their grip, allowing me to stand on my own as I regained what little composure I had.

"Bullshit," I replied. "Jacobson said there were other attacks. This was a coordinated effort. Who put them up to it?"

"ISIS," Tompkins said with a shrug.

"OK, but who radicalized them here? Who funded them? Who trained them?" I pressed. "Have there been any arrests?"

"The FBI has the case now," Davis said, sidestepping next to Tompkins. "But from what I've heard, they're not sharing anything with us."

"Who has the case now?" I asked.

"From our side?" Tompkins asked.

"Yeah."

"Well, after Abbott, it was Detective Morris, but like Davis said, when the FBI took over they pretty much shut us out," Tompkins replied.

"And the Sheriff is OK with that?"

Tompkins shrugged. "He didn't really have a choice. It became a federal matter as soon as it was tagged an act of terrorism, and more so when we learned that they were from Mississippi. We helped them as much as we could, but they shut us out about three weeks ago. I don't think Morris is even working with them on it anymore."

"So that's it? They take out a school bus full of kids in our jurisdiction and they tell us to fuck off when they get what they need?" I asked. My heart rate was starting to climb again. Tompkins nervously looked down at my clenched fists.

"Do you want to go talk to Morris yourself?" Tompkins asked. "Would that help?"

"I don't give a fuck about Morris!" I snapped. "I want justice for my family!"

"Maybe you should just get some rest," Claiborne offered. "You need to eat something."

"No," I said as I took in a deep breath and exhaled slowly. "Let's go talk to Morris."

"Fine," Tompkins said. "But you have to be nice to him."

"What?" I asked.

"I know there's a history between you two," Tompkins said cautiously. "And you're rightfully pretty upset right now, so-"

"So, nothing," I said. "Let's go."

CHAPTER NINE

I could feel the stares of everyone as we walked into the Law Enforcement Center. The large substation was the home office of the Special Operations Division, Investigations Division, and Criminal Patrol Division for the western side of the parish. We walked into the bullpen where a few detectives in plain clothes stopped in their tracks as they recognized me.

The sudden work stoppage was followed quickly by a gauntlet of people rushing to me to give their condolences and ask how I was doing. Their faces started to blur as I pushed past them and headed toward the man I had come to see. As I moved toward the back of the bullpen where the sergeants of Investigations sat, I could see uniformed deputies enter the room out of the corner of my eye. The few deputies that weren't out on the road had come to see me as word spread that I was in the building.

Tompkins and Claiborne mingled with the crowd as I pushed through. Captain Clint Levy, the head pilot of the Air Wing, stepped forward and extended his hand as he blocked my path to the truth.

"It's good to see you, Alex," Levy said as I shook his hand. "I was there that day. I am so sorry we couldn't do more."

"It's not your fault," I said. I could see the sincere regret in his eyes as he shook his head. "I failed my family."

"You did the best you could," Levy replied. "We all did."

"It wasn't good enough," I said solemnly. "Excuse me; I have someone I need to speak to."

Levy pulled out a business card from the breast pocket of his tan flight suit and handed it to me. "If you need anything at all, don't hesitate to give me a call," he said as I accepted the card.

"Thanks," I said as I stuffed the card in my pocket and continued walking past the sea of deputies.

"Hey, Shep," a booming voice called out from behind me as I continued my march toward the back offices. I turned to see Lieutenant Jacobson standing on the other side of the row of cubicles near the door to criminal patrol. I had lost track of the days, not realizing my team was on shift.

"What brings you back here?" he asked as he walked toward me. I stopped and faced him, not sure of what to say. "How are you, buddy?" he added.

"Just wanted to talk to Morris," I said nodding toward the back offices. Through the glass, I could see Detective Morris on the phone with his feet propped up on his desk.

Jacobson frowned. "You need to be getting some rest at home," he said. "You don't need to be agitated."

"Agitated?" I snapped. "You think I'm just agitated?"

"Easy, Alex," he said. "You know what I mean. You've been through hell. You need to be resting, not here dealing with someone that will just set you off."

"I just have some questions," I said as I turned back toward Morris. "I'll be fine."

"I'll go with you," he said as he caught up with me. "Just in case."

"Whatever," I said. I didn't care about the history between Morris and me. He was a world class prick. I had watched him claw his way out of criminal patrol and step on as many people as he could to further his career. I didn't like the guy, but as long as he told me what I wanted to know, I didn't really care about history.

I walked up to his office and looked through the glass as I knocked on the door. He held up a hand and waved me off as he continued his phone conversation. I ignored him and walked in.

"Give me a minute, will you?" he asked as he held his hand over the handset. Jacobson stood in the doorway as I walked in and sat in the leather chair across from his desk. Morris gave me a disapproving look as I sat there staring at him, waiting for him to hang up.

When he realized I wasn't going anywhere, Morris made a pained expression and said, "Sir, I have someone who just walked into my office, can I call you back? Thanks."

"That was the Chief Deputy, but I'm sure whatever you have is much more important," he said snidely as he pulled off his glasses and rubbed his shaved head. "How can I help you, Corporal?"

"What is the status of my case?" I asked flatly.

Morris let out an exasperated sigh. "Look, Shepherd, I am very sorry for your loss, but you know it's more complicated than that."

"Complicated? It's been over two months. What progress have you made?" I growled.

"Easy, *Corporal*," he said, holding up his hands as he looked at Jacobson for help. "It's an active terrorism investigation, and the FBI has primary jurisdiction."

I leaned forward to the edge of my seat. "Do I look like someone you want to be fucking with right now, *Sergeant*?"

"Is that a threat, Corporal?" he asked as he smugly leaned back in his chair and adjusted his striped tie against his beer belly.

"Alex," the Lieutenant said from behind me. "Relax, buddy."

"I am relaxed," I said with clenched teeth. "My family was brutally murdered right in front of me. This is as relaxed as I get. I just want answers."

"The people who did this to your family are dead, Shepherd," Morris said, shaking his head. "The FBI is now trying to prevent more attacks. I know you want justice, but that's just the shitty part about terrorism. There will never be justice."

"What about the people who sponsored them? How did they get here? Someone had to set them up. Train them. Fund them," I replied.

Morris shook his head. "It's a dead end. These cells get their training in the Middle East and are funded by ISIS, so unless you want to hitch a flight to Syria or Iraq, you'll never find the people responsible."

"Let me see the report," I said.

"You know I can't do that," Morris replied.

"I won't ask again," I growled as I stood.

"Are you threatening me, Corporal?" Morris asked with a nervous laugh as he leaned toward me. "You think you're some badass just because you're SWAT?"

There it was. He always managed to show his true colors. He had washed out of SWAT tryouts and had a chip on his shoulder about SWAT operators. Everyone on the team knew he still held a grudge, but no one ever did anything about his attitude.

"Last chance," I said as I put both hands on his desk. I glanced over my shoulder to see Jacobson turn around. He knew what was about to happen and had no intentions of stopping me. Even the brass hated the smug little prick.

"Fuck you," he said with a smirk. "Show some respect, Corporal."

I lunged toward him, grabbing his tie and wrapping it around my hand as I pulled him toward me. The sudden shift in his weight caused his chair to roll out from underneath him. He fell to his knees, his head and throat just above the desk as I leaned forward and pulled him close.

"You think I've got something to lose?" I shouted. "You think I fucking care about your rank?"

"Please!" Morris pleaded as he gasped for air and tried to regain his bearings. "You're crazy. I can't breathe."

"You wouldn't be talking if you couldn't breathe," I said as I took my free hand and wrapped it around his fat wattle. He choked as I squeezed it tightly.

"Now, I'm going to ask you one more time," I said as I released my grip. "Please give me the report."

Morris squirmed as I pulled down on his tie. Moments later, Jacobson rushed over and pulled me away while yelling for me to let go of Morris.

"You're going to jail, motherfucker!" Morris said, regaining his confidence as Jacobson pushed me against the wall.

"Shut up," Jacobson barked. "No one is going to jail."

"Bullshit!" Morris replied.

Jacobson let go of me and squared his brawny shoulders toward Morris. "Excuse me?"

"Sorry, Lieutenant," Morris replied sheepishly as he slunk back into his chair.

"I just want the report," I said calmly. "That's all."

Jacobson nodded to Morris. After a bit of hesitation, he opened his locked filing cabinet and pulled out the thick brown folder. "You'll have to sign for it."

"I'll take care of it," Jacobson said as he handed me the file. "Now get back to work."

"Thank you," I said as Jacobson ushered me out of Morris's office. I started thumbing through the folder as we walked out.

As we cleared the office, Jacobson pulled me out of view of the other detectives that had been watching the scene unfold.

"You need to get it together, son," Jacobson said, making his best attempt at a whisper with his deep voice.

"I'm sorry," I said.

"Look, I know you've been through the shit, and we're going to get you someone to talk to," Jacobson said, putting his beefy hand on my shoulder. "But you have to get your anger in check before you wind up in prison, or dead, or both. You can't go off half-cocked like that anymore. Next time, I won't bail you out. Got it?"

"Ten-four, sir," I replied, trying to control the rage growing inside me.

CHAPTER TEN

Jacobson dropped me off at my house with my own copy of the report in hand. I had thumbed through it on the fifteen-minute drive to my house, trying to avoid the gruesome pictures as I found the name of the FBI agent that had taken over the investigation. Jacobson had warned me that trying to help along a federal investigation would just lead to more trouble, but I shrugged him off. I needed to keep moving forward in order to hang on to what little sanity I had left.

I went into the house only long enough to grab my truck keys and a bottle of water. The screams of my daughter haunted me as I walked through the empty house. I tried to force them out, to keep moving forward, but the knot in my chest grew larger. Chelsea's toys were still scattered about, and I could still smell

Lindsey's perfume. I half expected them both to come walking out of our bedroom, smiling and laughing as they always had.

Shaking it off, I grabbed my keys off the key rack in the kitchen and headed for the front door. As I reached the front door, Chelsea's stuffed police bear caught my eye. She had given it to me for Father's Day earlier in the year. I squatted down and picked it up, remembering the day she had proudly presented it to me, along with breakfast in bed.

"It's you, Daddy," she had said, jumping into the bed with me as Lindsey walked in with a tray of bacon, eggs, pancakes, and orange juice.

"It's me?" I laughed as I sat up and squeezed my baby girl.

"She picked it out herself," Lindsey said as she put the tray on the nightstand while Chelsea squirmed away.

"He protects people just like you do, Daddy," she said proudly as she pointed at the stuffed bear's badge. "See?"

"He sure does," I replied. "Thank you, sweetie." I kissed her forehead as she bounced on the bed playing with the bear.

"His name is Maggots!" she said proudly.

"Maggots?" I asked as I turned to Lindsey, trying not to laugh.

"Maddox," Lindsey corrected with a hearty laugh. "From the books."

"Do you like Maggots, Daddy?" she asked, jumping into my lap and holding the bear six inches from my face.

"I love him!" I said as I gave her another big hug. "Thank you, sweetie."

"We made you pant cakes too, Daddy. I helped!" she said as she crawled over me to the tray.

Pant cakes.

"Don't ever grow up," I said as I gave her another hug and kissed her cheek.

I picked up the bear and gently placed him in my cargo pants pocket as I walked out. Chelsea had loved that bear so much that she ended up keeping it. It was always so funny watching her parade around the house with "Maggots" and Buttons. In her little world, Buttons was her best friend and the police bear kept her safe, just like her daddy, she said.

But I had failed, and my request for her to never grow up had become reality. I felt like throwing up again as I unlocked my truck and put the bear on the dash. I went to the backseat and opened the locked under seat storage container. I grabbed my Glock 19 and holster, tucked it in my pants, and covered it with my shirt tail. Most of my weapons were in my patrol unit that had been taken back to vehicle maintenance while I was in the hospital, but I always kept body armor and an M4 in the hardened storage container in my truck in case of a SWAT call-out while off duty.

I didn't even turn on the radio as I made the forty-five-minute drive across the Lake Pontchartrain Causeway Bridge into New Orleans. The news didn't interest me anymore. It would never be the whole story, and I was sure they would find a way to blame law enforcement anyway. They always did.

I pulled into the parking lot of the FBI building and found a parking spot near the back of the lot. I took a deep breath before picking up the folder from the passenger seat. I knew I had to put aside my feelings as a father and husband and get back to being a cop. It was the only way to survive.

Detective Abbott's initial report had been thorough. Our crime lab had done a good job of analyzing both scenes. I started with the hijacking report on Highway 1088 first.

They had found eighty-seven 7.62mm casings at the scene. Based on ballistics and crime scene analysis, it was determined that the bus had stopped normally ten feet from the Toyota Camry. Aaron Miller's autopsy results indicated that he had been shot in the back of the head at point blank range using a 9MM handgun. His body had been further mangled from the school bus crashing into the parked Toyota Camry at slow speed.

The Toyota Camry was a rental car out of Jackson, Mississippi. It had been rented to a Mike Ritz using a credit card and ID bearing the same name. Surveillance cameras confirmed that it had actually been known terrorist Siddiqui Ghalib using an alias. The car was mostly empty, except for the empty gasoline containers they had used to build their Molotov cocktails.

I skimmed through the pursuit and went to the analysis of the movie theater parking lot crime scene. The savages holding those children hostage had used Molotov cocktails consisting of motor oil and gasoline to burn the children alive. They had rigged the bus with C4 on a central remote detonator – the dead man switch one of the men had been carrying. He had attempted to detonate his vest as well, but the wiring had failed. The blast I had felt had been the bus exploding. As I read the report, I wished the terrorist hadn't been so incompetent. The ball-bearing vest he had been wearing would have killed me instantly at such close range, keeping me from the hell on earth I found myself in afterward.

I forced myself to read through the autopsy reports. Some of the children had been killed by the blast, while others had burned alive. My little Chelsea had died of severe burns before the blast. I didn't look at the pictures. *I couldn't.*

I found the autopsy analysis on Lindsey. Her body had been severely burned, and she had suffered multiple gunshot wounds. The probable cause of death had been blood loss due to gunshot wounds, but the autopsy report was inconclusive due to her beheading. I was numb to it. I couldn't get the image of her lifeless face out of my head. The love of my life was gone. Everything I had ever wanted in life had been taken from me. I felt dead inside.

The report stopped there. The last pages were nothing more than chain of custody statements, handing the case over to Special Agent Daniel Gibson of the Federal Bureau of Investigation. Detective Abbott had been removed from the case, and Morris had been assigned to liaise with the FBI for any further inquiries.

I closed the folder and put it back on the seat. I wiped the tear from my cheek and stepped out into the humid air. There was a slight breeze coming off the nearby lake, but it wasn't enough to quell the stifling heat. I could hear a few passing boats on Lake Pontchartrain as I made my way to the main entrance.

As I reached the lobby, I slid my credentials through an opening in the one-way glass and told the receptionist I was there to see Special Agent Gibson. The woman behind the glass told me to have a seat in the lobby. Moments later, a very muscular black man with a shaved head appeared wearing khakis and a polo shirt. The ID hanging from his neck read GIBSON.

"Deputy Shepherd, I wasn't expecting you so soon after getting out of the hospital," he said as he approached with an outstretched hand. "I am so sorry for your loss."

I shook his beefy hand. "Do you have time to chat?" I asked.

"Of course!" he said. "Please, let's go to my office."

I followed him through an open room full of cubicles that looked very similar to our investigations division at the LEC. There were only a few other agents in the office, and most were idly clicking through reports on their computers. None of them acknowledged us as we continued past the cubicle farm toward a narrow hallway.

Gibson stopped at a door marked COUNTERTERRORISM INVESTIGATIONS and swiped his badge on a nearby keypad. After a beep, the light turned green, and the door made a metallic *click* sound. I followed Gibson down another hallway and into his office where he offered me a seat across from him.

"I'm sorry you drove all this way," Gibson said as he sat behind his cherry oak desk. "I would've been more than happy to drive up to the Northshore to see you, especially after all you've been through."

"How many arrests have you made on this case?" I asked abruptly.

Gibson frowned. "On this particular incident? None. Nationwide? Five."

"Why none?" I asked.

"It's complicated," Gibson said, shaking his head.

"I have all day, Agent Gibson," I said as I sat back in the chair and crossed my legs. "Enlighten me. How has it been almost two months without a single arrest?"

Gibson smiled. "I understand your frustrations, Deputy Shepherd, but it's not simply a matter of time."

"It's very simple," I snapped. "A school bus full of kids, two school workers, and a police officer were killed. Where is their justice?"

The smile vanished from Gibson's face. "I'm afraid when it comes to terrorism, there is no justice. Just like 9/11, the people who did this died in the attacks. The arrests we've made so far have been to stop copycat attacks. Unfortunately, all we can do is try to prevent more of them."

"Who financed them? Who trained them?"

"ISIS has claimed responsibility," Gibson replied. "Their financing network is classified, and we are working on dismantling it as we speak."

"How did they get here? Who housed these people? Who gave them shelter? Who gave them a base of operations here?" I asked.

"I appreciate your concern, Deputy, but you need to let us do our job," Gibson replied calmly. "I can't imagine how I would feel if I were in your shoes, and I know you're hurting. This investigation is much bigger than you or me. I'm sorry we can't bring your family back, but I promise you that we will do everything we can to stop future attacks from happening."

"Please," I said. I could feel my face turning red as the anger grew inside me. "Just tell me what you know about these people."

Gibson let out a long sigh. "OK," he said as he logged into the laptop on his desk and pulled up the report.

"Muhammad al-Iraqi, Siddiqui Ghalib, and Kamal Hamid Salman were the three involved in the school bus attack. They were part of a cell that we think was based out of Jackson, Mississippi. Another four attacked the mall in Southaven. They were also killed in the attack, so we don't have any direct intelligence from them."

"But based on the rental vehicles at both scenes, we traced everything back to Siddiqui Ghalib who was killed in the school bus attack. We think he was responsible for recruiting and planning this operation, much like Mohamed Atta was in the 9/11 attacks," he continued.

"What about Texas?" I asked.

"Different cell," Gibson replied. "And from everything we've found, they operated autonomously. Those that we have arrested had no idea of the others beyond the knowledge that more attacks were taking place."

"So you think it ends there?" I asked.

"Not necessarily," Gibson said. "That is as far as we've gotten to date, though."

"What does that even mean?"

"A lot has changed in the last few years," Gibson replied. "It is a lot harder to get warrants than it was even five years ago."

"Forty-four kids died!" I yelled.

"I know," Gibson said, holding up his hands. "But the NSA scandals have set us back, especially with the gutting of the Patriot Act. I'm not saying it's a bad thing, but it makes an investigation like this more difficult."

"So what's the problem?" I asked.

"There's a mosque in Jackson where we think Siddiqui Ghalib might have stayed," Gibson said, looking back at his computer. "As soon as the incident happened and they found out we were in town, they lawyered up. No one will talk, and we can't get a FISA court to issue a warrant."

"FISA?"

"Foreign Intelligence Surveillance Act court," Gibson explained. "It's a secret court that allows us to get a surveillance warrant without tipping our hand."

"So now what?"

"We drag it out in Federal Court until we can get a warrant," Gibson replied.

"Fuck that!" I said.

"Exactly," Gibson said. "I wish it were easier, but you know how this goes."

"Yes," I said as I stood to leave. "I do."

CHAPTER ELEVEN

It was late afternoon when I passed the city limits sign for Jackson, Mississippi. School buses peppered the moderate traffic as I made my way into the city. Each bus was like a punch in the gut, reminding me of what these animals had taken from me. My heart was broken, but my blood boiled.

I found the address for the mosque that Agent Gibson had mentioned. It was on a large plot of land in an isolated suburban neighborhood. The satellite view from Google Maps showed access by a lone road lined with tall trees. There was no good way to do surveillance except from the air. I opted for the direct approach instead.

Trees provided ample shade for the quarter-mile winding driveway. It would have made for a perfect ambush location, but

I wasn't worried about that. Seeing my family didn't sound all that bad anyway. After years of worrying about coming home alive to my family, it felt slightly invigorating to have no fear.

I drove right up to the front of the mosque and parked my truck next to a silver BMW. I could hear them in prayer as I walked up to the front door. The building appeared to be a two-story structure that had been recently renovated. It looked more like a small apartment complex than a house of prayer.

Adjusting my shirt over the Glock 19 concealed in my waistband holster, I walked up to a large wooden door. There was a sign on it listing the day's events in both English and Arabic. After checking my watch, I guessed that they should just be finishing their evening prayers. Although, honestly, I had no idea how long those should last. I assumed an hour would be sufficient.

I tried pushing the door open only to find that it was locked. I had never been to a church with locked doors, but then, I'd also never been to a mosque. I used the large metal knocker and slammed it against the door four times before stepping to the side, a habit from years of police work and being taught never to stand in front of a door.

After a few minutes, the door swung open. A man with a thick, black beard emerged. He was wearing a black turban and what looked to be a white bedsheet. He was barefoot as he stepped out of the mosque.

The familiar smell of marijuana and incense suddenly hit me. This guy had been toking up as part of his afternoon activities. His eyes were bloodshot, and he appeared as high as a kite, but he still scowled upon seeing me.

"Are you police?" he asked angrily. "I have lawyer."

"Easy, buddy," I said as I instinctively moved my hand toward my weapon. "I just want to talk."

"You talk to my lawyer!" he said as he pumped his fist at me. "This is harassment!"

"I ain't a cop," I said as I held my left hand up. "I just came by to talk."

"No cop?" he asked. "Then you trespass! I call police!"

I could see movement behind him in the mosque. A fellow worshipper had taken an interest in our conversation and had moved to within a few feet behind the angry gatekeeper. I could see his left hand, but his right hand was hidden. My hand was now resting on my hip against the butt of my concealed gun.

"OK," I conceded. "I just have one question, and then I'll leave."

"One question?" he asked.

"Just one."

"What do you want?"

My eyes were fixed on the man behind him. He was creeping forward as the two waited for my question. I would have to drop both of them if he drew on me. I calculated my movements in the event of a shootout.

"Siddiqui Ghalib," I said slowly. "Did he worship here?"

After a pause, he smiled and said, "Sorry, I'm afraid I do not know that name."

He was lying. The tell had been quick, but he had curled his lip slightly upon hearing the name and then briefly grimaced before smiling to conceal his lie. The other man moved next to him. His right hand was still hidden behind his back. He was much larger than the lying gatekeeper.

"Don't watch the news, huh?" I asked.

"This is a place of worship," the man said. "We do not pollute it with such trivialities."

"No TV at all?"

"No," he said. "Not at all here. This is a place of prayer. It would not be appropriate."

"But Allah is cool with a Bimmer?" I asked, nodding my head to the BMW parked out front.

"I believe you said you only had one question," he said. "My car is not of your concern. You leave now."

"Fine," I said. "But what about the big man next to you?"

"What about him?" he asked. The buzz was wearing off. I could tell he was starting to get angry.

"Did he know Siddiqui?" I asked.

"You are trespassing," the man said angrily. "I do not have time for this. I have an appointment. I am calling the police."

"Fine," I said as I slowly stepped back. "You fellas have a good evening."

I watched them over my shoulder as I walked to my truck. The big guy stayed outside, staring me down while the smaller man went back into the mosque. The big guy was obviously muscle for whatever operation they were running. Part of me wanted to kick the door in and knock the little shit's teeth in for lying to me, but the cop in me had a better plan.

I drove slowly down the long driveway and then turned to the right into the subdivision. I passed a few apartment complexes before emerging out onto the main highway that fed into the interstate. I had a feeling the gatekeeper would be leaving soon in his BMW, giving me the perfect opportunity to isolate him and get the truth.

As I reached the highway, I found a bottling plant across from the subdivision. It was a perfect place to hang out and wait. I pulled into the parking lot and killed the engine after rolling down the windows. I had a night-vision capable spotter scope in my go-bag. The sun was starting to set behind me, giving me a little more concealment as darkness fell.

Traffic into and out of the subdivision was light. I stayed vigilant, waiting for the BMW to appear. Each time I found myself drifting off or losing interest, the image of my family brought me back. The anger fueled me. It pushed me forward.

As darkness fell, the BMW suddenly appeared and turned left toward the interstate. The little gatekeeper was alone, having left his bodyguard behind at the mosque. I waited a few seconds before starting my truck's engine and turning on its lights. I was fairly certain he would be oblivious, but I couldn't risk alerting him. I needed to catch him by surprise.

I pulled out onto the two-lane road as a couple of cars passed me. The BMW sped east toward the interstate and merged onto I-55 South a few miles later. I followed at a safe distance, watching as he held a cell phone up to his ear for most of the drive.

Traffic was light as we continued toward downtown Jackson. He didn't seem to be worried about anyone following him as he cruised southbound at ten miles per hour over the speed limit. We passed the downtown area and continued past I-20. Had he been spooked? Was he bailing and heading toward New Orleans?

My questions were answered as we reached the McDowell Road exit. The BMW signaled and then exited east toward what looked like a warehouse area. There appeared to be a UPS processing facility nearby. Maybe he was expecting something coming through Customs.

He passed the processing facility and then turned left into another parking lot. I had to do a double-take as I saw the bright pink neon sign flashing above the building.

Seriously? A strip club?

CHAPTER TWELVE

I took up a position in the parking lot of a warehouse across the street and watched the little gatekeeper get out of his BMW in the parking lot of the strip club. He had changed out of the bedsheet he had been wearing, into slacks and what appeared to be a dark silk shirt.

Moments after he exited the vehicle, a dark Mercedes pulled up next to him. Even with my night vision spotting scope, I couldn't get a good look at the driver. The man from the mosque had his back to me and was blocking the driver's side window. The gatekeeper appeared to pull something out of his back pocket and hand it to the driver before the driver sped off.

The Mercedes turned left out of the parking lot and headed back toward the interstate. I copied down his plate information as

I followed him through the scope before turning my attention back to the gatekeeper.

He strutted into the strip club and out of sight. There were very few patrons going in and out of the club, but I kept close watch. A few hours later, the gatekeeper emerged from the club with a chubby brunette wearing too much makeup and too little clothing. She was clinging to his arm as they staggered out into the parking lot.

She didn't look to be one of the strippers, although it was an establishment in Mississippi, so there was no telling for sure. It seemed to be too early in the night for one of the dancers to be getting off work. I guessed that she was an escort of some kind. The two stumbled to his car together as he fumbled with his keys. Finally unlocking the doors, they got in and sped off, heading back toward the interstate.

They went north for a short distance before exiting near a truck stop. I kept my distance as the silver BMW pulled into the parking lot of a shady-looking motel, and the couple stumbled to the front office while sticking their tongues down each other's throats and groping each other.

I watched as they walked out of the office a few minutes later. The gatekeeper was holding a key in his hand while escorting his mistress to Room 210 on the second floor. It had been a while since I had seen a motel room of any kind use an actual key to get in, but the gatekeeper fiddled with it for a second, then opened the door and jerked his mistress inside by the arm.

As they closed the door behind them, I put away the scope and went to the under seat storage in the back of my truck. I pulled out my Taser X26 and snapped an extra cartridge into the grip. I put it into the cargo pocket on my left pant leg, grabbed my Glock 19, and clipped the paddle holster to my right hip. Sufficiently armed, I retrieved my bandana and covered my face before putting on my tactical gloves and slamming the door shut.

The parking lot was empty as I walked across and headed for the breezeway stairs. I could hear another couple fucking a few doors down. The motel was apparently the go-to place for people to seal the deal with their hired lovers.

I reached the gatekeeper's room and knocked five times before stepping to the side. The blinds were closed, but I could see the light on through a crack in the side.

"Who is it?" the woman yelled after a long pause.

I knocked three more times without saying a word as I leaned against the cinder brick wall.

"I said, who's there?" the woman shouted.

This time I used my fist to beat against the door four times. I heard movement and a string of expletives from the gatekeeper.

"What do you what?" the man said this time.

"It's me!" I said, disguising my voice slightly.

"Who?" the man asked as he opened the door slightly. The safety chain was still latched. As he strained to see me through the narrow gap, I could see something hanging around his neck, but couldn't quite make it out.

Stepping in front of the door, I kicked it open with my boot, snapping the flimsy chain. The door hit him in the face as he stumbled back. I moved swiftly and violently as I entered, grabbing him by the throat as his hands shot up to protect his face.

As I walked in, I kicked the door close behind me, driving the little man toward the bathroom as I carried him by his throat with my right hand. The woman shrieked and then went for the phone.

I stopped and drew the Taser with my left hand, centered its laser on the black leather corset she had changed into and squeezed the trigger. I heard the familiar pop of the CO_2 cartridge deploying the prongs as they buried into her back.

The woman took a five-second ride before dropping to the ground. I held the Taser up with my left hand as the timer on the back of the gun counted down to zero while continuing to squeeze tightly around the man's throat with my right.

Turning my attention back to the man, I noticed he had a ball gag hanging loosely around his neck. He was shirtless and wearing white underwear. He tried to fight against my grip, but I kicked his leg out from under him as I drove him into the ground head first. His mistress tried to get up again, but another trigger squeeze sent her on another five-second ride as her body tensed.

"Move and I will pull the trigger again," I warned as I rolled the unconscious gatekeeper onto his chest, pulled out a pair of zip ties, and secured his hands behind his back.

"OK!" the woman yelled.

With the man's hands bound behind his back, I ordered the woman onto her stomach and zip tied her hands together.

"If you scream, you're taking another ride, got it?" I warned.

The woman nodded cautiously, but I didn't take her word for it. I pulled the ball gag from around the gatekeeper's neck, stuffed it in her mouth, and cinched it down. I didn't want her inviting anyone to the party that was about to start.

As I was finishing, the gatekeeper began to moan behind me.

"Let's go over your answers from earlier," I said as I turned to face him.

CHAPTER THIRTEEN

W ho are you?" the man shrieked as he came to. After securing his lady friend, I had put him in the bathtub. The cold water of the shower snapped him out of his dazed state. I held the Taser X26 ominously as I sat on the edge of the tub, while the water washed the blood from his face and neck.

"You first," I said as I drove the Taser into his abdomen and gave him a five-second drive stun while covering his mouth with my gloved left hand.

"What's your name?" I asked as I removed my hand.

"My name is Abul Farah," he said as he caught his breath. "What do you want from me?"

"You lied to me earlier," I said. "I don't like liars."

"What are you talking about?" the man asked with wide eyes. He was afraid, completely naked in the bathtub with his hands zip tied behind his back and his ankles taped together.

I flicked the safety off the Taser and turned digital display toward him so he could see the yellow 94 displayed on the back. "See this? Ninety-four percent left. You'll give out long before this Taser does."

"Please," he said. "I do not know what you are talking about."

"Siddiqui Ghalib," I said. "You know him, yes?"

"Yes," Farah admitted. "I do."

"What is your involvement with him?" I asked.

"I pray with many people," Farah said while looking away.

"Wrong answer," I said as I drove the Taser into his neck and squeezed the trigger, riding out the writhing and screaming as the five-second shock timer counted down on the gun.

"Still over ninety percent," I said. "Try again."

"The police will come for me," Farah said as he tried to regain his composure. I could tell the cold water beating down on his face from the shower was also starting to get to him.

"In this dump?" I scoffed. "Ha! I'm sure this isn't half as kinky as some of the stuff that goes on here. Hell, you've probably been involved in most of it. Are hookers part of the Quran?"

"How dare you judge me?" he asked with a wild look. "You are an infidel!"

I set the Taser aside gently as I rotated toward him. I stood momentarily before driving my fist into his face with all of the force I could muster. There was a satisfying crack as my clenched fist impacted his orbital bone and drove his head into the back of the tub.

As he lay dazed, I stood and grabbed a towel, wiping the water and blood splatter from my hand as Farah struggled to breathe with blood and water pouring into his nose and mouth. He coughed and choked as I walked back over and sat back on the edge of the tub. I was still seeing red, but I had to calm myself. I needed answers, not vengeance. *Yet.*

"First of all," I said as I picked up the Taser. "Fuck you."

"Second," I said as I drove the Taser into his neck again and squeezed the trigger. "Fuck you again."

When he finally recovered, I put the Taser aside. "I have all night. You don't, but I do. What was your involvement with the attacks?"

"Please," he said. Tears were starting to stream down his face. Like most criminals, the tough talk was merely a façade. Deep down, they were all pussies. "Please stop!"

"Answers, Abul," I said. I held up the Taser and pulled the trigger. The crack of 50,000 volts between the two prongs caused Abul to jump.

"I gave them a place to stay," he said finally. "That's it, I swear."

"Who planned the attacks?"

"Tariq Qafir."

"Who?" I asked.

"He was a brave warrior for Allah," Abul said smugly.

"You're not a very fast learner, are you, Abul?" I asked as I drove the Taser into his chest and squeezed the trigger.

"Please!" Abul pleaded.

I turned off the water. "Tell me everything."

"I let the men stay with me. Tariq came to this country through Mexico and trained the men. He planned the attack, but he was killed by the Americans a year ago. The plan was delayed as Siddiqui took over and brought in new men," Abul said, as he tried to catch his breath.

"How did these men get here?"

"They came in as refugees from Syria and Libya."

"And they stayed here?"

"I just gave them a place to stay and ensured the money was handled," he said. "Please, I didn't have anything to do with the attacks."

"Where did the money come from?"

"Kaleed Adid," he replied, wincing as he waited for my response.

"Who is Kaleed Adid?"

"He runs the Southeast Division of the Coalition of Islamic-American Cooperation," Abul replied, wincing again.

"You're lying," I said as I turned the cold water back on.

"I am not!" he yelled.

"Why do you keep flenching when you talk about him?"

"CIAC is very influential in your government," he said. "If he knew I had spoken of him he would surely have me killed."

"So the money comes from him alone?"

Abul nodded slowly.

"How?"

"Small wire transfers to various accounts," Abul replied. "Small increments over the last two years so as not to alert police. I distributed the cash to Siddiqui, and he did the rest. Just like tonight."

"So that's the car that met you? You were giving him money?"

Abul nodded.

"Is there another attack planned?"

"Only Kamal knows what is planned next," Abdul said, turning his head to the side to avoid the shower.

"Kamal is dead," I growled. "So you're going to have to think real hard and figure out what is planned."

"No, he was very much alive when I handed him the money he asked for," Abdul replied.

"When?"

"Tonight."

I turned the water off. "Kamal is dead. I killed him during the attack."

"You killed his brother, Ali Husain," Abul said with a laugh. "The dumb one."

"Bullshit," I said as I flicked the safety off the Taser and aimed its laser at his crotch. His eyes suddenly widened. "We had DNA analysis done."

"They were twins!" Abul shouted as he tried to turn away from the Taser. "I swear!"

"What?"

"Ali was Kamal's twin brother. He carried out the attack that Siddiqui and Kamal planned. He had cancer and wanted to die a martyr so that Kamal could continue the Jihad," Abul said proudly.

My left hand went straight for Abul's throat, squeezing until his eyes seemed to pop out like a cartoon. His left eye was already starting to swell shut from my previous hit.

"Where is he?" I growled.

He tried to speak, but my grip was crushing his trachea. I loosened my grip as he mouthed the words.

"He has a training compound near Utica off Highway 18," Abul choked. "That's where he goes to train and plan. I'm sure that's where he went after we met."

"Where?"

"Chapman Road," Abul said.

I released my grip and stood.

"Please," Abul pleaded. "I've told you everything. Release me."

"Don't worry," I said with a forced smile. "You'll get your wish."

"Thank you," Abul said with a sigh of relief.

"But you may have to share a few virgins with your boy Ali."

CHAPTER FOURTEEN

It was late afternoon when the doorbell woke me up. I half expected the wiener dog to start barking like the vicious attack dog he was until I remembered that Lindsey's parents had taken him on the day of the attack. It was better that way. I could barely take care of myself, much less a dog.

I had driven straight through the night to get home and then slept most of the day. I hadn't eaten in twenty-four hours. I wasn't hungry either, but I knew I'd have to force myself to eat again eventually. I would need strength to finish what I had started.

I rolled off the couch and stumbled to the door, peering out a nearby window through the blinds to see who was at the door. I saw two Sheriff's Office Tahoes parked out front and immediately thought they were there to arrest me. I had been careful in Jackson, but getting caught wasn't out of the realm of possibility.

I considered my options as I saw Deputy Hyatt and Deputy Parker standing near the door. Cops don't really do well in prison. Eating a bullet was a much better option. I wouldn't make those two do it either. Suicide by cop was a coward's way out. It was definitely a do-it-yourself job.

I walked back to the living room where I had left my Glock 19 sitting on the coffee table. The knocking continued as I gripped the handle and picked it up. I was probably headed straight to hell, but anything was better than the hell on Earth I was living – or would be living in prison.

"Alex, it's Cindy," Parker shouted. "Open the door."

I stood there, gun in hand, weighing my options. I kept picturing my teammates kicking the door in to see my brain matter splattered all over the walls. It was just as bad as the thought of getting into a shootout with them. They were like family to me. None of this was their fault. They didn't deserve to be put through that. "Strippergram!" Hyatt yelled. "We love you long time!"

I froze. *What the fuck?*

"C'mon, Alex, we know you're home," Parker added. "I'm here to check on you, and Hyatt…well, that's between you two."

"Housekeeping!" Hyatt yelled. "We fluff pillow?"

"Alex, if you don't open the door, we're going to call Fire and let them kick the door in," Cindy warned. "And you know how much they love that."

They have no idea. I exhaled, quickly putting the gun back on the coffee table and wiping my eyes. *Holy fuck.*

I walked to the door and regained my composure before opening it. Parker smiled as she saw me.

"You look like shit," she said. "You OK, boss?"

"Just trying to get some sleep," I said as I rubbed my eyes. "Until you two showed up."

"It's almost two," Hyatt said, looking at his watch. "You up all night snorting coke off hookers' asses or something? And if so, why didn't you call me?"

"You're still an idiot, Hyatt," I replied. "I just don't sleep much anymore."

"I get it," Cindy said. "The Lieutenant said he came by last night to check on you and you weren't around. Said your phone was turned off too, so he wanted us to check on you."

"I don't even know where my phone is," I said as I checked my pockets.

"Are you going to make us stand out here in the heat, or are you going to invite us in?" Hyatt asked as he adjusted his vest under his uniform. Cindy punched him in the arm and said something under her breath as they waited for my answer.

"Of course," I said, stepping aside. "Come on in, deputies. No meth labs to see here."

"Jesus, what happened to your hand, Alex?" Cindy asked as she walked in.

My right hand was bruised and slightly swollen, a holdover from the night before. I shoved it in my pocket as I closed the door behind them.

"Hitting the bag to let off some steam," I said sheepishly.

"Damn man," Hyatt said. "I'd hate to see the bag."

"You guys want a beer?" I asked as I went to the fridge. "Oh, that's right, you're on duty."

"Ha ha," Hyatt replied. "Dick."

"So what are you doing here again?" I asked while popping open my beer and walking back. "You're telling me you're both all caught up on your reports and you had nothing better to do?"

"Welfare check," Cindy replied. "You can check with dispatch if you like. It's in the system."

"I'll take your word for it, but if you must know, I spent most of yesterday across the lake talking to the FBI," I deflected.

"Sounds like a great day," Hyatt said. "I would've been more impressed if it had involved strippers though."

As I waited for Cindy to hip check Hyatt for being a dumbass, an unmarked Tahoe pulled into my driveway. Seconds later, the vehicle rocked as the Lieutenant exited and slammed the door shut.

"What is this, a goddamned party?" I asked as I went to the door. I took a long swig from the beer before opening the door. I didn't need all the attention.

"Alex!" Jacobson said as he approached. Like Hyatt and Parker, he was wearing the STPSO patrol uniform. "You had me worried. Where the fuck have you been?"

"Across the lake in New Orleans," I replied as I ushered Jacobson in. "Beer?"

"Just had one, thanks," Jacobson joked as he stepped through the doorway. "And I heard about your little trip to the FBI."

"Word travels fast," I said before downing the rest of the beer.

"It does when certain detectives find out you've gone around them," Jacobson said with a frown. "You know, chain of command and all that."

"That prick ain't in my chain of command, and you know it," I snapped.

"True," Jacobson replied. "But Detective Morris is still the liaison with the FBI on this case and would have preferred you liaise with him first."

"Fuck Morris," I growled.

Jacobson smiled. "Relax, Alex. I took care of it."

"He can kiss my ass."

"Well, he did give me an update on the case if you're interested," Jacobson said.

"Really? Did he just figure out that ISIS is behind it?"

"Sort of," Jacobson said with a grin. "But slightly better than that."

"What?"

"They found the money man behind the operation last night," Jacobson said.

"Really?" I asked, feigning shock. "Almost three months and someone finally did some police work?"

"Well, not exactly," Jacobson said, shrugging off my jab. "He was room temperature when they found him."

"Good," I said.

"Not even a little bit interested in who it was?" Jacobson asked with a raised eyebrow.

"Fuck no," I shot back. "Each and every asshole involved in killing my family deserves to be room temperature."

"Well, I'll tell you anyway," Jacobson said. "It was the Imam of the local mosque they had suspected the cell of operating from. Abdul or Abul or Kabul...Farah was his last name."

"Fuck him."

"Funny you mention that," Jacobson said. "He was into some really weird sex shit and died fucking, or at least that's what they think. They found his naked body dead of asphyxiation in a hotel known for prostitution flow-through. He had some pretty bad electrical burns and bruises on his face and a plastic bag over his head. He was into some really messed up stuff. They haven't found the hooker, but the desk attendant said he saw her enter the room with him."

"Again," I said, holding up a finger. "Fuck. Him."

Jacobson smiled. "I agree. I just thought you'd like to know."

"Is that it?"

"That's it." Jacobson shrugged his broad shoulders.

"No leads on any of the others?"

"Dead men don't do well in interrogation, Alex," Jacobson replied.

"What about the mosque? The other players? Finding Kamal Salman? Future attacks? You know, police shit," I said. My blood was boiling.

"Finding Kamal Salman?" Jacobson said, keying in on what I had just let slip. "He's dead, remember? *You* shot him."

"You're right," I said, shaking my head. "But you can't believe they were going to stop with just one attack."

"I don't know, Alex," Jacobson replied. "That's the FBI's investigation."

I let out a frustrated sigh.

"Do you know something, Alex?" Jacobson asked.

"I know there will never be justice for my girls," I replied. "Not with bureaucrats running this."

Jacobson put his giant hand on my shoulder. "You've been through hell. No man should see his child die. I am so sorry for your loss."

"Sorry doesn't bring them back," I said angrily.

"It doesn't, you're right," Jacobson said.

I walked to the door and opened it. "I think I want to be left alone now," I said.

"Fair enough," Jacobson said. Hyatt and Parker followed close behind "But do me a favor."

"What?" I snapped.

"The grief counselor will be at the LEC tomorrow," Jacobson replied softly. "Please talk to him. Just for a few minutes. It'll be good to get out of the house."

"Fine," I said motioning for them to leave.

"And, Alex," Jacobson said as he stopped at the door.

"Yeah?"

"Keep your phone on," he replied. "You had us all worried."

"Fine," I said as I ushered him out and closed the door behind him.

CHAPTER FIFTEEN

As expected, I couldn't sleep that night. I spent most of the night finding out everything I could about the names and addresses the fat Imam had given me.

The compound in Utica was the first area of interest. I pulled up satellite imagery, ownership information from the tax assessor's office, and anything else I could find on the internet.

It was buried deep within the Mississippi woods, accessible only by a small dirt road that snaked for two miles away from the main highway. There was an open field on an adjacent property, but otherwise, it was completely surrounded by trees – a perfect place to train and hide away from civilization as they planned their attacks.

The imagery was not great, but I could see that they had created a makeshift range in the back. They also had what appeared to be a mock-up of a school bus off to the side. They had practiced the operation long before executing it. It made my blood boil.

The tax assessor's website showed that the property was owned by the Mississippi Freedom Foundation. A two-minute search revealed that this was just another arm of the Coalition of Islamic-American Cooperation. I wondered if the Feds knew this yet. Or if they even cared, for that matter.

As my anger continued to build, I turned my attention to Kaleed Adid. Based in Atlanta, he was the Chairman of the Southeast Division of the Coalition of Islamic-American Cooperation. There were thousands of search hits to wade through.

The son of a Saudi Prince, Adid had been very vocal in the American Islamic community. There were hundreds of articles relating to his role in lobbying Congress for improved treatment of prisoners in Guantanamo Bay during the Iraq and Afghanistan wars. There were also conspiracy theory websites claiming his involvement with the oil lobby to give Iraqi oil contracts to the Saudis before the U.S. troop withdrawal.

Adid had also played a large role in the relocation of Syrian and Libyan refugees to America. He had called upon the current Administration to render aid and give shelter in America to those affected by "illegal American wars for oil." The more I read, the more convinced I was that Adid was everything the Imam had claimed him to be.

At 7 a.m., I headed to the Law Enforcement Center in Covington. There was much less fanfare when I entered this time. Aside from a few head nods and people asking how I was doing, no one made a big deal of my return. Everyone had seemingly moved on.

I saw Detective Morris near the coffee pot chatting it up with the front desk receptionist. He glared at me as I navigated the cubicles toward Lieutenant Jacobson's office where I was to meet the department's psychologist.

"You're here early," I heard Jacobson's booming voice say behind me as I neared the office. I turned around to see Jacobson holding a fresh cup of coffee. "Your appointment isn't for another half hour."

"Couldn't sleep," I said as I turned to shake his hand.

"You look like shit, Alex," Jacobson said. "Coffee?"

"Please," I said.

"I'll be right back," Jacobson said. "How do you take it?"

"Black," I said as I took a seat in a chair across from his desk.

"I heard that about you," Jacobson quipped with a hearty laugh.

I watched Morris scurry away as Jacobson poured the coffee into a styrofoam cup for me. Moments later, Jacobson returned and handed me the cup before closing the door and taking his place behind his desk.

He took a sip of his coffee and placed it on the desk as he leaned forward. "How are you, Alex?"

"How do you think?"

"As fucked up as any of us would be in your shoes," Jacobson admitted.

"So why ask?"

"Fair enough," Jacobson said. "Do any more late night field trips last night?"

I shifted uneasily in my chair. *Did he really know what I had been up to? Had I been that careless? Had Jacobson just been toying with me at my house the day prior?*

"I was home all night," I said flatly, trying not to open that can of worms.

"Good," Jacobson said. He seemed satisfied with that answer. "You need to get some sleep."

"I can sleep when I'm dead."

"At the rate you're going, that might not be too far off," Jacobson said. His forehead wrinkled. "Alex, I mean it. You can't let this kill you. Your girls wouldn't want you to give up like this."

"Have you talked to them lately?"

"No, but-"

"But nothing," I snapped. "They were murdered, and no one seems to want to do anything about it. Everyone has just moved on."

"That's not true," Jacobson said, shaking his head.

"Isn't it? Then why haven't there been any arrests?"

"Alex-"

"I'll tell you why," I barked. "Because of politics, that's why."

"Alex, the men behind the attack are all dead," Jacobson said.

"Who funded them? Who got them into this country? Do you think they just magically appeared?"

"It's terrorism, buddy," Jacobson said softly. "It's not that cut and dried. You take out one cell and three more pop up in their place."

"And you're cool with that? It's just the way the world works? That's it?"

"Hell no, I'm not OK with it. I'm furious that it happened, especially here. But you're fighting demons, Alex. You can't obsess over the who and the why. You have to work on picking up the pieces and moving on with your life before it kills you," Jacobson said.

I sat quietly, staring at the floor as the images of losing my wife and daughter that day raced through my head. The sounds of my daughter's helpless screams were deafening. I started to see red as the rage built inside me.

"It already did," I said without looking up.

"What do you mean?" Jacobson asked. He stood, walking around to the front of his desk where he sat and leaned over to get closer to me. "You're not dead, buddy. You still have a lot of life ahead of you."

I looked up at him, staring through him as the images continued to haunt me. "I died with my family in that parking lot."

Jacobson nervously looked at his watch. "Dr. Narby will be here in a few minutes, and you really need to talk to him. We can help you. You know I'm here for you."

I stood and tossed the empty styrofoam cup into the trash can by the door. "I'm done talking," I said calmly. I turned to walk out. Jacobson stood and followed me to the door.

"Where are you going?" Jacobson asked.

"Thank you for everything you've done for me, boss," I said.

"Alex, I can't let you leave," Jacobson said as he grabbed my arm.

I turned and looked at his hand before looking back up at him. "Let go," I said. He was twice my size, but he knew I would give him a fight if it came to it.

"You know I can't let you leave talking like that," Jacobson said. "I'll PEC you before I let you go home and off yourself."

A Physician Emergency Certificate, or PEC, was a certificate completed by a physician on a person exhibiting unsafe behaviors or suicidal or homicidal thoughts. We often used them in law enforcement to commit someone who demonstrated intent to kill themselves and needed psychiatric evaluation.

"I'm not going to kill myself," I said as I pulled my arm back and squared off with him.

"Talk to Dr. Narby then," Jacobson said. "If he says you're good to go, then that will be the end of it."

"So that's how it's going to be?"

"It's only because I care about you, Alex," Jacobson said. "You know I'm on your side."

"One chat," I submitted.

Jacobson shrugged his brawny shoulders. "Fine, but if I find out you clammed up on him, I'll call for a PEC."

"Whatever," I grunted. "Where is this guy?"

Jacobson looked out the glass behind me into the cubicle farm. "Good timing," he said as he pointed to a bald man with black glasses and a neatly trimmed beard. He looked to be about the same height as Jacobson and was wearing blue jeans and a peach-colored button-down long-sleeve shirt.

"Him?" I asked.

"He likes guns and race cars, so you two just might hit it off," Jacobson offered as he opened the door for me.

"Let's get this over with," I said as I followed Jacobson out.

Jacobson led me into the cubicle farm where he introduced me to Dr. Narby. We shook hands and then moved to one of the interview rooms. As we entered, I unplugged the hidden listening devices and covered the hidden cameras. I didn't need anyone spying on me.

"I didn't even realize those were there," Narby said as he pulled a notepad and pen out of his ledger and sat down.

"That's the point," I said as I sat down across from him and folded my hands on the table.

"My dad was a state trooper in New York," Narby said. "He always talks about how much he hates the way technology has changed things."

"Times have changed," I said. "He also didn't have to deal with terrorists killing his family."

Dr. Narby frowned. "You're right; the political landscape has changed in the last twenty years. I am sorry for your loss."

"Thanks," I mumbled.

"I'm not here to adversely affect your career, Alex. In fact, my goal is just the opposite. I'm here to listen and offer suggestions to help give you tools to deal with the stresses of what you've been through," Narby said.

"You think I care about a career?"

"You were a corporal and member of SWAT," Narby replied. "You have commendations and a very impressive resume. I think you did care very much at one point."

"Things change."

"I've spoken to many SWAT guys from different agencies, but never anyone from this one. What is the selection process like?" Narby asked.

"It sucks, but I don't see how that's relevant," I replied, annoyed by his attempt to change the subject.

"Humor me," Narby replied.

"I applied, went to the tryout, and they picked me," I said.

"That's it?" Narby asked.

"That's it."

"Wow," Narby said as he scribbled something on his notepad. "Cakewalk compared to other agencies. The guys across the lake made it sound like Hell Week in SEAL training."

"Jefferson Parish?" I scoffed. "Not even close."

"No?"

"No," I replied. "The tryout was sixteen hours of constant movement. They told me I was selected and then called me in the middle of the night to try out a few days later. We had to do the entire obstacle course in full kit for an hour straight. Some guys didn't even make it that far."

"Then what?" Narby asked.

"Then they loaded us up in the Bearcat and took us to the range. We had no idea where we were going. We had to do shooting drills. Running. Push-ups. Then they told us to navigate through the woods to a nearby range where they gave us more drills. And pull-ups, lots of pull-ups. Some guys puked. I didn't. I hadn't eaten anything."

"Did you want to quit?"

"Hell yeah, I wanted to quit. Especially when they made us run up and down the fire tower. It was something like ten stories.

There were ten of us, and only four made it through the whole thing. They only selected two."

"But you made it."

"Yeah. Then I went to Sniper School, which was another kick in the nuts," I said, remembering the endless pushups and running at the FBI's Sniper School.

"That sounds brutal," Narby said, still scribbling notes.

"It wasn't a picnic; I'll tell you that."

"What made you keep going?"

"My family," I said, closing my eyes. "My wife was the most beautiful woman I had ever known. I couldn't bear the thought of telling her I had failed."

"So you pushed on."

"I pushed on and kept going," I said. "I would have had the tryout kill me before going home to tell my wife she had married a quitter."

"Are you a quitter?" Narby asked as he looked me squarely in the eyes.

"No," I said flatly.

"A lot of people in your position would be, especially after what you saw," Narby replied.

I thought about it for a second before answering. "I wanted to die," I said as I watched his eyebrows rise. "But if you're asking if I would do it myself, the answer is no."

"And now?" Narby asked.

"What do you mean?"

"You said 'wanted' as in past tense. What about now?"

"That part of me is already dead."

"I see," Narby said as he went back to taking notes.

"Do you think I'm some crazy nut job that's going to off himself?" I asked as I watched him take notes.

"No," Narby said thoughtfully. "I think you're a man who's been through hell and back. Someone used to taking action and seeing things through, but you're now in turmoil because there's no closure here."

"No closure?" I asked.

"It's your personality type," Narby explained. "You're driven by righting wrongs. I read the personality profile from when you joined the agency. You seek justice for wrongdoings, but in this case, you can't."

"Can't?"

"It's the worst part of suicidal terrorists. Unlike a typical crime where you can arrest the perpetrator, there is no one to seek out here. The people responsible for the death of those children and your family died in the attack. Beyond that, you're fighting an ideology that has no face. There's no way to seek justice or closure due to the very nature of the crime."

"What am I supposed to do?" I asked.

"Find closure from within," Narby said. "Accept what is, so that you can let go of the injustice."

"So, you're saying just deal with it?"

"In a manner of speaking, yes," Narby replied. "But not alone. There are support groups that I think can help you with this."

"Don't bullshit me, Doc; are you going to send me to the hospital?" I asked impatiently.

Narby laughed. "No, I don't think you're a threat to yourself or anyone close to you, but I am going to recommend that your medical leave of absence with the department be extended while you work this out."

"Fine," I said.

"Take this time to find a support group. Travel if you feel up to it. While the rest of the world has had two months to deal with this, your wounds are still fresh. It's going to take time," Narby said.

"Travel," I repeated softly.

"Sometimes a change of scenery can help greatly."

"No, I like that, Doc," I replied. "I think I'm going to do some traveling."

CHAPTER SIXTEEN

The cemetery was buried deep in the woods, accessible only by a narrow asphalt road. I snaked slowly around the minefield of potholes as the rain pelted my truck's windshield. The first cold front of the fall had finally arrived, causing severe storms as it moved through the area.

As I turned onto the gravel drive of the small cemetery, the rain slowed to a steady drizzle. I followed the horseshoe path to the place where Jacobson had told me their graves would be.

I pulled up next to the site and killed the engine. I grabbed Maddox the Police Bear from the front seat and stepped out into the rain. The grave sites were covered with flowers, wreaths, and small flags.

I walked slowly to the foot of the graves. There were three headstones – two large ones and one smaller one. To the far left, I saw my own name. It showed my date of birth, but the date of death was blank. I guessed that Lindsey's parents had used the insurance money to buy a family plot. They hadn't given me much hope of survival. It was fitting.

The rain pouring down my face concealed my tears as I moved on to Lindsey's grave. It was adorned with flowers, both engraved and real.

A Beautiful Soul Who Loved Children, the epitaph read. Lindsey was a beautiful soul. She was the best person I had ever known. Every day she made me want to be a better man - *for her.* She gave me a reason to get up every morning and put on the uniform, knowing that I was keeping her safe.

But I had failed. I hadn't kept her safe. I had let very bad men come right into the area that I patrolled. Very bad men who killed her in the most horrific way possible as she tried to protect those children – as she tried hopelessly to pick up where I had failed.

I fell to my knees as I moved to Chelsea's little headstone. I sobbed uncontrollably as I saw the picture of her beautiful smiling face leaning next to it. She was my little angel.

As I sat on my knees crying, I pulled out my Glock from my concealed holster and held it loosely in my hand. My life had long been over. I had taken everything for granted – a loving wife, a beautiful daughter, a good job. And there I sat, staring at my own headstone. All that was left was to lay my body to rest.

I closed my eyes as I pressed the cold barrel against my chin. The wedding, the birth of Chelsea, the first time she said "Dadda," and all of the beautiful memories seemed to run through my mind. I imagined that's what heaven would be like. I adjusted my grip and moved my finger to the trigger.

As I started to apply pressure to the trigger, the images suddenly changed. I heard Chelsea's screams. I saw Lindsey's lifeless head in the hands of the madman. I saw the burning bus and Chelsea's little hand reaching up toward the windows.

I started to apply the three and a half pounds of pressure against the Glock's modified trigger when suddenly a wave of calm came over me. I saw Chelsea holding her stuffed bear as she proudly showed it to me.

He protects people just like you do, Daddy.

The calm turned to anger as I pushed the Glock away from my chin and opened my eyes. Chelsea's stuffed bear lay on the ground in front of me. I had dropped it as I had fallen to my knees.

I put the gun down and picked up the bear. I had spent my entire life trying to protect people, sometimes even from themselves. I wanted so badly to pull the trigger and join my family, but I realized that my work on earth was not done just yet.

I tucked the Glock back into its holster as I stood.

"I am so sorry, girls," I said softly as I stood clutching the bear in my left hand. "I let you both down."

I walked to Chelsea's little headstone and perched the bear on top as I squatted down. "I still have people to protect, baby girl. But I'll see you soon."

I walked back to my truck as the rain started to let up. I looked back one more time before opening the door. I knew the next time I'd be there was in a wooden box. It was a strangely comforting feeling.

I cranked the engine and started toward the exit of the cemetery as I set my GPS. My truck would be my new home. I had taken everything I needed and locked up. No cell phone. No radio. No way to communicate with the outside world. I had pulled enough cash out of my accounts to last for months – if I survived that long.

I headed toward Mississippi. It was time to go to work.

CHAPTER SEVENTEEN

It was early evening when I arrived in the sleepy Mississippi town of Utica. A lone patrol unit sat working radar on the side of the road near the town's only red light. The Crown Victoria looked to be about fifteen years old, which was at least three decades more modern than the rest of the town.

I checked my speed to ensure that I was adhering to the strict twenty-five mile per hour speed limit down the main drag. I didn't know how long I would need to operate out of Utica, but I certainly didn't want to draw the attention of law enforcement – especially with out of state plates.

The officer looked up and eyed me as I drove by. We made eye contact momentarily before he returned to whatever novel he was reading. If Islamic terrorists had been operating nearby, I wondered how they had evaded attention for so long. I couldn't imagine them blending in very well in a town like this.

Just as I had dropped my guard, I saw the Crown Vic spin around behind me with his blue and red lights activated. He chirped his siren, and I put my turn signal on to acknowledge him. I pulled into a nearby parking lot of an auto parts store as the patrons all seemed to stop and observe the traffic stop.

I lowered my window as I put the truck in park, keeping both hands on the steering wheel as I watched the officer behind me. His car rocked as he rolled out of the car and put his Smokey Bear hat on. He was wearing a light blue shirt and tan pants with a blue stripe. The man had to be pushing four hundred pounds.

I waited for him to waddle up to my window. He stopped at the tailgate of my truck and appeared to write down my plate information, an unusual tactic as far as officer safety was concerned, but I didn't intend to give him a lecture. I pulled my wallet out of my pocket and put it on my lap.

"Good evening, sir," he said with a thick drawl. "I'm Officer Tagnan with the Utica Police Department. Do you know why I pulled you over today?"

I cringed. As a Field Training Officer, it was a pet peeve of mine when police asked that question. We always taught our people to be courteous and direct when executing a stop. Tell them who you are and why you stopped them. Leave the guessing game out of it.

"Good evening, officer," I said with a smile. "No, sir, I do not."

"I had you doing twenty-eight back there," he said as he adjusted his oversized duty belt. "This is a twenty-five mile per hour zone."

"I didn't realize that, sir," I said. I opened my wallet, revealing my silver star. "For your safety and mine, you should know that I am carrying my duty weapon at this time and I have other weapons in the vehicle."

"Aw hell, you're a cop?" he asked as he pulled down his aviator sunglasses. He reached for the badge. I handed it to him and waited as he studied my ID.

"St. Tammany Parish, Louisiana?" he asked. "You're a little far from home ain't ya?"

"Yes, sir," I replied.

"What brings you this way?"

"Just doing a little traveling," I said.

"Traveling?" Officer Tagnan asked with a frown. "Nobody *travels* through here. What's really going on?"

I had to hand it to him. Despite his lax demeanor, he had a decent bullshit filter. I decided to come clean with him.

"I'm looking for this address," I said, handing him a piece of paper with the address I had scribbled down from my searches.

Officer Tagnan studied it for a moment and then handed it back to me. "That's the County Sheriff's case now. They've been pretty tight-lipped about it."

"You mean the FBI?" I asked, thinking the Feds had actually beaten me to the punch.

"No, I mean the Hinds County Sheriff's Office," he said, speaking slowly as if I had been having trouble understanding him. "And the Fire Marshall of course."

"Why? What happened?" I asked.

"Somebody burned the place down yesterday," Tagnan said, shaking his head. "Killed eight people."

"It was a Muslim retreat, wasn't it?" I asked.

"Something like that," Tagnan replied. "It's outside of town. They never bothered anybody here. I never even saw them pass through. There were rumors, of course. But I never saw any of them."

"What kind of rumors?"

"That they were terrorists," Tagnan replied.

"What did you think?"

"They never came near my town, so I didn't really care one way or another. The Feds came through here about a year ago to check it out. Said they found a fella dead on a fence post. I don't think anything ever came of it. Then a few months ago, after them attacks in Louisiana, Texas, and up north in Southaven, the Feds came back sniffing around, but from what I heard, they didn't find anything," Tangan said, shaking his head. "I'm sure they'll be back out here to investigate this too."

"What makes you say that?" I asked.

"Because it's a 'hate crime.' They love to stick their noses in stuff like that. I'm just glad it's out of my town," Tagnan replied.

"Is there anyone on the scene now?" I asked.

"Not as far as I know. Their camp is pretty far into the woods. They have the roads blocked off and a unit sitting on the road, but last I heard they finished their initial crime scene processing," Tagnan explained.

"I really appreciate the info," I said.

"You're welcome," Tagnan replied. "But I still need to see your license, registration, and proof of insurance."

"You do?" I asked, having been convinced that the reason for his stop was to simply see what an out-of-stater was doing in his town.

"Yes, sir," Tagnan replied. "We don't take speeding lightly in this town."

I handed him my information with a confused look on my face. He accepted it and said, "I'll be right back with you," before waddling back to his patrol car.

A few minutes later, the officer returned with a ticket for doing twenty-eight in a twenty-five in hand. He had me sign it with the familiar reminder that my signature is not an admission of guilt and then instructed me on how to mail in the fine should I choose to do so.

"I would turn around and go back to Louisiana if I were you," he said ominously, as he stuffed his pen back into his shirt pocket.

"Yeah?" I asked innocently, as I tossed the ticket onto my passenger seat.

"You're looking for trouble," he said. "I can see it in your eyes."

"Thanks for the advice," I replied. "But trouble has already found me."

Officer Tagnan shrugged his huge shoulders. "Suit yourself," he said. "Have a nice day."

I raised my window as Officer Tagnan returned to his patrol unit before killing his lights and heading back to his perch by the town red light. I stowed my information back in my center console and slowly merged back onto Main Street, headed out of town.

I pulled into a diner at the edge of town and had dinner as I waited for the sun to set. When it was dark, I paid the tab and made my way to the address I had for the compound.

I found the address off Highway 18. As Officer Tagnan had mentioned, there was a Sheriff's Department Tahoe blocking the driveway entrance. I maintained my speed as I continued, trying not to draw attention to myself. As I passed, I saw the road to the adjacent property was unguarded.

I drove two miles past the driveway and then turned around. The nearby property's entrance was about a quarter mile from the deputy standing watch. I turned onto the road and killed my lights, using my night vision scope to guide me down the winding road toward the open field I had seen on Google Earth.

Upon reaching the end of the road, I put my truck in park. Grabbing my scope, gloves, and handgun, I exited and locked the vehicle. I crept through the tall grass, careful not to make any noise as I headed for the nearby woods.

Using the scope to guide me, I moved slowly through the woods to the compound. There were no lights on, and the thick trees made it impossible to see without night vision.

As the compound came into view, I found a barbed wire fence. I briefly used my flashlight and found that someone had cut out a very small opening. There were also sensors of some kind on the top of the fence posts that appeared to have been disabled. *Military? SWAT?* It looked like the work of a tactical team.

I stepped through the small opening and continued toward the edge of the trees. I used my scope to scout the clearing. Only parts of the frame of the building still remained. It had been reduced to ash and rubble. It looked like a bomb had gone off.

I scanned for any sign of investigators. There were spotlights set up. They had probably worked well into the night before. Crime scene tape was tied to a small fence surrounding the remains of the compound. I followed it to the north side of the compound. There appeared to be targets set up. And then I saw the school bus.

I remembered it from the Google Earth imagery. There was half of a bus set up. There was no doubt that this was where they had trained to take down the school bus. My blood boiled as the flashbacks of that day came rushing back. *Chelsea. Lindsey.* My heart was racing.

I put down the scope and tried to catch my breath. I was almost hyperventilating as I felt the flood of emotions. *Sorrow. Sadness. Despair. Anger. Rage.* I focused on my breathing as I tried to calm down.

When I finally calmed down, I stepped slowly out into the open area. The ground was wet and muddy from the earlier rain. I walked toward the rubble. As I shined my flashlight on it, I could see markers where the debris looked different. I assumed that that was where the bodies had been dug out. There were seven markers.

I walked under the frame of the building and into what once was the main entryway. The odor was pungent. It still smelled like burning flesh and hair. I covered my mouth and nose with my shirt as I moved toward the north side of the building.

The back part of the building seemed to be much more open from what I could tell. I assumed the back was where they did most of their planning and work, while the front was used for living and sleeping.

The fire seemed to have affected the back area more than the rest of the building. I found the necks of glass vials. It reminded me of a meth lab that had burned to the ground. I wondered if this was where they built their explosives.

I kicked around the debris while shining my flashlight. I didn't know what I expected to find, but it didn't stop me from looking. I assumed the investigators had taken most of the worthwhile information before leaving the scene anyway.

As I searched the area, something glossy caught my eye near the corner of the room. I walked over to it. It was part of the room that hadn't been burned as badly. I bent down and pushed some of the debris out of the way, revealing a small photo that still had a thumbtack in it.

Shining the light on it, I studied it. It was a picture of a school bus picking up children at a stop. I wiped away the ash covering the side of the bus. The decals on the side read ST TAMMANY PARISH SCHOOLS in big block letters. I dropped the charred photo as my hands started shaking.

I started having another panic attack. I tried to take another deep breath, but the smell was still overwhelming. I ran out into the open area on the north side, coming face to face with the school bus. As I looked down, I saw casings for rifle rounds everywhere. They had used the area as a shooting range.

I finally caught my breath as I bent down and picked up a round. It was 7.62, just like the rounds used in the attack. The evidence was clear, but where were the perpetrators? What had happened to them?

I shined my light around some more, finding another evidence marker on the west side of the outer courtyard. I walked over to it and shined my light on it. There was no chalk outline, but blood stained the grass. It was the eighth body, confirming what the town cop had told me.

I had more questions than answers. *If it were a federal operation to take down the terrorists, why did it look like a murder investigation? Had there been a standoff? And if it hadn't been a takedown op, who had done it? Had someone beaten me to the punch?*

I killed the light and headed back toward the tree line and my truck. I decided that it was time to get the hell out of Mississippi and move on to my next objective.

CHAPTER EIGHTEEN

Good afternoon and thank you for coming to the second annual Islamaphobia Conference in Atlanta," Kaleed Adid said as he took the podium. "I am honored to speak to you all today, As-salamu alaykum."

I sat in the back of the crowded auditorium at the Islamic Center in Atlanta. I watched as the man with the dark black beard waited for the round of applause to cease so that he could begin his speech.

After leaving the terrorist training compound, I had driven through the night to Atlanta, the last known location I had found for Kaleed Adid. I paid cash for a room in a shady motel outside the city, using their spotty WiFi to find that Adid would be speaking at a conference the next day.

Despite my three-day stubble, I stood out like a sore thumb among the hundred or so Muslims gathered to hear Adid speak about their oppression in America. He went on about how Islamaphobia was a growing concern in their community, detailing his efforts with local government agencies to combat it.

I was about fifty feet away, but I could see the evil in the man. He had financed the murder of innocent children, my wife, and my daughter. In my mind, he deserved more than perceived oppression – he deserved extermination.

I scanned the room as Adid rambled on about the injustices and hardships that American culture placed on Muslims. The people in the room – almost all men – seemed captivated by the man. I wondered how many of them actually bought into his lies, how many were just there because they felt obligated, and how many were planning the next terror attack. It made my blood boil.

"We will continue to encourage common sense measures to stop American imperialism overseas, strengthen our relations at home, and continue humanitarian efforts here in America," Adid continued.

He went on to explain each item, lamenting the U.S. support of Israel and "foreign wars for oil." He spoke of legislation he had proposed that would enhance penalties for "hate crimes" and further restrict law enforcement from what he called "illegal spying on places of worship."

"We must care for our brothers from Syria, Libya, and Iraq – victims of American foreign policy failures. We have been successful in giving their women and children safe haven here in America, but we must not stop there. We must ensure that anyone who wishes to flee the war-torn regions can come here safely and worship in peace," Adid said.

Refugees. Jacobson had mentioned that some of the attackers had been thought to have come to America as refugees from Iraq and Syria. The attackers that killed my family had managed to blend in amongst the women and children that flooded into New

Orleans. It was clear to me that Adid was using it as a channel to get battle-hardened soldiers into America.

Adid finished his speech with a call to living life in America in strict accordance with the Quran. The room erupted in applause as he thanked everyone for attending and exited the stage. I watched as he embraced several of the more senior members in the audience and made his way toward the exit.

I had parked my truck on a side street with a good view of the front entrance of the Islamic Center. As Adid said his goodbyes, I disappeared into the crowd and made my way to my truck. He and his entourage were just arriving at his makeshift motorcade parked out front as I started the engine.

I watched as the three-vehicle convoy comprised of white Cadillac Escalades sped out of the parking lot. I pulled out behind them at a safe distance, allowing cars to get between us on the four-lane highway.

I tailed them through the side streets of Decatur and onto I-285. They sped along the highway at speeds in excess of ninety miles per hour, ignoring the posted speed limits as they headed south.

They slowed only to merge onto I-20 before resuming their ridiculous speeds. I kept my distance, but at the speeds they were traveling, I had no choice but to pace them. I kept an eye out for Georgia Troopers. The last thing I needed was more attention from law enforcement.

When they were well out of the city, the motorcade exited the interstate and blitzed down back roads. I followed them until they turned off into a narrow driveway. I watched as iron gates closed behind the last vehicle. The driveway looked to be about a quarter mile long before it opened up to a circular drive in front of a huge mansion. The son of the Saudi prince wasn't hurting for money.

I passed the driveway slowly as I took it all in. The gated mansion was a tactical nightmare, especially with the security Adid seemed to have. If I wanted to get some one-on-one time, I'd have to either grab him at an event, or launch a night time assault. Neither option seemed to give me great odds of success.

I continued past the drive and pulled into a neighboring driveway to turn around. As I passed the mansion one more time, I tried to take in as much as I could. Surveillance would be a pain in the ass. I found myself wishing I had the Sheriff's Office air unit available. It was nice for SWAT to always have real-time airborne imagery, and the Cessna could remain airborne for hours before and during an operation. If I decided to assault the compound, I'd be flying blind.

I wrote down Adid's address on my scratch pad and headed back toward the motel. As much as I wanted to kick the door in and put a gun in Adid's mouth, I needed to step back and evaluate the tactical situation first.

CHAPTER NINETEEN

I spent a week doing surveillance on Adid. I had found a place outside his compound to watch his movements in and out of the area on a daily basis. After a week, I felt like I had a good handle on his daily routine.

Adid was a man of strict habits. Every morning, I watched as he went to morning prayer at a nearby mosque from 7 a.m. to 9 a.m. From there he would return home, and then his motorcade would assemble and take him to the city.

He had an office in downtown Atlanta. It was the headquarters for the Coalition of Islamic-American Cooperation, Southeast Division. He would spend anywhere from four to six hours there before returning to his compound unless he had a speaking engagement or other event.

I waited patiently in the woods as I watched the one-lane road beneath me. It was a spot I had picked due to its relative isolation, concealment, and elevation. It gave me a good vantage point from which to view the trap I had set up.

I squatted in the brush as I checked my watch. It was 0645. My adrenaline surged as I mentally walked through my plan one more time. It was the same feeling I had gotten just before every SWAT roll. The anticipation. The nervousness. The excitement. I stretched my finger against the trigger guard of my Daniel Defense M4 rifle.

I had rented a Honda Civic earlier and parked it on the road below my position. I had left its hood and trunk open, removed the back left wheel, and leaned it against the side. The hazard lights were also flashing.

I heard a vehicle in the distance. I shouldered my rifle and checked the bait vehicle one more time through the Trijicon 4 x 32 ACOG scope. I would have preferred a Remington 700 sniper rifle for the task at hand, but my SWAT weapon had been taken, and I didn't want to risk the purchase. At just over a hundred yards, the M4 would be more than sufficient.

The sound of the approaching vehicle grew louder, and I could see its headlights in the distance. Although the sun had started its upward trek, the trees cast shadows over the narrow road, keeping it in relative darkness. I watched through my scope as the Cadillac Escalade came into view. The SUV slowed to a crawl as it approached and then stopped behind the Honda.

The SUV sat still for what seemed like an eternity. I imagined Adid's men debating about what to do next as they assessed the threat. I was counting on the fact that Adid traveled with a small security detail of only two men when going to morning prayer. I could picture them arguing over who would go out and check the disabled vehicle.

The driver exited and walked toward the rental car. He stopped at the left rear tire and studied it for a moment before cupping his hands against the window and peering inside. I followed him through my scope as he realized no one was in there and walked around to the front of the Civic.

As the driver looked around for signs of the owner of the disabled vehicle, the passenger exited the front seat of the Escalade. He was much less casual about the vehicle. I watched him draw his weapon as he approached the passenger side and waved at the driver to step away.

I slowly started making my way down the hill as I kept watch for any additional guards. The unarmed driver turned back toward the Escalade. I flicked the select fire switch to SEMI and dropped to a knee. As he stopped again at the removed rear wheel, I steadied the crosshairs on his head and squeezed the trigger.

The crack of the rifle echoed through the shallow valley. The armed passenger instantly spun around and fired wildly in my direction. I calmly shifted my aim and acquired him in my sights, aiming for center of mass, just below the throat. I fired twice, striking him as he managed another unaimed shot before falling face first onto the pavement.

I quickly traversed down the remaining fifty yards of the hill, keeping my rifle up as I watched for additional men to emerge from the SUV. As I reached the bottom, the passenger door was suddenly flung open and Adid emerged.

I stopped as we made eye contact. Adid tried to take off running toward the front of the Escalade, but I stopped him with a well-placed round to the back of his knee. I approached slowly, clearing the interior of the Escalade as Adid screamed in agony and tried to drag himself away from me.

Satisfied that there were no remaining threats in the vehicle, I dropped the M4 against its single-point sling and retrieved my flex-cuffs. I grabbed Adid by the back of his shirt and shoved my boot into his bloody leg. I drove him face first into the ground and put my knee on his neck as I went to work.

"Who are you?" he screamed as he grunted in pain.

"We'll get to that," I said as I secured his hands behind his back.

I picked him up and dragged him to the Escalade, tossing him in the back, slammed the open door shut, then took my place in the driver's seat.

"Where are you taking me?" Adid demanded. "This is kidnapping!"

"Nothing gets by you," I said sarcastically as I flipped the car around and pushed the accelerator to the floor.

CHAPTER TWENTY

I took Adid to a nearby construction site I had found during my surveillance. It had been abandoned, and a cursory internet search had revealed that the project to build the isolated distribution warehouse had gone bankrupt and the property was in foreclosure.

"Where are you taking me?" Adid again demanded from the back seat as I approached the locked gate. *Duct tape. Damn it. I knew I had forgotten something.*

Without slowing, I charged through the flimsy gate and onto the construction site. The frame of the warehouse was mostly finished, but there were only three walls. It was enough to keep me concealed from any passersby.

I drove around to the back of the site to hide the Escalade. Adid tried to squirm away from me as I opened the back door, but I grabbed him by the hair and dragged him out into the bright sun.

"You can't do this!" Adid screamed. "I have rights! Do you know who I am?"

"Yeah," I grunted as I hauled him into the building. I had pre-positioned a folding chair and supplies in the center of the room earlier that morning. I walked him to the chair and shoved him down onto it. I flex-cuffed his feet together, then used a third cuff to anchor the hand and foot cuffs together. His back was arched in a stress position. He grunted in pain.

"What do you want from me?" Adid asked nervously.

"You're the money man, right?" I asked as I stood over him. "For terrorists."

"I don't know what you're talking about! I am an advocate for Muslim rights!"

I flicked open my Gerber tactical knife and drove it into the thigh of his good leg and twisted the blade around. The leg I had shot was still bleeding. He screamed out before I covered his mouth with my gloved hand.

"Shut the fuck up," I said. "You don't know pain, yet."

"Who are you?" Adid demanded.

"Who am I?" I repeated.

"CIA? FBI? Mossad?" Adid asked frantically. "Do you know who my father is? Do you know how much money we give your governments every year? You cannot do this to me!"

"My name is Alex Shepherd," I said as I walked over to the five-gallon gas can I had staged nearby. "I'm currently unemployed."

"What do you want?" Adid asked. "What is your price?"

I picked up the gas can and twisted open the spout. I carried it to Adid as he squirmed, watching me. I poured the gasoline into the fresh, open wound as he screamed in pain.

"I want my family back," I said as I watched Adid writhe in pain.

"Who are you?" Adid shouted.

"Did you recognize the disabled car routine?" I asked as I put the gas can back down. "I learned it from you."

"What are you talking about?"

"August 27th, a school bus full of children, a retired principal, and my wife were killed when your thugs staged a disabled vehicle and took control of the school bus in Mandeville, Louisiana. Sound familiar?"

"I heard about that on the news. It was awful!" Adid yelled, avoiding eye contact.

I punched Adid in the gut, causing him to flip backward in the chair. As he landed, I put my boot on his chest.

"You funded it," I said.

Adid shook his head in denial as he gasped for air.

"You're going to lie to me?" I asked as I stared down at him.

"You are going to kill me either way," Adid said defiantly. "Why should I tell you anything?"

I pulled out my Glock 19 from my drop leg holster and pointed it at his forehead. "Because if you don't, I'm going to make you wish you were dead. So you can either die quickly or die a slow, painful death. Doesn't matter to me. I have all day."

"Fuck you, infidel!" Adid said angrily. "You don't scare me."

"Suit yourself," I said. I removed my boot from his chest and walked back to the gas can. I returned, putting my boot on his throat as I poured the gasoline onto his face. The odor was intense. Adid choked and coughed as he turned his head away to avoid the waterfall of fuel in his face.

With the gas can half empty, I stepped away from Adid's throat and put the can down. Adid coughed and choked on the fuel. His eyes watered. He tried to spit out the fuel that he had ingested.

"We can do this all day," I said calmly as I squatted down next to him.

"Yes! Ok!" Adid shouted. "I did!"

"You did what?"

"I funded it. Are you happy?"

"Who directed the operation?" I asked.

"What?"

"Where did you get your orders? Where did you get the money?"

"ISIL"

"Who?" I asked.

"The Islamic State!"

"Give me a name. A person," I pressed.

Adid laughed. "The Islamic State is more than a person. It is the future. It is the caliphate!"

I gave Adid a quick heel stomp to the sternum. "Don't get cocky, dumbass. Who was in charge of planning this?"

"Tariq Qafir," Adid said as he recovered from the blow.

"Where is he?"

"Dead. You Americans killed him in Mississippi a year ago. He is a martyr for the glory of Allah!"

"Who killed him?" I asked.

"CIA? FBI? You? You Americans fight with no rules like the devils that you are," Adid said.

I squatted down and grabbed Adid by the hair. I could feel my heart beating in my chest as the rage built. "No rules? Like killing innocent women and children? And burning them alive? Those kind of rules, you sick fuck?" I snarled.

"It had to be done," Adid said. "You Americans are all the same. You send your mercenaries to fight wars overseas for money and oil. You never see the cost of war. You idolize war."

"Who sent Tariq whatever his name is? Who is in charge? Who sent Tariq here?"

"Ayman Awad al-Baghdadi," Adid replied weakly.

"Who is he?"

"He is the head of Foreign Operations for the Islamic State," Adid replied.

"How do I find him? How do I stop him?"

"You want to kill al-Baghdadi?" Adid laughed again. "Naïve Americans. You cannot hope to stop us. For every one you kill, there are a hundred more holy warriors that will rise up to take his place. It is the will of Allah!"

I slammed his head into the concrete floor. There was a loud crack, but Adid maintained consciousness.

"Where is the other one from the attack in Mississippi? The twin? What is he planning?"

Adid was dazed, but still somewhat coherent. "He's dead. Your men killed him."

"At the training compound in Mississippi? Who killed him?"

"American Special Forces," Adid said. "CIA. A kill team. You?"

"Wasn't me," I said.

"What do you want, then?" Adid asked. "I have told you all that I know. Release me and I will pay you double whatever your government is giving you."

"I'm doing this for free," I said.

"No one does anything for free," Adid said. "What do you want? I have a family!"

"So did I," I said. "I loved my wife and daughter more than anything in the world."

The realization suddenly became apparent in Adid's face. "I didn't kill them!"

I stood and picked up the gas can. I poured the remaining gasoline all over Adid from head to toe.

"You are going to burn in hell for this! Just like your family!"

"Poor choice of words," I said as I pulled out a lighter, flicked it open, and tossed it on Adid.

Adid screamed in agony as he burned alive. I turned and walked out. As satisfying as it was to watch him burn for the murder of my family, I still felt pent up rage inside me. I knew there were more vile terrorists than just Adid responsible for the death of my family, and Ayman Awad al-Baghdadi was at the top of that list.

I decided to do some more traveling.

CHAPTER TWENTY ONE

My thirst for vengeance wasn't quenched with Adid. After ditching the Cadillac, returning the rental car, and retrieving my truck, I headed out of town.

I stopped at a café with WiFi access and read up on the attack that had killed my family. I had avoided the news and internet since it happened. I didn't want anything to do with it, but after talking to Adid, I had to know more about the sick coward that had taken responsibility for the murder of my family.

Ayman Awad al-Baghdadi was that lowlife thug. I found videos he released shortly after the attack. They showed a man very proud of himself as he condemned the "infidels" and rejoiced at the victory struck against the "Great Satan." It showed the media footage from the news helicopters that filmed the burning bus. Al-Baghdadi vowed that it would be the first of many victories in their fight to secure the Middle East.

There were more videos, but not from the attack. Al-Baghdadi loved the camera, especially when it involved bragging about some horrific act. I watched them all. He burned children in cages, beheaded Iraqi soldiers, and drowned a Kurdish fighter. It was horrific. As the camera zoomed into his face on the last image, I saw the evil that lived within. His eyes were as black as night. He showed no remorse whatsoever.

In a related search, I found a video of an interview of a man who traveled from New Jersey to Iraq to fight with the Kurds. He talked about the injustices he had seen and the American government's unwillingness to do anything about it, and how that had driven him to act. He described some of the battles he had been in and the warrior spirit of the Kurdish People's Protection Units that fought ISIS.

At the end of the video, there was a link to a Facebook page called the Lions of Rojava. I clicked on it, finding a call to recruit foreign fighters with instructions on how to discretely contact them.

I took down the contact information as I finished my coffee. I conservatively guessed that I only had a few days before someone would discover the bodies of Adid and his men, and I would become a person of interest. I had no intention of going to jail.

I wanted to continue the fight. I knew the U.S. military wouldn't take me. I was too old, and it would take months for me to get to the front lines. My thirst for the blood of more terrorists was steadily growing.

I left the coffee shop and went to a nearby shopping center. I found a store selling prepaid cell phones and bought two. After I activated the first one, I called the number on the Facebook page.

"Hello," a man with a thick southern drawl answered.

I froze. What do you say to someone seeking mercenaries? *Yes, I'm calling about your ad to go kill terrorists?*

"Hello?" the man repeated.

"I'm responding to your ad," I said. "The one on Facebook."

"What state are you in?" the man asked quickly.

"Georgia," I replied.

"Do you have a vehicle?" the man asked.

"I do."

"Go to this address at 7 p.m„" the man said. I scrambled to write down the information he relayed before he hung up abruptly.

The address was outside of Atlanta near the airport. I decided to do some surveillance since I had several hours before my appointment. I ditched the phone and started driving.

I arrived shortly after 4 p.m. The address appeared to be a small car repair shop. I double-checked it against my GPS several times and decided that however suspect the shop looked, it must be the place.

I went to a nearby chain restaurant and ate a long dinner, agonizing over the decision as I downed beer after beer. *Was this a trap? What if they were really ISIS? Could I really go to a foreign country and fight? Was I ready to die?*

The answer to the last question was the easiest. It was a resounding yes. In fact, I hoped it killed me. I couldn't imagine growing old with the memories of my family haunting me. Going down in a hail of bullets was the best way for me, and I wasn't about to attempt "suicide by cop" like a coward.

The other questions weren't as easy to answer. I had nothing holding me from going overseas. My family was dead. My friends would move on. My in-laws already had the wiener dog. As far as they were concerned, I was already dead anyway. They hadn't even bothered to make contact once I had gotten out of the hospital. No one would shed a tear.

The question of whether I was walking into a trap, or not, really bothered me. I couldn't imagine the recruiting process being so simplistic. I had read hundreds of reports of Americans getting hemmed up by the Feds for trying to provide material aid to ISIS. Prison scared me more than anything. If this turned out to be an FBI sting, I would have to go down shooting, risking innocent agents just trying to do their jobs. I didn't like it.

I paid my tab and walked back to my truck. I was slightly buzzed. In the past, I never would've even considered driving, but with no career and nothing left to live for, I didn't care.

I drove back to the car repair place. The OPEN sign in the window had been flipped to CLOSED. I checked my watch – I had fifteen minutes before the 7 p.m. meeting time. I parked across the street and waited, watching for signs of movement inside the office. There were none.

At five minutes to seven, I started to second guess the address again. The place looked empty. Was that part of it? Were they waiting for me to show up? The hair was standing up on the back of my neck.

As the clock in my truck hit 7 p.m., I put my truck in drive and started to drive off. I watched the office as I drove away for any signs of life, but to no avail. It was still empty. As I turned my attention back toward the road, I slammed on my brakes, coming within inches of hitting two men crossing the street. I waved apologetically as they glared at me and continued toward the shop. I sat in the middle of the street, watching them.

The two men walked through the gravel parking lot and headed toward the west side of the building, away from the office. They disappeared behind a parked SUV near the side of the building.

A car honked its horn behind me. I pulled over to the side of the road and parked. I killed the engine and exited. I checked the Glock 19 concealed on my right hip and grabbed a spare magazine from the door of my truck, stuffing it into the cargo pocket of my 5.11 tactical pants as I slammed the door shut.

I cautiously walked across the street, following the same path as the two men I had nearly hit. I could see a light on near the back of the shop as I passed the parked SUV. I continued to the back where I found an open door. I peered inside to see a tall, slender man standing in front of four others.

The man stopped as he saw me. "Please, come in," he said with a warm smile. I recognized his voice as the man from the phone call. I stepped in slowly as the others turned to look at me.

They were mostly young. Two of them had full beards with light eyes. One appeared to be old – close to sixty. And the fourth man had a Mohawk and several tattoos on his neck.

"You are in the right place, friend," the man said as I stopped near the door. I kept my right hand loose by my side, ready to draw if I had to.

One of the bearded men stepped toward me and extended his hand. "I'm Chase Robbins," he said. "We're all here to kill us some goatfuckers."

I reluctantly shook his outstretched hand. He had a Confederate Flag tattooed on the inside of his wrist.

"We spoke on the phone, yes?" the man in front asked.

I nodded as my eyes darted to the hands of each man in the room.

"Then we are all friends here," the man said. "Please, join us."

I motioned for him to continue, staying firmly planted where I was near the exit.

"As I was saying," the man continued. "My name is Jordan Watson, and I am helping to recruit for the Kurdish People's Protection Units. I would like to thank you all for coming here. As you can imagine, your discretion is also very much appreciated."

"Come with me," Watson said, motioning for the group to follow.

I trailed behind, keeping an eye out for potential threats and escape routes. The situation had sobered me considerably. I was on high alert, and my adrenaline was pumping. It felt like an undercover operation.

Watson led us through the mechanic bays of the repair shop into another room. It looked like a break room. There was a coffee pot near the sink, a muted TV playing the evening news in the corner, and a table with six chairs.

"Please, have a seat," Watson said. The others immediately took seats and faced him. Watson watched me as I hesitated.

"It's OK," he said as if coaching a nervous child on his first day of school.

I sat at the head of the table, opposite where Watson stood. I had a good view of the others, and my back wasn't to the door. It was the best I could do tactically, given the situation.

"I am here recruiting for this mission because I have been there," Watson continued. "I spent a year in the Kurdish territories in Iraq and Syria before coming back here to help recruit. I have seen the many horrors of that war, and what our government fails to do."

"Did you kill any of them fuckers?" one of the bearded men asked.

"Killing is not something I enjoyed doing, but yes, I did. I have killed many of the Daesh fighters, and they have killed many of my friends. Make no mistake; this is nothing like the movies," Watson explained.

"Daesh?" the older gentleman asked.

"It's the true name for the Islamic State, or at least, the one we use to piss them off. They hate it because it's the Arabic acronym for ISIS, but the word also means bigot, which they hate. They have threatened to cut the tongues out of anyone who uses it. So, Daesh it is!" Watson replied.

"Should you choose to join the fight," Watson continued, "we will arrange for your travel. You could leave tomorrow or three months from now. The choice is yours. Once you arrive, you will be picked up by one of our fighters and taken to your base. Don't worry; we tend to group Americans with other English-speakers. From there, you will train with the Kurds before you are sent to fight."

"What is the training like?" the man with the Mohawk asked.

"What's your background?" Watson asked.

"Five years as an Eleven Bravo before I got discharged for smoking weed after coming back from Afghanistan," the man replied.

"Eleven Bravo, that's infantry, right?" Watson asked.

The Mohawk gentleman nodded.

"Shouldn't be more than a week or two," Watson replied. "You may even be asked to train the newer fighters yourself. Make no mistake; you are not going to war with Blackhawks and air support and the finer things the American military brings. This is a pick-up game. You're fighting for something more than that."

"Why are we fighting?" I asked.

"Have you seen what Daesh has done?" Watson asked.

"Firsthand," I said. I leaned back with arms folded, waiting for Watson to continue his speech.

"Then you know why we fight. I've seen them brutally murder men, rape women and children, and burn their bodies. They are sick, and they will not stop until they push their agenda on the entire world," Watson said. "They are a threat to the Kurds, Israelis, Christians, Jews – anyone who stands in the way of the caliphate."

"Just to be clear," Watson continued, "if you sign up for this, you're not fighting for America or the Brits or NATO. You're fighting for a common good to stop a violent and brutal regime from continuing their push to overtake the Middle East. The U.S. government won't bail you out. If you die, they won't play taps at your funeral or give your families a neatly folded flag. As far as they're concerned, you're signing your own death warrant. Are you ok with that?"

Watson paused and looked at each person in the room, waiting for a nod or gesture of agreement. "What about you?" he asked as he got to me.

"I'm counting on it," I said. "When do we leave?"

CHAPTER TWENTY TWO

I was the first of the group to leave for Iraq. I stayed with Watson for two days in his small two-bedroom apartment as he made my travel arrangements.

He was a single guy, no family, no kids. He had flown to Iraq after seeing mass executions of Christians on the news. He was a very religious man. "A man finds God in war," he said often.

He gave me a good idea of what to expect. With my training and experience, I would be one of the first to go out on the front lines. He had been intentionally vague in the recruiting pitch in describing the organization of the Kurdish militia. He guessed that only a few of those that went would actually see direct action.

Watson explained that when he first arrived, it was the wild west. The Kurds were taking anyone that could hold a rifle. They would use them in combat regardless of experience or training.

But they soon found that the system was unsustainable. The foreign fighters, however well intentioned, had trouble integrating with the People's Protection Units or Yekîneyên Parastina Gel (Y.P.G). Most of the foreigners only spoke English, some not even that. When they started dying, changes had to be made.

The first change was to establish training. Watson had mentioned it in his recruiting briefing. All new fighters were given two weeks' worth of basic infantry training – training the Kurds had picked up from American Special Forces and American Army field manuals. It wasn't enough to make a civilian with no experience a warrior, but it was enough to at least instill some structure.

The second change was to create units for the foreign fighters. The fighters were given a rank structure and reported directly to their Kurdish counterparts. These units consisted of ten to twelve fighters. They were sent on missions with the Kurdish YPG based on experience and skill level.

The final change was to limit the direct action of the foreign units. The less experienced units were relegated to staying behind to guard villages and places of interest while the Kurds engaged ISIS on the battlefield. They were given more administrative functions, like stocking supplies and burning trash. The men with more training and experience were allowed to integrate with the YPG only on a case-by-case basis.

Watson described some of the men that joined – former military, drifters, Iraqis, criminals. They ran the gamut from willing and able to distracting and divisive. He said that sometimes, with all the different characters, it felt like a really bad Spaghetti Western.

I asked Watson about his combat experience before heading to Iraq. "I was a travel agent," Watson had said in his thick southern accent. "The most action I had seen was in video games." He told me about the first time he killed a man and the nightmares that followed. He hadn't been sure if he could do it again, but sure enough, he did. Time and again, until he became a well-respected fighter.

"Respect is important in their culture," Watson told me. "More so than here. If you earn your keep and do well, they will treat you like a brother."

After the arrangements and coordination had finally been completed, Watson drove me to the airport on Saturday morning. I wasn't nervous. That feeling had finally subsided. I was just ready to get to work and face the evil that had taken everything from me.

"Don't burn yourself out over there," Watson warned as he helped me with my bags. "PTSD is a real thing. If you don't take some time and come home, you'll lose yourself over there."

I knew that I had nothing left to lose, but I thanked him for the advice anyway. He left me at the ticketing counter and headed back to his car, presumably to help the next set of recruits with their journey. He never mentioned if they were paying him for his services or if the money was coming from somewhere else, but I never asked either.

I was nervous as I went through security. I kept waiting for one of the TSA agents to pull me aside and cuff me as Atlanta PD took me into custody for the murder of Adid. It was a feeling that would repeat itself going through every customs checkpoint along my route.

I flew from Atlanta to Norway, where I had a six-hour layover. I got a nice buzz off the Norwegian beer in the airport, figuring it would be the last time I'd ever partake. I had always heard that the Middle Eastern countries were very dry, both in climate and alcohol consumption.

From Norway, I flew to Dubai where I got my first glimpse into the new culture. Although Dubai was a very modern city, it felt like I had traveled to another dimension. The smells, the sights, the sounds – all were very different than anything I'd experienced growing up in rural Louisiana. It was the first of many culture shocks in my journey.

It was dark when my flight from Dubai to Sulaymaniyah landed in Iraq. I located the fake taxi – a beat up Mercedes C-class – as Watson had instructed. The driver introduced himself as Kara and told me to put my duffel in the trunk.

He was silent as he took me to a safe house just outside of Erbil. Despite my jet lag, I was on high alert for the entire drive, worried that he might really be a Daesh fighter that had come to kidnap me.

Kara stopped the vehicle in front of a run-down wooden house. By the time I was out of the vehicle, he had already retrieved my bag from the trunk and tossed it into the dirt.

"You stay here," he said in broken English.

"What time is it?" I asked.

Kara shrugged his shoulders as he returned to the car and sped off. *So much for a hero's welcome.*

I walked up the steps as the wood creaked beneath my boots. I took a deep breath and knocked on the door. Seconds later, a man opened it.

"You're the last one?" the man asked. He was young – I guessed in his early to mid-twenties. He had sandy blonde hair, blue eyes, and pale skin. He was wearing cargo pants and a Superman t-shirt.

"I suppose so," I said. Another man appeared behind him – much older. He had a full salt-and-pepper beard and balding head. They both appeared to be Americans.

"I'm Dave Frost," the younger man said, extending his hand. "That's Abe."

I shook his hand quickly as I walked inside. The house was empty except for six cots, an ice chest, and a portable stove. It couldn't have been more than a thousand square feet. It was dusty and bare.

"Alex Shepherd," I said as Frost closed the door behind me. Abe waved politely and went back to his cot. He picked up a knife and started sharpening it, ignoring Frost and me.

"They said they'd come get us in the morning," Frost said as he took my bag from me. He walked it to a cot and put the bag down next to it. "This is where you can rest."

"What time is it?" I asked. I hated the displaced sense of time. My body was telling me it should be daytime, but it was pitch black outside.

"Almost midnight," Frost replied. "Where are you from?"

"Louisiana," I said as I took in my surroundings.

"I'm from Michigan," Frost said before turning to Abe. "He's from Ohio. Abe doesn't talk much."

"Me neither," I said.

"Do you want water?" Frost asked, pointing to the cooler. I nodded and he opened it up. There was no ice, just a dozen or so water bottles standing upright at the bottom. He handed it to me and smiled. As I twisted the cap, I realized that the bottle had been refilled previously.

"You get used to it," Frost said as he saw my hesitation. "First time in country?"

"Yeah," I said. "You?"

"First time as a civilian. I came here in 2012 with the Army," Frost said.

"2012?" I asked. "What were you…twelve years old?"

Frost laughed. "I get that a lot. I'm twenty-four. Joined when I was seventeen. We didn't see any action, just helped pack up Baghdad. I was an Information Technology Specialist. What's your background?"

"I'm a cop," I replied.

"I fucking hate cops," Abe grunted from the back, still working on his knife.

"Great," I said.

"Well, on that note, I think I'm gonna hit the rack and get some shut eye before Cotkar gets here," Frost said.

"Who?" I asked.

"Cotkar," Frost repeated. "Didn't they tell you anything? He's going to take us to Kirkuk tomorrow. That's where we'll start training and learn our assignments."

"I guess I didn't get the memo," I said.

"Don't worry, I'll help you," Frost said warmly before retiring to his cot.

I sat on my cot and unfolded the wool blanket sitting on the meager pillow. I could see Abe eyeballing me when he wasn't studying his knife.

I could tell it was going to be another long night.

CHAPTER TWENTY THREE

I was still awake when the front door was kicked open and the single halogen light bulb was flicked on. Three men stormed in, doing their best impressions of Marine drill sergeants as they yelled at us.

I was on my feet before the last man entered. I saw the other two men sit up in their cots. Frost sat up and started putting his boots on while Abe lazily stretched. I had slept in my clothes – khaki 5.11 tactical pants, a polo shirt, and boots – the night prior. I was exhausted and jet-lagged, but my heart was racing. It felt like the first day of the police academy.

"Get up! This is war!" one of the men yelled. He had a Middle Eastern accent. Two of the men had thick, black beards and were wearing bandannas. The third appeared to be American. His beard was lighter. They were all wearing desert camo fatigues.

"Rise and shine, princess!" the third man yelled. He sounded like a Texan. Unlike the others, he had a sleeveless shirt. There was a Marine globe and anchor tattooed on his right shoulder.

I stood with my arms to my sides, waiting for the yelling to inevitably turn my way. The Marine turned toward me and stepped to within a few inches of my face.

"What about you, sweetheart? Are you scared? You just gonna stand there?" the Texan asked.

"No, sir," I said calmly. I looked over to see Frost and Abe standing by their cots, holding their duffels at a modified position of attention.

"Then what are you waiting for? Grab your shit and let's go!" the Marine said.

I casually picked up my duffel. The wannabe drill instructors herded us into a straight line by the door.

"Gentlemen, this is a war zone," the Marine said as he paced back and forth sizing each of us up. "I don't care what your background is or where you're from. You've never seen shit like you'll see in this country."

"Welcome to Iraq – the frontline in the war against evil," the Marine continued. "My name is Derrick Lee. I have been in this country for the last year. I'm a former Marine and infantryman, so you'd better listen to me if you want to stay alive."

Lee turned and motioned to the two other men standing beside him. "This is Cotkar and Rebin. They are your senior officers in this militia. You will do what they say or be sent away. Getting home is your own problem. We welcome your volunteerism, but we don't have time for quitters."

"Grab your shit and let's go," Lee said abruptly as he turned to walk out.

Welcomed with open arms. They led us out to a double-cab pickup truck. Lee directed us to load up into the bed of the truck, while he and the other two men piled into the cab. It was still dark out when we sped away from the small safe house.

"I love this shit!" Frost yelled over the truck's buzzing V6 engine.

I leaned back against my duffel, staring at the stars as we bounced along the dusty dirt road. I had never seen the stars so bright. It was like being in a different world. I closed my eyes and tried to get some sleep.

As I drifted off, I saw Chelsea and Lindsey. They were trying to tell me something, but I couldn't hear them. I told them I would be joining them soon. They turned and walked away, suddenly disappearing as I tried to follow.

I found myself back in SWAT tryouts. The instructors were yelling at me, telling me never to give up. My feet were bleeding and my body aching, but I kept going.

I woke up as the truck suddenly stopped. I could see the sun starting to rise behind a nearby mountain. The air was still crisp and cool but smelled of burning trash and dust.

The men exited the cab and yelled for us to follow. I hopped over the side with duffel in hand as the three of us filed in behind Lee. The two other men disappeared in different directions.

We were in a village outside of Kirkuk. The houses were all small, making the safe-house look like a mansion in comparison. Lee led us through the center, taking us to another building with more cots.

"This is where you'll stay," he said as he opened the door. We walked in to find a large bay with a dozen or so empty cots. Most had bags and gear around them. Lee instructed us to find an empty one and toss our bags on it.

"You're already late," he said, as we dumped our bags and walked back out. He led us outside to what appeared to be a training area. There were cardboard targets set up near a dirt pile, a few makeshift obstacles, and a set of badly welded together monkey bars. I counted seven other men of various ages and nationalities already doing jumping jacks in the center.

"Fall in!" Lee yelled.

We joined the back of the line just as the Kurdish instructor had the group drop to the ground. He counted slowly as we started doing push-ups. Some of the others were already grunting and groaning as we made it through the first ten. I was physically and mentally exhausted from the travel and lack of sleep, but I had it easy in comparison.

After twenty pushups, the instructor yelled for us to get back on our feet. He made us run in place and then had us drop to the ground and get back up before continuing to run in place. We repeated this about ten times before he led us on a two-mile run.

I always hated running. My general philosophy was that the only time I should be running was toward bad guys or away from bombs. "Jogging for pleasure" was not in my vocabulary.

We kept a steady pace. Several of the larger guys had trouble keeping up and tried walking before Frost and a couple of more motivated young guys fell back to push them forward. My lungs started to burn. I had never run at elevations higher than sea level, and it felt like I was breathing through a straw. I stayed in the middle of the pack so as not to draw attention to myself.

At the end of the run, they made us run the poor man's obstacle course. We had to run through a set of dry-rotted tires, jump a ditch, and low crawl under a set of ropes before swinging through the monkey bars. They creaked, and the structure swayed dramatically as each person went through. I was waiting for the whole thing to collapse as some of the others went through it.

Of the ten of us, two made it to the end of the course and started vomiting. Two others didn't even make it through the entire course, falling out shortly after the low crawl. Abe had been one of them. I watched him throw up on himself as he tried to get up after crawling through the dirt. His rugged demeanor had been broken down by an amateur obstacle course.

The six of us that remained were given AK-47s as the fall-outs were taken away. I cleared the weapon and checked that it was safe. It was dirty and worn out. I didn't have much experience with Kalashnikovs, but I knew the basics.

I watched the others as they studied their rifles. Frost easily cleared his, keeping the muzzle downrange. A few of the others, however, were far less proficient.

One of the foreign kids pointed the weapon directly at the Kurdish instructor with his finger on the trigger. He was reprimanded and his weapon was taken away before the instructor forcibly showed him how to hold the rifle when not shooting at someone.

Another guy with an American accent dropped his rifle muzzle-first into the dirt and then tried to stare down the barrel as he attempted to clear the mud from the flash-hider. The instructor could do nothing but just shake his head with the rest of us.

I was starting to understand their frustration, and the reason Watson had mentioned that most recruits stayed behind to do menial tasks. They weren't exactly getting the best and brightest, but any additional manpower was better than nothing.

They gave us quick ten-minute academics on how to operate the rifles. I paid special attention to the operation and location of the fire selector since it was a bit different from the M4s I had been used to. They showed us how to aim and basic body positioning – or at least, their version of it.

As they had us practice taking aim with the weapons, I could see them take note. I had a bit more training with rifles than the others. Frost and I appeared comfortable and fluid in our movements while taking aim, while some of the others were more awkward. One guy insisted on "chicken-winging" his elbow out like Johnny Appleseed.

After we practiced dry firing the rifles, they gave us two magazines each and placed a bucket of 7.62 rounds in front of us.

They showed us how to properly load the magazines and gave us a few minutes to load our issued magazines. When we were finished, they took us to the makeshift firing range.

They started us out at twenty-five yards. The iron sights on the weapon I had took some getting used to, but it wasn't unmanageable. My groupings were the tightest of the new shooters. Frost came in a close second. Some of the others had trouble even hitting the paper targets.

We had neither hearing nor eye protection. Range safety seemed to be more of a suggestion than an absolute requirement. I avoided the two that had demonstrated absolute idiocy with the weapons early on. I was convinced that they would end up shooting themselves or one of us before it was over.

We shot the two thirty-round magazines from twenty-five yards. When we were done, the instructor took each of us to the targets to discuss errors and fixes. When it was my turn, he introduced himself as Zirek and walked with me to the target. He stuck his finger in the grouping and nodded.

"This will do well," Zirek said. "What is your background?"

"Law enforcement," I said as I nervously kept an eye up-range to make sure the two mouthbreathers weren't about to start throwing rounds at us.

"What is that? Police?" Zirek asked.

I nodded.

"This does not look to be the work of a simple policeman," Zirek said with a raised eyebrow.

I shrugged. "I guess I'm just lucky."

Zirek smiled through his thick beard. "We will see."

Zirek directed us back to the ammunition bin. We reloaded our magazines and headed back to the range. This time, Zirek had us shoot from about fifty yards. It seemed pretty ambitious for our group, but it wasn't my show.

The problems some of the others were having were amplified at fifty yards. The two simpletons at the far end continued missing the target altogether. On the second magazine, one of them switched from SEMI to AUTO on the select fire and emptied his magazine Rambo-style from his hip.

As before, Frost and I were the two leaders of the class. My grouping was less than two inches. Frost only had a few errant rounds. Once again, Zirek went to each individual and debriefed shots.

Between the two of them, the men at the end only hit the target three times, and I wasn't sure they hadn't hit each other's targets. I watched Zirek shake his head in disappointment as he ordered them off the range. I assumed they were going to the same place as the guys who couldn't make it through the obstacle course.

After debriefing the other two and Frost, Zirek grinned as he saw my target. We walked together to the target as he shook his head. He laughed as he stuck two fingers in the hole I had made beneath the 25-yard grouping.

"Just a policeman," Zirek said with a laugh. "Tell me, Mr. Policeman, why are you here?"

I considered the question for a moment. To be honest, even I wasn't sure why I had traveled halfway around the world to enlist in a rag-tag militia.

"To help out," I said finally.

Zirek laughed derisively. "To help out!"

"You don't believe me?" I asked.

"Friend, I have seen many people come through here. They all come for many reasons. Some seek adventure. Some believe in our cause. Still others come here to escape their situation in America. But you. You are not here for any of those reasons. You are not one of them," Zirek said, poking his finger in my shoulder.

"Is that so? What makes you say that?" I asked.

"You have significant training," Zirek said. "Like the American CIA and Green Berets that trained me. The way you shoot. The way you hold a rifle. Even the way you conduct yourself. You are not one of them." Zirek pointed to the others.

"I'm just a cop," I said.

Zirek studied me. He laughed again before throwing up his hands. "Whatever you say you are, I believe you. But you are not here just to help. I can see that much in your eyes."

"Just tell me where to shoot, boss," I said.

"Come," Zirek said, looking back at me over his shoulder and waving for me to follow as he walked away. "We have more training to do."

CHAPTER TWENTY FOUR

T he second day of training started much like the first. Zirek and his fellow instructors stormed into our makeshift barracks just before 6 a.m. Although this time, I felt significantly more rested.

The day prior had been long and grueling. After the range, they had given us lunch and then taken us to do more PT. After PT, we started basic unarmed combatives – something I did well in, given my experience with the Sheriff's Department. We ended the day with dinner, and I got to take my first shower since leaving Atlanta.

It wasn't much. The Kurds had set up field showers outside our barracks. They were the ones the Americans had left behind.

The water was cold, and the water pressure was abysmal, but it felt good to get some of the sweat and grime off me.

After the shower, we were given U.S. Army Field Training Manuals to study and sent back to the barracks. I made it fifteen minutes before I was out. It was probably the most I had slept continuously since getting out of the hospital. My body just couldn't go anymore.

The morning PT was easier with a good night's sleep. Frost and I led the smaller pack. We had found out the night prior that the men that had been removed from our group were being used for more menial tasks – burning trash, guarding gear, and driving ambulances. They could be given the opportunity to try again if they did well in their new tasks.

The four of us that remained would be eligible to join the fighting ranks of the Kurdish militia if we continued to do well. Frost and I were the only two that had any training. The burly guy named Foster had been a football player in the Arena Football League before an ACL injury ended his semi-professional career. And the scrawny kid named Vince had never really held a job but claimed to be an Airsoft enthusiast. I called him a kid, but he was probably Frost's age.

They added moving and shooting drills after the basic range day. After every drill, Zirek would just give me a knowing smile as he shook his head. "Policeman!" he would scoff.

After our range training, they gave us Meals, Ready-to-Eat for lunch. As we sat in the training area eating, Zirek suddenly came running up to us. "All of you, come with me," he said.

We put down our food and jogged behind him. I could hear the whine of a siren in the distance. We followed Zirek through the village to a large tent on the north side. In the distance, I saw flashing blue lights and a dust trail as an ambulance sped toward us.

The sound of the European siren grew louder as the ambulance approached. It skidded to a stop in front of the tent as two Kurdish women rushed toward the back door. A Western-looking doctor followed, putting on a pair of purple nitrile gloves as he approached the ambulance.

The women reached the ambulance as the driver got out. He appeared to be one of the foreign fighters. They opened the rear doors, revealing a man on a stretcher.

The man screamed in pain as they lowered the stretcher's legs and locked them. He appeared to be in his mid-thirties. His head and face were covered in blood. His left leg was missing and wrapped below the knee. He had a tourniquet on his thigh.

The doctor went to work assessing the man as they wheeled him into the medical tent. The four of us stared in shock as they disappeared inside. I watched Vince look away and steady his breathing. He looked like he was about to lose his lunch.

"That man is British. He is a volunteer like you," Zirek announced. "Follow me. You need to see what you are signing up for."

We followed him into the field hospital and stood in the corner. The doctor looked like he was prepping the British fighter for surgery. The man's heart rate monitor was beeping furiously as he screamed for someone to help him.

We watched in silence as the doctor shouted out commands. He had an Australian accent by my guess. He worked fluidly with the women as he tried to remove a piece of shrapnel and stop an arterial bleed.

Despite the doctor's efforts, the patient's condition worsened. The heart rate monitor beeped faster and faster as the doctor unsuccessfully tried to stabilize the patient. The man flatlined, and the doctor jumped onto the stretcher, straddling the patient as he pumped on the man's chest.

He barked out more orders. One of the women intubated the patient and then injected him with something. The doctor coolly continued to work on the patient. Vince and Frost both stood with their jaws dropped. Foster didn't seem phased by any of it. I could feel Zirek watching me for a reaction, but I just watched the scene unfold.

After several minutes of CPR, the doctor jumped off the patient. He removed his gloves and shook his head with disgust. "He's dead," he said as he threw his gloves into an open trash can. "Goddammit!"

"Let's go," Zirek said softly. He motioned for us to follow.

We solemnly walked out with him. He said nothing as he led us back out to where our MREs littered the ground. "Have a seat," he said.

We sat back down in the dirt. No one touched their food. We didn't have the stomach for it.

"That man's name was Chester Martin," Zirek said. "Former British SAS. They were out on a patrol when they were ambushed by Islamic State fighters. He was the only one of his six-man patrol to live long enough to have a shot with the doctor, and you just saw what happened."

Zirek paused as he studied us. "We train you for this reason. If you do not make the training, we will not bring you to fight. The stakes are far too high."

"That is not to say we don't appreciate your help," Zirek continued. "Your contributions are appreciated no matter how you help. But this is a Kurdish fight. We send our own out to fight and die. We have been fighting for many years."

Zirek pointed to the untouched MREs on the ground. "Finish your meal. In battle, you never know when the next time you will get food or water. Never pass up such an opportunity. I will be back in fifteen minutes, and we will continue training."

"Well, that sucked," Foster said before shotgunning a cheese packet from his MRE. "This shit ain't checkers."

"You ok, Vince?" Frost asked.

Vince was staring at the ground. I wasn't sure he had ever seen anything like that outside of movies and video games. He was in a state of shock.

"Vince?" Frost asked as he shook the kid. "You there, buddy?"

"What have I gotten into?" Vince mumbled, still staring at the ground.

"First time seeing someone die?" Foster asked.

Vince nodded without looking up.

"I remember my first time," Foster replied. "Baltimore. Watched one of my buddies capped in cold blood. We were just kids that got caught in the middle of a gang war."

"How old were you?" Frost asked.

"Fourteen," Foster replied, shaking his head.

"I was in this very country," Frost said. "Two of my squad mates were blown up by an IED just outside of the Green Zone. It was gruesome."

"How do you deal with that?" Vince asked. "What if it happens to us?"

"You honor the dead and move on," Foster answered. "That's all you can do."

"What about you, Shep?" Frost asked, turning to me. "Have you ever seen shit?"

I tried not to think about my family, but the images kept flooding back. I had seen plenty of death as a deputy, but nothing compared to watching my family die. It was the worst thing I had ever experienced.

"Shep?" Frost asked again.

"Yeah," I replied.

They were all staring at me, waiting for an explanation.

"Yeah," I said again as I saw Zirek and the Marine trainer approach.

"Let us continue!" Zirek yelled as he approached.

We went through the same regimen of PT and combatives. The group had a different feel to it in the wake of the hospital visit. Frost and Foster seemed more focused. They tried to motivate the group whenever possible. Vince had lost the edge. I could tell he was reconsidering his participation.

After the field showers, Zirek gave us our final talk for the evening before chow. At the conclusion of his speech, he asked me to join him for dinner. "We should talk," he said before giving me instructions on how to get to his home.

I showed up promptly at 6 p.m. It was a small hut near the western edge of the village, far away from our barracks and training room. Zirek opened the door and welcomed me in. He appeared to live alone in the small hut. There was a small kitchen and dining area with a separate bedroom. It felt like a one-bedroom apartment.

"Please," he said welcoming me in. "Tonight, we dine as friends."

I smiled graciously and walked in. He offered me a seat across from him at his table. A glass of water had already been poured. He brought in a rack of lamb and placed it in the center of the table. It smelled delicious. I hadn't had a real meal in days.

"Help yourself," he said as he served himself.

Zirek was an older man. There were pictures of a younger woman with a small boy in various places of the house. I wondered where they were.

"Thank you for having me," I said as I enjoyed the first bite. It was just as delicious as it smelled. "This is great."

"You are quite welcome," Zirek said. "My wife was a much better cook than I am."

Was? I frowned. "Do you mind if I ask what happened?" I asked, putting my fork and knife down.

Zirek's brow furrowed. "Much the same that happened to your family," he said solemnly.

As my family? My face felt flush. I had told no one about what happened, not even Watson. "Excuse me?" I asked.

"Your name is Alex Shepherd of Louisiana, is it not?" Zirek asked.

"It is," I said. I had not tried to hide my identity throughout the process, but I didn't think anyone would research it either. Perhaps I had been too naïve.

"Last night, I researched you," Zirek said. "As meager as our village may be, we do have the internet here. I wanted to know how a simple policeman could be as proficient as you. I found your story, Deputy Alex Shepherd, SWAT Sniper, and hero on a very dark day in your country's history."

"I'm not a hero," I said. The images of my little girl burning came rushing back. My fists clenched.

"I understand, Alex," Zirek said. "I felt the same way when they killed my family."

"You did?"

Zirek nodded. I could see his eyes start to water. "I was a teacher when Al Qaeda came to my village four years ago, before any Americans knew what the Islamic State was. I had gone to Mosul for the week – to bring back teaching and humanitarian supplies that the Americans were giving out before leaving. There were many of us gone that week," he said softly.

I listened intently as Zirek cleared his throat.

"When we returned, our houses had been burned to the ground. The men had been executed. Our women had been raped and burned alive in cages. Our children had been crucified, dying as they watched their mothers burn," Zirek stopped as he wiped a tear from his cheek.

"I'm sorry," I said. I knew exactly how he felt. The rage. The sadness. The helplessness.

"The CIA showed up as we tried to pick up the pieces," Zirek continued. "They offered training and aid. They told us they couldn't fight Daesh themselves, but that they could help us. I joined the People's Protection Group the next day."

"And now you're here?" I asked.

"War is a young man's game," Zirek said. "After four years, it was time to teach others to carry on."

"But we're not real fighters," I replied. "The militia barely uses us on the front lines."

"I speak fluent English," Zirek replied. He shrugged. "The militia are not real fighters either."

"How do you mean?"

"We fight fiercely. We are better trained and organized than Daesh and have had many victories, but we are no American Army," he replied. "We are not *you*."

"I'm nobody," I replied. "Just a man with a score to settle, like you."

"Even so, there is nothing I can teach you here," Zirek replied. "You remind me of the Green Berets that worked with us."

"What does that mean?" I asked.

"Why are you really here?" Zirek asked.

"To kill Ayman Awad al-Baghdadi, or die trying," I said.

Zirek laughed. "The man from the videos?"

"Yes."

"And then what?"

"I don't know."

"Alright," Zirek replied. "You may one day get that chance, but are you prepared to fight and die here?"

"Does death scare you anymore without your family?" I asked.

"I suppose not," Zirek replied.

"Then you have your answer," I said.

Zirek finished his last bite of lamb and then pushed his plate aside. "Tomorrow, you will not be training with the others. You will be issued a rifle and be part of a security detail for a convoy headed to Makhmur."

"What about the others?" I asked. "Frost seems like a sharp kid."

"They will have their day in due time," Zirek said. "Do you accept?"

"Just show me where to shoot, boss," I replied.

CHAPTER TWENTY FIVE

It had been a sleepless night. I tossed and turned in the tiny cot, haunted by the specter of loss. I couldn't get the images of my dead wife and daughter out of my head.

At 5 a.m., I quietly folded my blanket, grabbed my duffel, and left the training barracks for the last time. "Good luck, fellas," I whispered as I closed the door behind me.

I walked to the center of the village where a line of militia fighters had already formed at the armory. As Zirek had instructed, I joined the tail end of the line. Two men stood at the entrance of a small building, handing out gear.

I heard chatter from the men in line in front of me. Most of it was in a language I didn't understand, but some of it was English. I picked up bits and pieces. They were discussing a raid from the night prior. The fighting had been intense, but from what I could gather, they had defeated the small company of ISIS fighters. They spoke very proudly of this fact.

By the time I reached the end of the line, a dozen or so men had fallen in behind me. They had a mix of M4s with optics and iron-sight AK-47s. The two men in front of me had each been issued an AK-47 and two hand grenades.

"Name?" the man asked. He was black with a British accent. The man next to him also appeared to be a westerner. He held up his clipboard, ready to search for my name. They were much better organized than I had expected.

"Shepherd," I said.

The little man with the clipboard flipped through the pages and said, "Alex Shepherd?" He had an American accent. Boston maybe? He sounded like a New England Patriots fan I had seen interviewed on TV.

"Is there more than one?" I asked.

"Just answer the question," the man repeated. *Definitely Boston.*

"Yes, sir," I said.

The British supply clerk picked up the AK-47, cleared it, and then handed it to me. "Do you know how to operate it?" he asked.

"Yes," I said as I accepted it and cleared it in a safe direction.

"Good," he said. He handed me a harness with two hand grenades and three magazines.

"And these grenades?" he asked, holding up the harness.

"Yes," I said. Although I had never used fragmentation grenades, I was familiar with their operation. In SWAT, I had used flash bangs and smoke grenades many times.

"You may proceed," the Brit said.

I followed the other fighters to the edge of town. A convoy of five vehicles – two pickup trucks with bed-mounted machine guns, two medium transport Mercedes-Benz Atego trucks, and a

Toyota Landcruiser – lined up on the main highway, preparing for departure as men loaded supplies into the transport trucks.

As I followed the herd toward the convoy, someone suddenly grabbed my arm. I spun around, retreating from the grip as I suddenly came face to face with Zirek. "Easy, friend," he said.

"I didn't expect to see you here," I said. "Come to wish me luck?"

"I'm going with you," Zirek said.

"I thought you didn't fight anymore?" I asked.

Zirek smiled. "Every new fighter must have an escort," he said. "I chose to be yours."

"I'm honored, but what about the others?" I asked. "You're a pretty damned good instructor."

"Mr. Lee will take care of them," Zirek said. "You have made me realize that my fight is not yet over."

"So what are we doing exactly?" I asked.

"We are taking supplies to Makhmur, an outpost near Mosul that has been set up on the edge of hostilities," Zirek explained.

"So once we get to Makhmur, then what?" I asked.

"We will then go to where we are needed," Zirek replied. "But for now, our goal is to safely get this convoy to Makhmur. It is a two-hour drive."

"What's the threat?" I asked.

"Daesh operates freely west of here, but they do not control anything east of Mosul. We have been told that the threat of attack is low, but one can never let his guard down," Zirek replied.

"Just show me where to shoot," I said, tapping the side of my rifle.

"We'll be near the back of the convoy," Zirek said.

I followed him to the Landcruiser parked behind the two transports. One of the trucks with bed-mounted machine guns was immediately behind us, bringing up the rear. Two other Kurdish militiamen took their places in the front seat of our vehicle.

Zirek said something to the men in Kurdish. They all laughed, most likely at my expense as Zirek slapped my shoulder. I ignored them, slapping one of the loaded magazines into the rifle and chambering a round.

"Don't worry," Zirek said to me. "They will watch out for you."

I turned my attention out the window as one of the vehicles honked its horn, and the convoy started rolling. The mission felt a bit rushed and piecemealed together. For something as preplanned as a resupply convoy, there had been no brief or plan issued. The militia seemed to just have the attitude of "Get in, shoot bad guys." I wondered if all of the units operated the same way.

The convoy moved at a surprisingly quick pace. The speedometer of the Landcruiser was in Kilometers, but it felt like we were doing at least sixty miles per hour down the two-lane highway. I had thought the big transport trucks would've been limited to forty or forty-five miles per hour.

The first hour of the trip was completely uneventful. The militiaman in the front passenger seat spent most of the time sleeping as Zirek and the driver told stories and jokes to each other in Kurdish. Every so often, Zirek would translate the punchline to me, but I spent the time scanning ahead and off to the side for hidden threats. I seemed to be the only one on high alert.

As we droned down the deserted highway, the handheld radio sitting in the center cupholder suddenly crackled to life. Someone yelled something in Kurdish. His voice sounded concerned, but not panicked as far as I could tell. I looked at Zirek for a translation as I saw brake lights illuminate on the truck in front of us.

"What's going on?" I asked.

"Goats in the road," Zirek said.

I shouldered my rifle and turned in my seat. Zirek tapped me as I lowered the window and started scanning for threats.

"It is of no concern yet," Zirek said. "Common."

"Nothing seems common here," I said as I rested my cheek against the stock and scanned outside.

The convoy came to a halt. There was more chatter on the radio. The hair was standing up on the back of my neck. I contemplated getting out in order to set up a perimeter.

"What's going on, Zirek?" I asked.

"Zirek?" I asked again, looking over my shoulder. He also had his window down now and his rifle up. He had an M-16A4 with optics.

There was another burst of chatter on the radio before Zirek yelled, "Set up a perimeter!"

"Shit!" I yelled. *I knew it! We should've been out long ago.*

I shot out of the door and into the desert heat. I heard a few sporadic pops of gunfire before the sound of the bed-mounted machine guns filled the air. There was more yelling in Kurdish.

I took a knee as I scanned with my rifle. I was at a major disadvantage, being unable to hear what the others were shouting as they traded gunfire with the unknown attackers. The gunfire increased near the front of the convoy. I scanned my zone, looking for flanking threats as I heard more shouting.

The gunfire was still sporadic. With no communications, I felt like I was flying blind. There was a sudden lull in the shooting before I watched the lead truck erupt in a fireball. I ducked instinctively, watching militia fighters run from the burning wreckage before I heard more gunfire.

As I went to turn back toward my zone, I heard a round zip by. I turned to see the driver of our Landcruiser lying face down in the dirt.

Time seemed to stand still as I assessed my options. We had been ambushed from all sides. *Was this how it would end? My first battle in country? Could I be so lucky? What about al-Baghdadi? What about vengeance?* My training suddenly kicked in as muscle memory took over.

"Contact left!" I yelled as I returned fire in the general direction I thought the shot had come from. "Man down!"

I didn't know if anyone would hear me, much less understand me, but I screamed it anyway. I ran toward the driver and took a knee, returning fire as I reached down to assess him.

He was bleeding from his shoulder and abdomen, groaning in pain. Another volley of rounds zipped by, causing me to spin around and take aim.

I found two men dressed in all black approaching in the distance. I flipped the fire selector on my AK-47 to single shot and fired, dropping the first man as the second ran for cover behind a dune.

"Cover!" I yelled. I grabbed the driver by his harness and dragged him back to the front of the SUV, out of the line of fire of the flanking fighters.

Flipping the select fire switch back to AUTO, I laid down suppressing fire in the direction of the fighters before turning my attention back to the driver.

"Is he alive?" Zirek asked as he appeared from the passenger side of the Landcruiser.

"He needs a medic," I said. I crouched behind the front bumper with my rifle against the quarter panel. "I'm contact two left side."

Zirek picked up his handheld radio and yelled something in Kurdish. He began to administer first aid as I continued to lay down suppressing fire. The machine gunner in the rear pickup suddenly turned and let loose a flurry of fifty caliber bullets. They shredded the remaining fighters.

There were a few more sporadic pops of gunfire and then another radio transmission. Zirek stood. "Let's get him into the back of the vehicle," he said as he slung his M-16 across his back.

"That's it?" I asked, still maintaining cover behind the truck.

"There were only five or six enemy fighters," Zirek said, nodding for me to grab the driver's upper body. "These are Daesh scouts."

I helped Zirek carry the man to the back of the truck as the front passenger arrived to help. Zirek and the passenger said something to each other and then closed the door. Zirek shook his head in disgust.

"What's wrong?" I asked.

"Ardalan was killed in the attack," Zirek said glumly.

"Who?"

Zirek scowled at me. "He was a brave warrior and the leader of our unit."

"Ah shit," I said. "I'm sorry."

"We must move on," Zirek said gravely. "You drive."

Zirek checked on the patient in the back one more time, giving him a bottle of water and checking his wounds. He returned to the front seat, having swapped with the previous shotgun rider. After a brief delay, while the dead and wounded were collected, the radio crackled to life, and the convoy started moving again.

I put the Landcruiser in gear as we slowly followed the transports. The lead truck was still on fire as we approached it. I tucked in behind the transport in front of me as we went off-road to go around it.

I couldn't help but stare at the burning truck as we passed it. I had found the war I had been seeking. It was nothing like I had expected.

CHAPTER TWENTY SIX

The convoy made it the rest of the way into Makhmur uneventfully. Upon arrival, the dead and wounded were collected and dealt with unceremoniously. It seemed to be a common occurrence for the people of the small outpost.

After helping Zirek get the Landcruiser driver into the field hospital, I followed him around like a brand new recruit on his first day out of the academy. There were many battle-hardened fighters milling about in the field hospital. Their injuries ranged from open wounds to missing limbs and eyes. It was sobering to see the toll war had taken on the people of this country.

The field hospital's patients weren't limited to the fighters, however. Women, children, and the elderly had also been taken in. I could picture Lindsey and Chelsea among them. It made me sad, but it also made my blood boil. The men that were doing this were animals.

We left the field hospital and went to another tent. Zirek appeared to be well known and respected. Several militiamen stopped and greeted him, or reverently moved out of his path. I was still unclear on exactly what the rank structure of the militia was, but he seemed to be well-respected.

At the second tent, we were served lunch. We had meat-filled dumplings on flatbread, vegetables, and juice. It was just as good as the meal Zirek had prepared for me the night prior. As I enjoyed the meal, I took a look around. The tent was occupied by mostly older fighters with rifles slung across their back. I wondered what Zirek's rank was as I watched more people reverently interact with him.

"Thank you for taking me under your wing," I said, breaking the silence as I sat next to him.

"You fought well," Zirek said. "You have earned your place."

"What exactly is my place?" I asked.

Zirek flashed a knowing smile. "This evening, we will travel to Rojava. You have earned a chance to fight with the Lions of Rojava."

"I have?" I asked. I felt that I had barely contributed to the fight that morning. I had been lost for most of it. It hadn't been my best performance.

Zirek nodded. "You fought bravely and saved a man. I expected nothing less from you."

"What does that mean?"

"Rojava is Western Kurdistan. It is where the YPG Units fight Daesh. It is where you will find your revenge," Zirek replied.

I was completely confused. I thought I had already been training with the YPG. I had obviously not done enough homework before traveling across the world.

"I thought I had been fighting with the YPG already."

Zirek laughed. "You have much to learn, my friend," he said.

"And you're not going to explain it to me?" I asked.

"In due time," Zirek said. "But for now, enjoy this honor."

"Ok, what country will we be in tonight?" I asked, frustrated by the Zirek's dodging of my questions.

"Rojava," Zirek said as he finished his juice.

"Let's pretend like I'm just a dumb American – because I am. What country would that be near?" I asked.

"Syria, Turkey, and Iraq," Zirek replied with a smile. He seemed to be enjoying my frustration.

"You're a pretty important guy here, aren't you?" I asked, changing the subject.

"How do you mean?" he asked as the smile disappeared from his face.

"You seem well-respected around here," I said before pausing to take a look around. "And this doesn't seem to be just any tent."

"You are very perceptive, Mr. Shepherd," Zirek said.

"Sometimes," I said. "So can you at least tell me that much?"

"Alright," Zirek said. "As I told you at dinner last night, I was trained by the Americans. I was one of the first to fight in the People's Protection Army, and I fought in many battles – in both Syria and Iraq."

"So you're a general?" I asked.

"I was a Commander during the Battle of Al-Hasakah nearly two years ago," Zirek said softly. "I had two hundred and fifty men under my command in that battle. It was a great victory."

"So why leave? Why go to training?" I asked.

Zirek flashed another smile through his thick beard. "You are very persistent."

"I'm just curious," I said. "I want to know the guy I'm fighting next to."

"I admire that about you, Mr. Shepherd," he replied. "The truth is, Al-Hasakah was a great victory, but there have been many defeats as well. As I mentioned last night, war has taken its toll on me. But the real truth is that what you were in was not training."

"It wasn't?" I asked.

Zirek shook his head. "No," he replied. "You see, when we first started receiving foreign fighters many years ago, we allowed anyone to fight with us. Ours was a great cause against evil, and we welcomed all. However, we soon found that this was not good. The people that came to help were of varying quality. Some were even criminals."

"Criminals?" I asked with a raised eyebrow.

"War is a very good way to escape society," he replied, nodding his head. "You see, the YPG is a secular force, committed to women's liberation, democratic confederalism, and the rights of all ethnic, religious, and cultural groups to live and prosper peacefully. Everybody with a democratic and antifascist mindset is welcome to join. But we found that rapists, fascists, racists, and sexists were coming out as well. They tried to rape our women. They did unspeakable acts on the battlefield. It could not be tolerated.

"So we changed how we screen people. Due to the nature of Iraq – the various factions of Peshmerga, the Iraqi government, and the ongoing Syrian Civil War, we could not recruit directly into the YPG, at least not at first. We developed a way to invite foreign fighters and screen them well away from the battlefield. What you participated in was part of that screening," Zirek said.

"I'm the only one that passed?" I asked. "Really?"

"No," Zirek replied. "I am sure others in your group will make their way to the battlefield, but what I told you last night was correct. I took an interest in you because of your story. I think you will fight well for the YPG, and you have already proven such."

"Was the convoy attack all staged?"

Zirek frowned. "Of course not! We are still in Iraq, and Daesh still operates within these borders. What happened this morning was very real, and should serve as a testament to what you have signed up for."

"And what's that?" I asked. "What really happens next, now that we're being honest?"

"At nightfall, we will travel to Al-Malikiyah, Syria, with other recruits. There you will receive actual training. You'll learn our language and customs. When you are ready, you will be assigned to a unit, and you will fight as one of us," Zirek said.

"Just show me where to shoot, boss," I said.

* * *

We left at dark in a convoy of three Humvees that Zirek told me had been abandoned by the Iraqi army. There were a dozen men in total – two other Americans, three Brits, an Australian, and the rest were Kurds.

Zirek and I were in the lead vehicle. I sat shotgun as two Brits rode with us. They introduced themselves as Cory and Nigel. I didn't ask about their backgrounds, but they both seemed very military-like in their demeanor. They were clean-shaven with very short hair.

My beard had finally started to fill in. I hadn't shaved in weeks. The patchiness was finally starting to give way to more hair. I was starting to look like a Special Ops guy from the movies, or at least, I thought I did.

"How long is this drive, mate?" Nigel asked from the back seat as we pulled onto the highway north toward Mosul.

"We'll be there in six or seven hours," Zirek replied. "Keep your guard up, though. We'll be passing through Daesh controlled areas."

I checked my AK-47 and spare mags. Before heading out, we all had been reissued gear. Zirek told me that once we were in country, I could expect better supplies. The U.S. government had been regularly airdropping supplies into Rojava, and U.S. Special Forces personnel were aiding some operations.

We made it through Mosul uneventfully. It was amazing to see all the burned out buildings and major areas that had seemingly been abandoned. It was like being on a different planet.

The convoy turned northwest toward the Syrian border. There were no other cars on the highway, except a few abandoned vehicles we cautiously passed. Otherwise, there were no signs of life. It was like a zombie apocalypse movie. It was eerie.

I started to doze off as I stared out into the clear night sky. The droning of the Humvee's diesel engine made for a nice lullaby as I drifted in and out. I was suddenly jolted awake as Zirek stopped the convoy.

I heard him say something on the radio in Kurdish as I looked up. I gripped my rifle as I tried to figure out what was going on that had him spooked. "What's up?"

"Do you see that?" he said, pointing to his left.

We were at an intersection. To our right was more darkness, but to our left, I saw fire out in the distance. It was several miles away, but it made the horizon glow orange.

"What is that?" I asked.

"Al Hugnah," Zirek said before exchanging more words over the radio with the other drivers in the convoy. "As of yesterday, it was controlled by Daesh."

"We're avoiding it, right?" Cory asked as he lowered his window.

I heard a loud thump and then saw another fireball erupt into the sky. An explosion?

"Ready your weapons," Zirek said as he picked up his radio. He gave an order in Kurdish and then accelerated as he turned left toward the burning village.

"Bloody hell," Nigel said as he slammed the bolt carrier shut on his AK-47.

Zirek headed toward the village. As we got closer, I could see several pickup trucks on fire. They looked like the same trucks with bed-mounted machine guns that I had seen in the morning convoy. Zirek stopped about a quarter mile from the village, and we dismounted.

The twelve of us walked toward the village in two lines of six. We kept our rifles up as we slowly advanced on the burning vehicles. I stayed close to Zirek as I cleared to his right with my rifle.

We saw the first of the bodies as we reached the first vehicle. There were two ISIS fighters dressed in all black laid out on the ground. Their heads had been split open by rifle rounds. There was blood everywhere.

We continued into the village. There were bodies everywhere. It was as if the angel of death himself had come in and wiped out every living thing in the village. It felt even more apocalyptic than Mosul.

As we reached the western end of the village, Zirek turned around and shook his head. "I do not understand," he said.

"Well if you don't, I sure as hell don't," I said as I surveyed the area with him.

Zirek's radio crackled to life. He took off in a jog toward the northern end of the village. I followed in close pursuit with my rifle ready, not sure what we were running toward.

We reached two of the other Kurds standing near one of the huts. As they stepped aside, I saw the body of another fighter leaning against the wall. His throat had been cut, and on the side of the hut above his head had been painted a skull with three interlocked triangles on the forehead. Beneath it was written, "Stamus Contra Malum."

"What the fuck is that?" I asked as I saw Zirek study it.

"Do you know who this is?" he asked as he tilted the dead man's head up with his rifle.

"Not the first fucking clue," I said.

"It's Abu al-Nasef," Zirek replied.

"Who?" I asked.

"He's the commander of Daesh in the Al Anbar province," Zirek replied as he removed his rifle from al-Nasef's chin.

Zirek and the other Kurds exchanged a look of disbelief. The two Brits arrived, stopping dead in their tracks as they saw the body.

"Who did this?" Zirek asked rhetorically.

"I bet it was the SEALs," one of the Americans said. "Same ones that killed Bin Laden."

"With the president we have? Shiiiiiit," the other said. "No way."

"Whoever it was wanted to send a message," Nigel said.

"What language is that?" the first American asked. "I don't speak Spanish."

"It's Latin, mate," Cory replied. "It means 'We Stand Against Evil.'"

CHAPTER TWENTY SEVEN

We arrived at Al-Malikiyah, Syria, just before midnight. Zirek showed me and the other six recruits to our new accommodations and then bid me farewell. He promised to find me again at the completion of my training.

For three more weeks, I trained. This time, the training was much more regimented and intense. Every morning, our group of foreign and indigenous fighters would wake up at 4 a.m., run up and down the mountains, and do group exercises. It felt like an actual boot camp.

The training was much the same as before, but with more academics. I gained a rudimentary grasp of Kurmancî, Kurdish, and Arabic – enough to not be completely lost during some of the group maneuvers we practiced.

As before, I was at the top of the class for all of the firearms training, both with the rifle and the handgun. I started to get the hang of the AK-47. It wasn't the most accurate rifle, but it was reliable. The handguns were all Beretta 92FS 9MM pistols that had been acquired from the Iraqi military. I cared for them a lot less than the Glock 17 Gen IV I shot with the Sheriff's Office, but they seemed to be reliable given their condition.

At the end of training, we were lined up in the middle of an open field with giant green and yellow YPG flags draped against the nearby trees. We stood at attention as the General Commander of the People's Defense Units gave a commencement speech.

With a chest full of medals, black beret, camouflage battle uniform, and dark sunglasses, the General Commander gave the entire speech in Kurmancî. I picked up bits and pieces that I recognized from my crash course in the language. I caught words like honor, courage, and warrior. Based on the roar of applause at the end, I guessed that it was the standard "rally the troops" kind of speech leaders often gave at graduations like these.

When the ceremony was finished, Zirek found me. It was the first time I had seen him in a military-like uniform. He also had a chest full of medals and brass on his collar. He walked up to me and shook my hand with a big smile.

"You have done well, my friend," Zirek said proudly.

"I guess you're kind of a big deal here," I said, nodding to his uniform. "*Sir.*"

Zirek ignored the gesture and turned to walk away. "Come with me," he said as he motioned for me to follow. "I have arranged a test for you."

"A test?" I asked.

"You will see," Zirek said without turning around.

I followed him out to the supply tent. I recognized "gun" as he spoke to the quartermaster. The man disappeared into the tent as I looked nervously at Zirek. Moments later, the man emerged with a rifle.

Zirek took the rifle from the man and cleared it in a safe direction. It was a Remington 700, the rifle I had used as a sniper with SWAT. I couldn't tell what kind of optics it had, but the scope appeared to be military-grade.

"You recognize this?" Zirek asked as he offered me the weapon.

"I do," I said as I accepted it. The rifle was desert tan with M40A5 stamped on the side, US GOVERNMENT. The scope said *Schmidt & Bender* on one side and 3-12×50 PMII on the other. It was a high-quality weapon from the US military.

"This is your final test," he said.

"Where did you get this?" I asked.

"Supply drop," Zirek said cryptically as the quartermaster handed him a pair of binoculars. "Come with me."

I followed Zirek out to the range. The normal cardboard targets we had been using were still standing. He walked me to the edge of the firing line and pointed at the ground. "This is good," he said.

"A shooting test?" I asked, holding the rifle as I looked downrange.

Zirek pulled out three 7.62 rounds from his pocket and handed them to me. "This was your job, no?" he asked as I accepted the rounds.

"It was, but…well…OK," I said as I reluctantly unfolded the rifle's bipod and took a prone position on the ground. The farthest target on this range was roughly two hundred yards away – tough with an AK-47, but it wouldn't make for much of a test with a military sniper rifle.

"Do you see the targets?" Zirek asked. I looked up to see him standing next to me, looking downrange as he focused his binoculars.

I set up my shooting position and adjusted the scope. The farthest cardboard targets were clearly visible. I could see the holes I had put in them the day prior.

"I think so," I said. I chambered a round and flicked off the safety.

"Good," Zirek said. "You have two minutes. The order will be King of Hearts, Ace of Spades, and Queen of Diamonds. Are you ready?"

"Wait, what?" I asked as I looked up to see him setting his watch.

"Begin," he said.

Shit!

I quickly went back to the scope, adjusting the focus as I searched for the target. All technique seemed to go out the window as I desperately searched for what I assumed to be playing cards.

I found a row of cards lined up on a fence post well beyond the normal targets just as Zirek called "One minute, forty-five seconds." There were at least two dozen playing cards affixed to the top of a fence outside the training area. I estimated it was roughly six hundred yards.

I quickly scanned, searching for the King of Hearts. *Slow is smooth, smooth is fast,* I told myself as I tried to calm down. I had done a similar drill in sniper school, but nothing quite like this.

"One minute and thirty seconds remain," Zirek announced.

The winds were calm. I did my best guess of the exact distance and took aim. I squeezed the trigger, letting it reset before I ejected the casing and chambered another round.

"Hit!" Zirek yelled. "One minute and fifteen seconds remain."

I scanned the fence post for the next target. There was no logical order to the cards. I struggled to find the Ace of Spades. "One minute," Zirek warned.

I found the card and took a deep breath, exhaling slowly as I steadied my aim. I squeezed the trigger and watched the card disintegrate through the scope.

"Hit!" Zirek yelled. "Forty-five seconds."

I chambered the final round. Flexing my finger against the trigger guard, I searched for the final target.

"Thirty seconds," Zirek said calmly.

I scanned the fence post, stopping on each card. There were three Queens, two of which were the Queen of Hearts, but I could not find the Queen of Diamonds.

"Twenty seconds," Zirek said. "New target, Jack of Clubs."

I felt the wind pick up slightly from right to left as I processed what Zirek had just said. I remembered seeing the Jack of Clubs earlier.

"Ten seconds," Zirek said with a hint of urgency in his voice.

Time seemed to slow down as I found the card. I adjusted my aim, eyeballing the slight wind correction as I fired.

"Hit!" Zirek yelled.

I ejected the spent casing as I let out an exhausted sigh.

"You had less than a second to spare, my friend," Zirek said.

I cleared the weapon and ensured it was safe before standing. Zirek slapped me on the shoulder with a big smile. I looked around to see several other fighters standing around. They had apparently been watching my test.

"I wasn't expecting that," I said, wiping the sweat from my forehead.

"You have done well," Zirek said. "Come; let us get the rest of your equipment."

"The rest?" I asked. "What does this mean?"

"You have earned the right to keep that weapon," Zirek said. "Tomorrow, you and I will go out and join the battle."

"A big wig like you?" I said with a wry smile.

Zirek let out a hearty laugh. "It is time for me to return to the battlefield. And, as you say, show you where to shoot."

CHAPTER TWENTY EIGHT

That night, Zirek and I left with a YPG brigade of around two thousand fighters. We headed south into the dark desert, on our way to retake the city of Ma'shūq from ISIS control.

Zirek and I were part of a four-man scout-sniper team sent ahead of the brigade. The other two men, Kurds from Northern Syria, spoke English relatively well – much better than I spoke their language. Their names were Ajwan and Terlan. They both appeared to be in their mid-forties.

As we cleared the city, we quickly left the brigade far behind. With the sheer number of vehicles in the convoy, they moved slowly. Our job was to advance toward the city and then ditch the Landcruiser a few miles outside it. We were to set up on the mountainside and provide overwatch as the fighters surrounded the city. As they pushed in, we would reposition to provide urban sniper support. It seemed pretty straightforward.

We drove for hours, passing through several Kurdish villages. The people cheered and waved as we drove through, as if sending off their heroes to war. For the YPG fighters, that's exactly what they were doing. They were going off to war to fight an army that detested their very existence. Defeat was simply not an option.

As we passed through the last YPG checkpoint in Kurdish-controlled territory, I could see the orange glow of a fire several miles in the distance. I had started to get used to the completely clear, star-filled night sky. Visibility was unlike anything I had ever seen. It was not unusual to see things miles away, and the fire was much farther than I expected.

"Enemy?" I asked as I turned to Zirek. We rode in the backseat as Ajwan and Terlan manned the front. Zirek frowned.

Despite the dark cabin of the Landcruiser, I could see the pained expression on Zirek's face. He said nothing, but I could tell he knew what we were about to run into.

As we drove closer, the glow became brighter. I could see that it was a village on fire. We stopped the vehicle about a mile out and hid it off road. The rest of our trek would be on foot.

We approached the village on foot. The terrain was rugged and hilly. The village lay in a slight valley a few miles outside of Ma'shūq. After an hour of hiking, we found a vantage point overlooking the village.

Zirek used the spotting scope he had brought to survey the village. It was a military-grade night vision spotter scope; another piece of equipment I assumed had come from the US Military.

I used the scope on my rifle as I crouched next to him. Although it wasn't night vision, I could see the burning huts and cars in the village below. Someone had set fire to everything.

"I don't see any movement," I said, scanning with my scope from the outer perimeter to the center of the burning village.

"They are long gone," Zirek said. "Let's move."

We moved slowly, zig-zagging down the hillside toward the village. Ajwan and Terlan kept a watchful eye out for ISIS fighters. They had come with us as security – the YPG often liked to send out four man sniper teams with a sniper, spotter, and two men that could watch their backs. It was a good system, but it also made us slightly less mobile.

As we reached the edge of the smoldering village, we spread out. The smell was the first thing I noticed. It was a mix of burning and rotting flesh. I knew we were about to find more gruesome evidence of the work of ISIS.

"Here!" I heard Terlan yell.

I turned to see him standing over a ditch of some sort. Zirek and I ran to his location. When we arrived, Terlan pointed and shined his flashlight at the trench beneath him.

I had seen plenty of dead bodies as a deputy, but the sight in the trench made me gasp slightly. There were at least a hundred bodies, all male. They were all blindfolded with their hands tied behind them. Most had fallen face first, but some had turned. Their mouths gaped open.

I turned to Zirek. He stood staring stoically at the mass grave beneath us. He had seen this before. "Where are the women and children?" I asked.

"In Ma'shūq," Zirek said without looking at me. "Daesh takes them as slaves. They will rape and kill the women that cannot be married and kill the children that cannot be made into fighters."

"My God," I said.

"There is no God on this battlefield," Zirek replied.

We skirted the rest of the village and continued toward our overwatch position. I imagined women and children being taken by ISIS. Their faces were replaced by Chelsea and Lindsey. I could see them struggling against their cowardly kidnappers. I wanted to kill every last one of those savages.

As we hiked toward the nearby mountain single-file, Ajwan suddenly broke the silence. "My cousin lived there," he said without stopping.

"In the village?" I asked, realizing it was a stupid question as soon as I asked it.

"She and her husband had their first son two months ago. It was a great honor for their family," he replied.

"Was her husband among the dead?" Zirek asked.

"No," Ajwan said gruffly. "He is a traitor. I will kill him."

I looked back at Zirek with a confused look. He was bringing up the rear of our four-man platoon.

"If he was not among the dead," Zirek whispered, "then he joined Daesh."

"Wow," I said.

It took us a little less than an hour of hiking to reach our overwatch position on the side of the hill. In the distance, I could see the headlights of the approaching convoy of YPG fighters. The battle for Ma'shūq was fast approaching.

We set up on a small cliff. Ajwan and Terlan took up positions on either side of us for perimeter security and Zirek unpacked his spotter scope. I used my backpack as a support for my rifle as I trained my scope on the outskirts of the city below.

"Checkpoint, five hundred meters," Zirek announced.

Once comfortable, I scanned for the checkpoint. A mile from Ma'shūq, ISIS had set up a roadblock on the single-lane road leading into the city. There were spotlights and two trucks with bed-mounted fifty caliber machine guns. I counted four fighters standing next to the vehicles.

I adjusted my scope for the shot. It would be tough to get all four before they were able to take cover and return fire, but at this range, it wasn't impossible.

"Scouts!" Zirek whispered. "Nine o'clock, two hundred meters."

I looked up from my scope to see where he was pointing. I shifted my shooting position to my right as I looked left. Walking to my left, there were two ISIS fighters wearing all black. One of the men was carrying a radio on his back. I could just barely make out the antenna whipping back and forth as he walked.

It was decision time. With unsuppressed weapons, the first shot would kick off the war. If we took out the scout too early, the men at the checkpoint would alert the others. If we waited too long, the scouts would do their job, and the battle would begin far too early.

"Show me where to shoot, boss," I said under my breath.

"Wait," Zirek ordered.

I watched the scouts continue toward the approaching YPG brigade. I focused on the man with the radio on his back, training my weapon on the back of his head. I was prepared to turn his head into a canoe if he even hinted that he planned to alert the others.

The two men continued for a few more steps and then stopped. The man carrying the radio lit a cigarette and then offered one to his partner. The two turned away from the direction of the approaching convoy, appearing to be content to shoot the shit in the middle of the desert.

I watched the two for what seemed like thirty minutes. As they finished their cigarettes, they turned back toward the approaching division. I could hear a jackal howl in the distance and then what sounded like the rumble of vehicles. I steadied my aim. The two men had simply run out of time.

"I'm taking them out," I whispered.

"No," Zirek replied.

"The militia is almost here," I whispered.

"Wait," Zirek insisted.

I watched the radio operator through my scope. As the sound of vehicles approaching grew louder, I saw him turn his head toward them.

"There's no time left," I said. As I exhaled slowly and began to squeeze the trigger, Zirek grabbed my shoulder firmly.

"Wait," he said.

I looked up at him, pissed that we were about to lose the window of opportunity. He pointed back down to the valley.

Returning to my scope, I saw a flash of movement behind the two men. I shifted my aim to see Terlan approach the radio man from behind. He jabbed a knife through the man's throat as Ajwan did the same to the radioman's partner. The threat had been neutralized without ever taking a shot.

"See?" Zirek said.

I watched as Terlan and Ajwan dragged the bodies out of sight and then sprinted toward our position. I was dumbfounded by what I had just witnessed. The very quiet Kurdish militiamen had just dispatched these two ISIS commandos without breaking a sweat. It was like something out of a movie. After everything I had heard, I had never expected to be fighting alongside such elite soldiers.

Satisfied that the scouts were neutralized, I shifted my shooting position and refocused on the checkpoint. The four men were still standing around, smoking and joking just as the two scouts had been.

The sound of the approaching YPG division grew louder. I set up my scope for the checkpoint fighter farthest from our position and mentally walked through the next three shots. The M40 rifle had a removable ten round magazine like the one I had used with SWAT. At that range, I felt confident in my ability to quickly reset my aim between each center of mass shot. My only concern was whether the rounds would effectively neutralize each threat.

"Fire," Zirek ordered as I lay in wait.

"Now?" I asked.

"Fire!" Zirek hissed.

I placed the crosshairs in the center of the man's chest, a few inches below his throat. I squeezed the trigger smoothly. The round hit. I cycled the bolt as I watched the man stumble forward and fall to his knees.

"Hit," Zirek whispered.

Zirek called off the range and wind correction for the next fighter. I had already mentally calculated the correction. The second fighter had barely turned to look at his friend as I squeezed the trigger. As with the first, the round hit true, dropping the man.

Zirek once again called off ranges. One of the fighters tried to react, firing off shots in our general direction. I ignored him as I focused on the fighter scrambling toward the fifty caliber machine gun mounted in the bed of the truck.

This time, I aimed for the fighter's head. As he reached the bed of the truck and stood, I squeezed the trigger. The round struck him in the left temple, causing him to collapse onto his ass. It was strangely satisfying.

Wasting no time as I chambered another round, Zirek talked me onto the final fighter. He was leaning against one of the trucks, trying to take cover and firing in the direction he thought we were. There was plenty of his body exposed, but I aimed for another headshot.

I lined up my sights once more, exhaling slowly as I squeezed the trigger. In the dim light of the spotlights, I saw blood and brain matter splatter against the white truck. It was even more satisfying than the first. I chambered a round and searched for more, realizing I had acquired an even bigger thirst for blood as my heart raced.

"We must move," Zirek said.

I shuffled to my knees while picking up my rifle and backpack. As I stood to follow Zirek, I saw headlights approaching quickly in the distance.

The battle of Ma'shūq had begun, and I had fired the first shots.

CHAPTER TWENTY NINE

O ur sniper team moved to the next overwatch position as the YPG fighters approached. They spread out and halted outside the city as they set up mortar tubes and began shelling the city.

Zirek called out targets as the fighting began. Neither side seemed to be all that interested in accurate fire. I picked off several ISIS fighters, dressed in all black, as they blindly fired their AK-47s from cover. I couldn't understand why the Iraqi Security Forces had run from these clowns. They were awful.

The fighting was sporadic until sunrise. More ISIS fighters seemed to emerge from the city as the firefight grew more intense. Slowly and methodically, Zirek and I picked off targets as a team. Ajwan and Terlan were content watching our flanks as we lay prone on the hill overlooking the city. They reloaded my magazines as I discarded them, keeping a fresh supply of rounds at my disposal.

I had just changed out my third magazine when Zirek suddenly tapped my shoulder and pointed.

"Two o'clock, five hundred meters, motorcycle," Zirek called out.

I found the motorcycle speeding toward the YPG fighters. The man was wearing a loose-fitting vest that bounced as he zigzagged toward a mortar position. *Suicide bomber.*

"Contact," I said, adjusting the windage and elevation settings on my scope. A moving target at five hundred meters posed its own challenge, but gusty winds had picked up through the valley.

"Five hundred and thirty-six meters," Zirek said, the urgency in his voice becoming more apparent. "Shoot!"

I had a ritual for every shot. Aim, adjust, breathe, flex, squeeze. But for this shot I rushed in, squeezing the trigger before I had a chance to breathe or flex my finger. The shot missed behind the suicide bomber as he continued toward the mortar position.

"Miss! Six hundred meters," Zirek announced without missing a beat.

I cycled the bolt as quickly as I could, chambering another round as I tracked the fighter headed toward friendlies.

"Six hundred and thirty-five meters," Zirek said.

This time I didn't allow myself to be rushed. *Aim.* Center of mass, with lead. *Adjust.* I steadied my shooting position. *Breathe.* I exhaled slowly as I continued to track him. *Flex.* I flexed my finger against the trigger guard before acquiring the necessary leverage on the trigger. *Squeeze.* The rifle recoiled as I sent the round downrange.

I heard the explosion as I watched the round hit. The vest detonated as the man fell from the bike. There was a cloud of dirt, debris, and smoke. I looked back toward the friendlies and saw that they had taken cover. I breathed a sigh of relief.

"Too close. Next target," Zirek said dryly.

Our routine continued through the morning. Zirek picked targets – mostly fighters threatening the mortar teams – and I picked them off. At noon, Zirek received a radio call that the YPG fighters planned a push into the city within the hour, so we packed up and started down the hillside.

I ate an energy bar from my MRE pack for lunch as we moved toward our next overwatch position. I slung my sniper rifle across my back and shouldered an AK-47 as we made our way into the city.

We moved in single file - Ajwan took point as Terlan brought up the rear of our column. I knew the fighting would be more intense as we approached the city. We would have to fight our way to the building we had selected as our overwatch point in the city, and quietly make it to the roof without alerting the remaining ISIS fighters.

We skirted the edge of town. In the distance, I saw YPG vehicles start to move into the city. I kept my AK-47 up, keeping both eyes open as I scanned for threats.

Our team moved fluidly given the limited training we had together. Ajwan held up a closed fist as we approached the first building. He peered around the corner as Terlan covered our six. When it was time to move, we moved in unison, each covering our zones.

We approached an alley, and Ajwan was nearly mowed down in a hail of bullets. I managed to pull him out of the way just as the truck mounted fifty-cal began firing again. I could tell this was where some of the training had broken down. The other three men seemed stymied by the perpendicular line of fire that this presented. There was no way around it.

Ajwan and Zirek tried blind firing around the corner to no avail. The fifty just returned fire, sending pieces flying from the building we were using as cover. I could tell Ajwan and Zirek were trying to figure out a way to safely look around the corner without being hit. I tapped Zirek on the shoulder.

As he looked back at me, I tapped my chest with my left hand and mouthed "Me" before tapping Ajwan and repeating the motion. He ducked as more pieces of the building exploded behind him.

Taking point, I motioned for Zirek to stay against the wall and continue to clear forward. Terlan maintained his position. I motioned for Ajwan to stand shoulder to shoulder with me.

I backpedaled as far as I could from the wall, careful not to get too close to the opposite building. With my rifle up, I began taking small side steps, leaning to my left as I approached the alleyway. It was known as "slicing the pie," a technique to clear a room or corner without exposing one's entire body.

I sidestepped, leaning left with my rifle as I shuffled around the arc. As I neared the splintered corner of the building, I saw the head of the ISIS fighter with his .50 pointed at the wall. It was just the side of his face, but it was enough to take a shot. I flipped the select-fire switch on my AK-47 to single and fired, dropping the man where he stood.

With the fifty disabled, I continued side-stepping around the corner. I found another man scrambling to replace the previous fighter. With two more shots, I dropped him as well. Ajwan also fired as I did, hitting a man I had not seen farther down the alley. We were beginning to operate as a cohesive unit.

Ajwan and I made it to the other side of the alley without further incident. I motioned for Zirek and Terlan to rejoin us, and we continued down the side street. When I tried to give the lead back to Ajwan, he shook his head, pointing for me to continue leading our small team. I had earned his respect.

We pushed deeper into the city. At each alleyway, I went through the same routine with the team, slicing the pie to ensure there were no hidden threats waiting for us. As we neared the final alleyway near the target building, I suddenly froze.

"Contact left," I said softly. I saw four Middle-Eastern men in jeans and sport jackets carrying rifles. For the most part, the YPG fighters all wore uniforms, but these men looked nothing like anyone I had seen in camp.

"Four males," I said as I peered around the corner and took aim for the nearest one.

"Stop," Ajwan said suddenly as he looked back over my shoulder to see what I was looking at. "No good."

"No good?" I asked. I looked to Zirek who was up against the near wall covering where we had just been. He looked back at me and said nothing.

"Syrians," Ajwan said.

"Yes, hostile," I said as I steadied my aim.

Ajwan broke formation and lowered his rifle. "Friend," he said.

He yelled something to the four men. They turned and looked, waving as they jogged in our direction. I had no idea who these men were.

Zirek stepped back from his cover position and approached. As he reached the corner and saw the men, he shot me a look. "You almost shot these men?" he asked.

"They looked hostile," I said, still with rifle up.

Zirek pushed down my rifle as the men reached our position. "They are Al-Sanadid Forces," Zirek explained. "We fight together."

"Just how in the fuck was I supposed to know that?" I asked, staring at four military-aged males in plain clothes. They didn't look like the men I was fighting with, and they were carrying rifles. *How could anyone tell who was friend and who was foe in this environment?*

The men exchanged greetings with Zirek and the others as I lowered my rifle.

Zirek pointed to the tactical vest one of the men was wearing. There was a red flag with a yellow inscription on it in Arabic. "This is their flag. Do you see?" he asked.

"I guess so," I said. "We should get moving to the next objective."

"They will help us," Zirek said.

Ajwan once again gestured for me to take point. We made it to the target building a few minutes later. The team of Al-Sanadid fighters seemed confused each time we approached an alley. One of them swept his muzzle across Zirek at least twice. They seemed very determined and serious, but it was evident that their training was lacking.

We reached the front door of the building. It was a multi-level apartment building. We had chosen it in pre-mission planning because it offered the highest and best vantage point over the YPG's ingress into the city. As with most of the city, we expected it to be empty since most of the civilians had fled with the arrival of ISIS, leaving only combatants to deal with.

Clearing a building potentially full of ISIS fighters, posed its own problem. We had been planning to clear a four-story building with just four men. Although we now had a team of eight, I wasn't convinced that our odds were any better.

I stacked up on the door, ready to be the breacher and kick in the door. Zirek pulled me away, shaking his head as he motioned to one of the Syrians.

"Bandar will go in first," Zirek said, pointing to the apparent leader of the Syrians.

"Who?" I asked. "Why?"

"They wish to be first," Zirek said.

"Is this a joke?" I asked.

"No joke," Zirek said. "Respect."

I readied my rifle as I stacked up behind Bandar and his men. I had no idea what kind of weird fighting rules these guys had, but I wasn't in a position to argue.

Bandar kicked the door open and then stepped back. His men surged in with me on the heels of the third fighter. The first man went left and fired, hitting an ISIS fighter. The second followed, also going left and firing at the same ISIS fighter.

It was here that things started to break down. The Syrian directly in front of me froze in the doorway, not sure which way to go. I pushed him forward, nearly trampling him as he fell to the ground and I button-hooked right.

I came face-to-face with a second ISIS fighter. I fired twice as he took a shot at the first two in the door. The rounds hit him in the throat and face, dropping him to his knees.

"Clear," I said as I scanned the room and headed toward the stairs.

I looked back to see Ajwan helping the third Syrian up while Bandar entered behind Zirek. Without wasting any time, I headed toward the stairs and started up. I figured I was better off alone than stumbling over scared Syrians.

I did a combat reload, swapping out my magazine for a fresh one as I paused on the first flight of stairs to wait for the others. I breathed a sigh of relief as I realized Zirek, Ajwan, and Terlan were behind me. At least I knew they wouldn't freeze in fear – or at least I hoped.

We cleared the second floor without incident. The third and fourth floors each had two fighters, but they proved to be little resistance for our four-man team. We were still operating well together.

We reached the roof and set up our perch. After a heated discussion with Bandar, Zirek convinced the Syrians to act as security for us on the first floor.

I had just finished setting up my shooting platform – an old crate – as Zirek returned.

"You shouldn't have done that," Zirek said angrily.

"Done what?" I asked, ignoring him as I put my AK-47 aside and unslung my sniper rifle.

"You were disrespectful to them," Zirek replied.

"You mean pushing him out of the way so we didn't all get shot?" I asked.

"Yes," Zirek said tersely.

"Fuck that!" I replied. "They would've gotten us and themselves killed if I hadn't. We don't have time for this shit."

"It is a fragile alliance," Zirek said.

"I think you'd be better off without them," I replied.

"You know not of which you speak."

I looked at my watch. "The rest of the men will be pushing into town any minute, we don't have time to argue," I said. "Let's get back to work."

Zirek waved his hand at me angrily as he set up next to my shooting platform. I still had a lot to learn about fighting in this culture.

CHAPTER THIRTY

The battle for Ma'shūq lasted well into the night. Zirek and I picked off fighters as the YPG pushed into the city. It was a bloody battle, but by the end of the night, the fighting had slowed to sporadic pops of gunfire.

I had lost count of my kills over the course of the battle. The people I shot weren't actually people to me anymore. They were simply targets. I felt nothing as I went through magazine after magazine, taking out ISIS fighters who were trying to maintain their foothold in the burned out city.

I didn't even feel anger anymore. The more I saw the atrocities of the war and what these savages were capable of, the more I realized that my story wasn't unique. It was just the horrible cost of war. I wanted to win.

So every target that Zirek had called out became one more step toward that goal. I wasn't fighting for vengeance anymore; I was fighting for their cause. I was fighting to win. For the first time since the attacks back home, I had a sense of purpose.

"You've done very well," Zirek said as I heard cheering in the distance.

"Is it over?" I asked, sitting back on my knees as I stretched. My body ached. I was physically and mentally drained from being up for nearly twenty hours straight.

"The cowards have fled west," Zirek said as he stood, holding the radio. "Ma'shūq has been returned to its people."

By the time we packed up and departed the building we had been using, the Syrians were long gone. I kept my AK-47 in a low-ready position just in case there were any pop-up threats, but Zirek and the others seemed pretty casual as we walked to meet the commander of the operation.

I saw bodies everywhere as we walked through the town. Several buildings were nearly collapsed – I assumed from the mortars earlier in the day, but it could have been from Daesh's initial capture of the city.

As we continued toward the center of town, non-combatants started to fill the streets. I had no idea where they had been hiding, but they showed gratitude. They were women, children, and the elderly, or at least what was left of them. I didn't see any able-bodied males. I wondered where they were.

"General Ibrahim will want to meet you," Zirek said as we neared the edge of the city.

There was a group of vehicles lined up near a large trench. I saw an older man with a thick beard and sunglasses standing in a crowd of much younger men. He had medals dangling from his chest. He looked like a caricature of a third world dictator.

He acknowledged Zirek as we approached. The two greeted each other and Zirek introduced me.

"Alex, this is General Ibrahim," Zirek said.

"An American?" Ibrahim asked as he shook my hand. There was a hint of condescension in his voice.

"He has fought bravely, General," Zirek said. "He has killed for our cause."

Ibrahim laughed skeptically. "And how many did you kill, American?"

I shrugged. I honestly didn't know. I hadn't bothered to keep count, and I didn't really care.

"Thirty-six fighters, General," Zirek answered.

"Thirty-six!" Ibrahim said with an exaggerated sigh. "In this battle?"

"It is true, General," Zirek said proudly.

"You are not like the other Americans," Ibrahim said, studying me. "Are you Special Forces?"

I shook my head. "Just a Louisiana boy," I replied.

"And why have you chosen to fight for our cause, Louisiana boy?" Ibrahim asked, butchering the pronunciation of Louisiana.

"To kill ISIS fuckers," I said as I looked around at the carnage from the battle. I watched as the YPG lined up a group of ISIS prisoners. They forced the prisoners to their knees with their hands on their heads.

"Is that so?" Ibrahim asked. "Come with me then."

I followed him to the prisoners. He asked for one of his men to hand him a rifle, and then he turned, handing it to me.

"These are Daesh," Ibrahim said, pointing at the dozen men on their knees. "Kill them."

"I'm sorry?" I asked.

"You said you wanted to kill ISIS," Ibrahim repeated. "Here they are. So kill them."

I looked to Zirek who nodded for me to go ahead.

"They are prisoners," I protested.

"Do you not think they would kill you if you were their prisoner? Would you keep your head?" Ibrahim asked.

"I'm not like them," I said.

"But you wish to kill them!" Ibrahim prodded. "So do it!"

As I struggled with the morality of such a decision, I heard Ajwan yell something behind me. I turned around in time to see him with his knife drawn running toward the prisoners. He stopped a few inches from one of the men in the middle.

No one said a word as Ajwan yelled at the man who bowed his head in shame. Ajwan drove the knife into the man's chest, retrieved it, and then slit the man's throat. He then wiped the blood off the blade and resheathed it as he watched the man die in a pool of his own blood.

"You see? No one is innocent," Ibrahim said as Ajwan returned.

Ibrahim motioned to his men. Two of them stepped back and fired their AK-47s in full auto, mowing down the prisoners. When they were satisfied they were all dead, Ibrahim's men dragged the bodies to the nearby ditch. I hadn't realized it earlier, but it was another mass grave like the one in the other village. It was horrific.

"It is of no consequence, however. Zirek is a good man, and if he says you killed thirty-six men, then I believe him," Ibrahim said. "Do you wish to kill more?"

I nodded.

"Zirek," Ibrahim said, turning to him. "You and your men will go to Hasud with Commander Zaweed. He and his men plan to rescue the women and children taken by Daesh."

"Yes, General," Zirek replied.

Ibrahim turned back to me. "And you will get your chance to kill more of them, American," the general said with a hearty laugh.

He turned back to his men.

"Let's go," Zirek said, leading us toward the other men.

"Ajwan, do you think your cousin is among the ones in Hasud?" I asked.

"Yes," he said unemotionally.

"Was that her husband that you killed?" I asked.

Ajwan nodded. "He brought great dishonor to his family," he said stoically.

Zirek looked at me disapprovingly. "We do not discuss these things," he said. "Focus on the mission."

"Yes, sir," I replied. "Just tell me who to shoot next."

CHAPTER THIRTY ONE

W e left Ma'shūq with Commander Zaweed and a force of about a hundred and fifty men. They were a rag-tag group, much less military-looking than some of the other units from the Battle of Ma'shūq. We set up camp about fifteen miles from Hasud in preparation for an early morning raid.

That night, Zirek took me to Commander Zaweed's tent. He and a few of his top lieutenants were busy poring over maps and sketches of the area where the prisoners were being held, planning the mission. We stood quietly in the back as Zaweed discussed the plans with his men.

The map showed the village surrounded by farmland. There were no clear avenues of approach. Zaweed seemed to be planning a full, frontal assault to retake the village and rescue the women and children.

"He's going to get them killed," I whispered to Zirek as Zaweed continued beating his chest over the battle he expected.

"Who?" Zirek asked.

"The hostages," I replied. "He's going to get them killed."

Zirek pulled me aside, getting us out of earshot from Zaweed. "Commander Zaweed is a very experienced commander. He will not do anything foolish."

"The compound that we think they're holding them in is on the south end of town," I replied. "If we try to capture the village before the hostages are freed, they'll kill them all."

"What do you propose?" Zirek asked with raised eyebrow.

"We take Ajwan and Terlan and free them ourselves," I said as I looked back over my shoulder toward Zaweed.

Zirek laughed derisively. "Four of us against nearly a hundred men? You are suicidal."

I shook my head. "No, we're not taking on a hundred men. But a smaller team can get in and free the prisoners quickly and quietly with less risk. Once they are free, then Zaweed's men can take the village."

"You have done this before?" Zirek asked.

"Well, not in the middle of the desert in a war zone, but I have done hostage rescues before," I replied.

"Very well," Zirek said, stroking his beard. "Then you will speak to Commander Zaweed and tell him of your plan."

"OK," I said.

Zirek led me back to where Zaweed was just finishing up his briefing. As he finished, I raised my hand timidly.

"Sir, if I may," I said as Zaweed looked at me. I could tell he was frustrated that anyone, especially a foreigner, had the audacity to speak up.

"What is it?" he barked as he looked to Zirek.

"Perhaps there is a better way to go about this," I said, trying to seem as non-threatening as possible. I could feel the eyes of everyone in the room turn to me. It was as if I had just insulted his mother.

"Commander Zirek, what is the meaning of this?" Zaweed asked impatiently, ignoring me altogether.

"My American friend has an idea that may help us save the women and children," he said. "His name is Shepherd. He was American Special Forces and has fought bravely as a sniper for us. I vouch for him."

The resume he gave the commander was a bit of an exaggeration, but I didn't intend to argue. It softened Zaweed's body language, causing him to relax his shoulders as he nodded his approval.

"Go on then, Mr. Shepherd," he said.

"Thank you, sir," I said, approaching the map. "The compound that we believe the hostages are being held in is located here, on the south side of town."

I pointed to the map and made a circle around the building with my finger. "As you can see, it is surrounded on all sides by dirt and farmland. Any approach we make with large forces will be recognized almost immediately, and they will kill the hostages."

"That is why we will strike swiftly and violently while they sleep," Zaweed interrupted. "They will not know what hit them!"

"I have no doubt that what you're saying is possible, sir, but it is a risky proposition. There is a far better way," I said.

"And what is that, Mr. Shepherd?"

"Sir, if you will allow Commander Zirek, Ajwan, Terlan, and myself to go in before the strike, we can free the hostages. Once they are safe, we will radio back to you to take the village," I said.

The commander scoffed. "Four people? Against a hundred?"

Zirek and I exchanged a look. I felt like I was reliving the same conversation I had just had minutes earlier. Although I agreed that more than four would've been desired, it was clear that this was a culture that didn't understand small teams.

"Four men to sneak in and rescue the hostages under the cover of night," I replied, shaking my head. "Your men will face the hundred. We will simply get the hostages to safety while you do so."

"Commander Zirek?" Zaweed asked. "Do you agree to this?'"

"I believe the American can be trusted," Zirek replied. "I am willing to try his plan."

"Very well," Zaweed yielded. "Please explain your plan in detail."

*　*　*

We moved methodically through the barren fields and mud toward the objective. Our team of four left camp a full two hours before the rest of the unit, parking our Landcruiser two miles short of the village to make the rest of the journey on foot.

It had taken more negotiating to convince Zaweed that my plan was the right plan, but by the end of the briefing, I was confident that he was on board. I just hoped he would hold up his end of the agreement. Our operation relied on timing.

I was confident that our four-man team could handle the mission at hand. With the help of Zirek, I briefed Ajwan and Terlan on what I expected. It was critical that we work together as a cohesive unit for this to be successful. I gave them a crash course in SWAT tactics in our own hour-long briefing before leaving the camp in the dead of night.

We completed our hike, stopping just short of the village and setting up at the edge of a drainage ditch. Our equipment was sparse – more so than I would have liked for an operation like this. On SWAT missions, we always had body armor and night vision devices, as well as perfectly-zeroed suppressed rifles. For the mission ahead, we only had harnesses carrying extra magazines, my AK-47, and sniper rifle.

I borrowed Zirek's night vision spotter scope and surveyed the village, focusing on the target building. There were two guards on the north end and one on the south. None of them seemed worried about the potential of an attack. The northern guards were smoking and chatting while the southern guard was leaning against the walls of the compound. I wasn't sure he wasn't sleeping standing up. He didn't move at all the entire time I watched him.

The village itself looked quiet. There were more vehicles with bed mounted machine guns and a few smoldering fires, but it appeared that everyone had gone to bed. Even without the benefit of suppressed rifles to aid our stealthy approach, it seemed like a pretty straightforward operation.

"I don't think we'll need Zaweed for this," I whispered to Zirek.

Zirek shook his head. "He will be here in an hour regardless of what you believe," he said.

I turned to the rest of the men. "Ok, it's just like we briefed. We'll meet at the front of the house, breach, gather hostages, and then get out through the south exit. Any questions?"

I asked Zirek to translate just in case Terlan or Ajwan had any issues. They both spoke English, but sometimes words were lost in translation. They both nodded their understanding.

"Let's roll," I said.

I raised my AK-47 to the ready position and took off in a jog toward the northern entrance of the compound as Zirek followed. Ajwan and Terlan separated from us, heading to the southern entrance.

I checked my watch as we approached the wall of the compound. In ten minutes, the fireworks would start regardless of our success or failure. I hoped Zaweed waited at least that long.

Reaching the corner of the compound wall, I slung my rifle and unsheathed my knife. I peered around the corner. The two guards were still smoking and chatting, facing away from us. I nodded to Zirek who drew his own blade.

I moved toward the two men in a crouch as I crept through the remaining darkness. They were standing under a lone light underneath the entrance, oblivious to their fate. Zirek followed close on my heels as I moved toward them.

I held the knife loosely with the blade pointed toward the ground. As I approached, the second guard caught sight of me. His eyes widened as he watched me grab the other guard's mouth with one hand and drive the blade into his throat with the other. He tried to raise his weapon, but Zirek was on top of him before he could, slashing his throat.

I had never killed a man with a blade. It was deeply personal, much more so than anything I had ever experienced. But I felt no emotion. It was just a means to an end. At some point, I had lost the ability to feel anything toward the people I fought. They were all just part of the mission.

As the man stopped struggling under my grip, I twisted the blade and withdrew it, sending blood everywhere. I dragged his lifeless body out of the light, wiped off my blade, and then re-sheathed it.

I helped Zirek move his guard and then held up my rifle as we stacked up on the entryway. I took a deep breath and then exhaled slowly. After a silent countdown, I bolted into the dark compound with Zirek close behind me.

I button-hooked left as Zirek went right. The courtyard of the compound was empty. I saw Ajwan and Terlan waiting by the entrance of the building. Two dead bodies lay at their feet. They had beaten us to the target building.

We stacked up on the door with Ajwan as the breacher. I took my place behind him as Zirek and Terlan brought up the rear. After Zirek tapped my shoulder, I tapped Ajwan's shoulder.

Ajwan pulled open the wooden door and I entered. The room was dark, lit only by a pair of lanterns. I could make out about two dozen silhouettes, either curled up, sitting, or lying on the floor. I turned right, looking for threats as I heard the others enter behind me.

As I turned back left, I saw a man stand from a cot in the back of the room. He yelled something before shots rang out. Terlan entered the room behind Zirek and dropped the man with two center of mass shots.

"Clear," I yelled.

"Clear," Zirek echoed. As he did, I heard muffled gunshots. Zaweed was right on time. They had begun their assault on the village.

I pulled out my flashlight, trying to get a better sense of the situation. There were women and children everywhere. I heard muffled cries as my ears stopped ringing from Terlan's gunshots.

Ajwan and Terlan covered the door as Zirek and I helped the women and children prepare to leave. As I went to the back of the room, one of the women said something to me. I leaned in closer to hear what she was saying. She seemed very weak.

"Give me a rifle," she said in English. *English*. I shined my light on her. She was dirty and disheveled, but I could tell she was very attractive beneath the grisly appearance.

"We're going to get you out of here," I said as I helped her to her feet. "You can barely stand."

"My name is Asmin," she said. "Let me fight."

I saw Zirek spin around, nearly dropping the woman he was helping as he heard the name.

"What did she say?" he asked.

"She said her name is Asmin," I replied. "We need to get moving."

"Give me a rifle," she repeated.

"No," I said sternly. "Let's get moving."

Zirek approached, shining his light in her face. "It's you," he said with a look of disbelief.

"Look, we can figure this out when we get to safety," I said urgently as I heard more gunfire erupt outside. "We have to get these people out of here."

"You're *the Lioness*," Zirek said, still standing there stunned by the woman in front of him.

CHAPTER THIRTY TWO

O K, so who is this chick?" I asked Zirek as Commander Zaweed and a group of his fighters gathered around the mysterious woman.

We had managed to get all the hostages to safety as Zaweed's men stormed the village. They were ruthless in their killing of ISIS fighters, taking no prisoners as they recaptured the area in under two hours. For as rag-tag as Zaweed's group looked, they were fierce and capable.

When the fighting subsided, we moved the women to a safe location. Ajwan was reunited with his cousin. When she asked about her husband, he told her that he had died fighting. She didn't even flinch as he broke the news. I guessed that she was over him too.

The attention of the camp had been drawn to the woman Zirek called *The Lioness*. He had personally escorted her to the hut that Commander Zaweed and his lieutenants had taken over for his command center. They treated her with reverence. Everyone seemed to recognize her.

"She is from the Yekîneyên Parastina Jin," he whispered as Commander Zaweed asked her to tell her story. "She has killed over one hundred and fifty men. Listen."

He pointed to the woman as she sipped on the water she had been given. The grit and grime had been wiped away from her face. She was even more attractive than I had originally suspected.

"We were in Ma'shūq to kill al-Amani," she said softly as she stared at the floor. You could hear a pin drop as everyone fixated on the woman.

"Someone told them about us," she said. "Everyone was killed. I managed to escape and blended in with the women they were taking."

"We thought you were dead," Zaweed said. "They played videos of your beheading."

Asmin nodded. "That was Lilan. I watched them do it. They searched all of the women looking for me. I was too weak to speak, but I remember her standing up and claiming to be me. She was very brave. She died for me."

"You were missing for three months," Zaweed said. "We will send you home and let the others know that you are OK."

"No," Asmin said, shaking her head. "Don't let them know I live."

Zaweed frowned. "You are more than just a brave warrior. You are a symbol for the YPJ and Kurdish people. They must know that you are alive."

Asmin shook her head once more. "Not until al-Amani is dead. He went back to Raqqa after they took us to Hasud. He must die."

She looked weary, but I recognized the look in her face. It was the look of someone with a thirst for vengeance.

"Your unit is gone," Zaweed said. "And I have no men to spare. You must go back. You may regroup once you've had time to recover."

I pulled Zirek to the side as Zaweed and Asmin argued the point. "What's next for us?" I whispered.

"We will go where we are needed," Zirek replied.

"What if we helped her?" I asked, nodding to the woman pleading her case to the commander.

"Commander Zaweed is right," Zirek said. "She must go home and prove that she is safe. It is the only way."

I suddenly felt connected to her cause. "She just lost her entire unit. Her friends died for her. You and I both know what she's going through. And if they bring her back, she may get killed anyway."

"What do you suggest?" Zirek asked.

"We have a good team," I said. "And if she's as good as everyone seems to think she is, she'll make a good addition. Let's go find this al-Amani guy ourselves."

Zirek laughed. "Do you even know where Raqqa is?" he asked.

I shrugged. I hated to admit that I knew less than I should have.

"It is the capital of Daesh territory. If he is there, he is guarded by ten thousand soldiers," Zirek said.

I thought back to my research on the Islamic State. *Ayman Awad al-Baghdadi*. If al-Amani was in Raqqa, I had a feeling he was either with al-Baghdadi or knew where al-Baghdadi could be found.

"We need to help her," I said sternly. "Let them fear her ghost."

Zirek sighed. "The war has changed you already, my friend," he said.

"You know this is the right thing to do," I said.

I waited to approach Asmin until Zaweed and his lieutenants had moved on to another hut to eat the breakfast prepared for them by the women we had rescued. As Asmin started to rise and follow them, I sat down across from her at the table.

She paused, studying me as she sat back down. "You're the one who wouldn't give me a weapon."

Her English was perfect. She had green eyes that seemed to stare right through my very soul with an intensity unlike anything I had ever seen. She reminded me a little of Lindsey, but with much more confidence and a more powerful presence.

I smiled sheepishly as I folded my hands on the table. "I'd like to help you," I said.

"Your accent...You're an American," she replied with a pained look on her face.

"I am," I replied.

Asmin let out a sigh. "You think you can help me?"

I looked up at Zirek who was standing behind me. I wondered why she seemed to have such a disdain for Americans. As far as I knew, there were many Americans fighting alongside the Kurds. I made a mental note to ask him about it later.

"Have you met Commander Zirek?" I asked.

Asmin looked up at Zirek. "I have heard of you, but I thought you left the battlefield long ago."

"I felt it necessary to return," Zirek replied.

Asmin turned her attention back to me. "And how do you believe you can help me?"

"You need a team to help you kill al-Amani," I said. "I think we can help you with that."

"The two of you?" she asked skeptically.

"Ajwan and Terlan are eating breakfast," I replied. "They will be joining us as well."

"It is not them that I worry about," she said, once again seemingly staring through me.

"You seem to have a problem with Americans," I said. "Maybe you'd rather go back to your hometown and wait for them to find a team for you."

I looked at Zirek and shrugged. As I started to stand, she grabbed my arm. "Wait," she said softly.

"Yeah?" I asked as I slowly sat back down.

"Your eyes," she said.

"What about them?" I asked.

"You're not like the other Americans I have seen out here," she said. "Your eyes tell a much deeper story."

"I don't understand," I said.

"The Americans I have fought with. They have no stake here. They fight for glory. For themselves. For fun. This is a playground to them," she said, shaking her head in disgust. "But you. There is much pain in your eyes. You fight for something much deeper."

"Is that so?"

"There is a certain sadness to your look," she said, speaking like a doctor examining a patient in a clinic. "You have experienced much pain that you try to hide, but your eyes betray you."

I closed my eyes, thinking of Lindsey and Chelsea. The woman across the table from me certainly wasn't wrong. I still carried the pain of their deaths with me, secretly wishing that the next battle would be my ticket to see them again.

"If Commander Zirek is willing to fight alongside you, then so am I," she said softly. "But the hatred and sadness in your heart are clearly visible in your eyes. Don't let them consume you."

Too late for that, I thought.

CHAPTER THIRTY THREE

I slept nearly twelve hours in the wake of the hostage rescue in Hasud. Despite the austere conditions, sleeping on the floor in one of the small huts in the village, I slept straight through the day and into the night. I was physically and mentally exhausted. My body just couldn't go anymore.

When I awoke, I found Zirek at the makeshift command center at the center of the village with Commander Zaweed. They were sitting casually at a table, laughing and telling stories over a cup of Qehweya Kezwanan- Kurdish coffee made of ground roasted terebinth beans. They looked like two old friends casually meeting at a coffee shop to catch up after years apart.

"You're alive!" Zirek said with a hearty laugh as I walked in. "I was beginning to think your spirit had left us."

"It sure felt like it," I said, scratching my head.

Zirek held up the pot of coffee. "Please join us. Would you like a cup?"

I graciously accepted. Zirek found a nearby cup and poured the caramel-colored liquid. I took a slow sip, letting the warm liquid linger in my mouth. I had tasted Kurdish coffee before, but this was much less bitter than I remembered. It was mostly sweet. A little too sweet for coffee, but it wasn't bad. I took a seat next to them at the oval table.

"Where's Asmin?" I asked, noticing that we were alone in the room. When I had left Zirek and Asmin, they had been discussing how we would go about finding al-Amani in Raqqa, after Zirek had talked Zaweed into letting her leave with us.

"A group of YPJ took her back to Al-Malikiyah this afternoon," Zaweed said. "She will be given a hero's welcome, and the world will know that Daesh cannot defeat our women."

I frowned and looked at Zirek. "But what of al-Amani?" I asked.

"He will be dealt with by the American Special Forces," Zaweed said matter-of-factly. "They are systematically eliminating Daesh's cabinet members."

"Come on," I said, shaking my head. "Seriously?"

"What is the problem?" Zaweed asked, exchanging a look with Zirek.

"That's bullshit," I said. "Why would you take her out of the fight?"

"Asmin is bigger than one fight," Zirek interjected. "She is a symbol."

"Of what? She wants to fight. Why not let her?" I asked. It was starting to piss me off. There was just as much bureaucracy here as there was in the sheriff's department back home. Keeping up appearances was more important than the actual mission, it seemed.

"It is not your place to question my decision," Zaweed said sternly. "Remember that you are a guest of the Kurdish people."

"Copy that," I said, standing as I downed the rest of the coffee and slammed the cup on the table. "Thanks for the coffee."

I stormed out into the cool night air. I didn't know why it bothered me so much, but the fact that Asmin was being used as propaganda just rubbed me the wrong way. There was something about her that I couldn't quite put my finger on, but she was different. Although she had said very little, somehow she made me believe in her cause.

I walked out to the center of the village where a group of fighters was standing around a bonfire. The two men nearest me moved aside to let me join their circle. I nodded in appreciation as they went back to their conversation.

"You're the American," the man next to me said in broken English as he studied me.

He was wearing a dirty Kurdish YPG uniform. After a few seconds of awkwardly staring at me, he smiled through his thick beard and elbowed the man next to him. They exchanged a few excited remarks in Kurdish and then pointed at me, saying *Gûr*.

I gave them a confused look. "Gûr?" I asked.

The man nodded. "Gûr!" he said excitedly. "It's you."

Suddenly all the men around the fire were staring in awe of me as they whispered "gûr" to each other. Was it some kind of insult for Americans? I had no idea what they were trying to say.

"I'm sorry, I don't understand," I said to the man who had started the unrest. "What is that?"

He pointed at me again. "Ma'shūq," he said. I knew that word. It was the city where I had fought with the YPG, but I still didn't understand what that had to do with me.

"Gûr?" I repeated.

"It means *wolf*," a voice behind me said. I turned to see Zirek standing with his arms folded.

"Wolf?" I asked, leaving the crowd of fighters now fascinated by my presence.

Zirek nodded as walked back toward the command hut. "That's the name they gave you after Ma'shūq. Like Asmin, your reputation is also much bigger than you are."

"Why? And how am I just now hearing about this?" I asked.

"You Americans already have enough ego, I didn't want you to be distracted," Zirek said. "You must focus on the missions ahead, not on your accomplishments."

"But what have I accomplished to earn a nickname like that?" I asked.

Zirek shook his head. "Nothing. There are no accomplishments in war."

"OK, I'm lost," I said with a shrug.

"You killed many ISIS fighters in Ma'shūq, hunting them like a wolf," Zirek explained. "Like anything else, your reputation exceeds your actual contribution. Many men believe that you are American Special Forces here to turn the battle in our favor."

"Oh," I said, not sure of how to respond to such a compliment.

"There is no doubt that you fight well. It is why I personally chose to fight with you. But I have kept this from you because I do not want you distracted. You must understand that the battlefield is a place of many such tales. Anything that stands out can become mythological in scope very quickly," Zirek said.

"Like the Lioness?" I asked, thinking back to Asmin.

Zirek frowned. "You should not have challenged Commander Zaweed," he said. "It was very unwise."

"That was bullshit though," I said defiantly.

"Perhaps," Zirek said. "But you are a guest here, and there is a chain of command."

I thought about it for a second as I looked up into the clear night sky. The stars were brighter than anything I had ever seen back home. Were this not a war zone, it might have been a beautiful place.

But it was a war zone, and not *my* war zone. Zirek and Zaweed were in charge. It was their show. If they wanted to focus on appearances over results, who was I to argue? My only goal was to kill al-Baghdadi or die trying. I decided that the politics of their decision was none of my business.

"You know, you're right," I yielded. "I'm sorry."

"Good, there is no place for ego here," Zirek said. "We have another mission tomorrow morning."

"What is it?"

"There is a convoy of oil tankers scheduled to be taken into Turkey through Nusbayin in two days. We are going to disrupt that shipment," Zirek said.

"Just the four of us?" I asked. It seemed like a pretty big task for a small sniper team.

Zirek shook his head. "In the morning, we will join a small unit of YPJ fighters in Sihel."

"YPJ? Women?" I asked, doing a poor job of hiding my skepticism.

Zirek nodded. "Patience, my friend," he said with a knowing smile.

CHAPTER THIRTY FOUR

The next morning, I set out with Zirek and company for Sihel. Commander Zaweed's men gave us food and ammo before assigning a four-door Toyota Hilux pickup to take us on our journey. This one didn't have the bed-mounted machine gun like the others, but it was newer and had Iraqi military badging in various places on the inside. I assumed it had been requisitioned from Iraqi Security Forces soldiers somehow, either through trades or outright abandonment.

Before leaving, I was able to pick up an M4 rifle, also presumably from the Iraqi military. It suited me much better than the AK-47 and had a Trijicon 4 x 32 ACOG scope on top. It was closer to what I had been used to in SWAT, but the downside was that I was the only member of the team now carrying 5.56 NATO rounds. Everyone else had 7.62, so in the event of getting into a firefight and exhausting both my M40 Sniper Rifle and M4, I would have to borrow another rifle or switch to the Beretta M9 I carried in my drop leg holster.

We drove through the farmlands of northern Syria. Some of it was very lush, green, and beautiful, with fields of bright red flowers. But most of the countryside was just desert and dirt like Hasud.

We passed through a few small villages. They seemed mostly abandoned. The area was heavily war-torn, a product of the war against ISIS that had been ongoing for years. They looked cratered and burned, like something out of an old war movie.

It was mid-morning when we made it to the village. Zirek parked, and we carried our gear toward the center of town. The people stopped and stared at us as we followed Zirek. Some seemed relieved to see us, but there was a palpable sense of guarded apprehension about our presence. I imagined it was another town that had grown weary of the fighting and the looming threat of ISIS.

"Pretty warm welcome," I said, breaking the silence as I watched a family retreat into their modest home.

"This is a Christian village," Zirek said. "Daesh has sent death squads to kill the men and rape their women. They all know."

"They all know what?" I asked.

"That those who stay behind are as good as dead," Zirek replied.

"So why do they stay?" I asked.

"To defend their homes," Zirek said. "Do you see any military here? If they leave, they either die or denounce their faith. At least here they have a chance to fight."

"These men don't look like the fighting type."

"No one does…until they have to."

He wasn't wrong. Before losing my girls, I certainly never imagined myself fighting a war. The most I had ever prepared for was shooting a suspect that threatened someone else or my ability to go home alive. War was still an altogether new concept for me.

It was apparently the same for Zirek – a school teacher turned military commander, trainer, and now the de facto leader of a sniper team. War just had a way of awakening the most primal instincts – fight or flight. For the people that stayed behind, despite the odds, they seemed to be choosing fight.

"I just see women, children, and elderly," I said as a few more people avoided us. "Where are the men?"

"Some fight with us. Others stayed behind to protect the village. They are likely out on foot patrols or sleeping so they can patrol at night," Zirek replied.

"How many fighters for a village this size?" I asked.

"Maybe a dozen," Zirek said.

"A dozen? They would get massacred."

"Why do you think it has come to this? This is not America. These people have no military or police to protect them. The Syrian government fights only to keep its power. Your government backs the rebels that have tried to overthrow Assad. Those same rebels support the Islamic State. That leaves the men of this village alone to defend against the growing Daesh Army," Zirek replied.

"I thought we were doing airstrikes and taking out top cabinet members of ISIS?" I asked. I remembered Commander Zaweed mentioning it, and I had heard bits and pieces of the airstrikes on the news.

"Daesh is like a garden full of weeds. For every one that you kill, another sprouts up in its place. The only solution is total elimination," Zirek said, shaking his head.

We arrived at a run-down building near the center of the village. Zirek knocked four times as Ajwan and Terlan took cover positions. After a few seconds, the metal door opened and an older woman appeared. Zirek said something to her in Kurdish, and she stepped aside, inviting us in.

We walked into the dusty room. I kept my M4 at the low-ready position, not entirely convinced that we weren't walking into a trap. Zirek casually followed the old woman through the house. The wooden boards beneath us creaked with every step.

She led us to one of the bedrooms and pushed aside the bed and then rolled up the rug beneath it, revealing a trap door that apparently led to a basement or cellar of some sort. The stairway was lit by an oil lamp. The woman moved aside, motioning for us to enter.

"You two stay here," Zirek said to Terlan and me, before nodding for Ajwan to follow.

I kept my rifle ready as I watched Zirek descend the stairs. I didn't like how cryptic he had been about this mission. He had told me that we were meeting with women fighters of the YPJ, but had failed to mention it involving secret knocks or hidden basements. The hair on the back of my neck was standing straight up.

I looked at Terlan for hints. He seemed alert but calm. I wondered if he was aware of the plan, or just naturally uninterested. I was sure he had understood the conversation between Zirek and the old woman. My limited proficiency in the Kurdish language had again put me at an extreme disadvantage. The only words I had caught were *woman* and *food*. It was hardly enough to gain an understanding of what was going on.

"He's been down there a while," I said nervously after checking my watch. It had only been a few minutes, but I had expected Zirek to return almost immediately with whatever he was down there for.

Terlan let out an uninterested grunt and went back to watching the hallway. He and Ajwan weren't very talkative in general. I wasn't sure he knew anything at all – or cared, for that matter.

"Do you know why he's down there?" I asked anyway.

Terlan looked annoyed as he turned back to me. I shrugged apologetically as he stared at me like the answer was stupidly obvious.

"To get *Keç*," he said finally.

Keç? I tried to remember the crash course I had in Kurdish. From what I could remember, Keç meant girl. *Girl? What girl?* My mind raced through the possibilities. Zirek had mentioned a dozen or so YPJ fighters joining us. *Was that what Terlan meant? Was it something else? A sex slave? A girlfriend?*

Terlan saw the confused look on my face and impatiently pointed down the stairs. I turned to see Zirek emerge, followed by a lone woman carrying a bag. As she neared the top of the stairs, the flicker of the gas lamp danced across her face. My face felt flush as I recognized her.

Asmin?

* * *

"Will someone please explain this to me?" I asked impatiently as we sat at the old woman's kitchen table eating meat pies called *kuki* and drinking black tea.

"We are going to kill al-Amani," Asmin said before sipping her tea.

"I get that, but what's with all the secrets?" I asked, staring at Zirek. "You told me we were coming here to pick up a dozen YPJ fighters."

"After your outburst with Commander Zaweed? How could I have told you?" Zirek asked calmly.

I was pissed. I didn't like going blindly into missions, and I *especially* hated being lied to. There was no excuse for not telling me what we were doing.

I slammed my fist down on the table, causing the silverware and bowls to rattle. "That's bullshit! You had plenty of time to brief me on the drive over here. Or – I don't know – anytime after!"

Asmin put her soft hand on my clenched fist, squeezing it gently. "Save your anger for the battlefield," she said.

Her touch was calming. The more time I spent with her, the more she reminded me of Lindsey. I pulled my hand away in a vain attempt to break her spell.

"Are we not a team here?" I asked.

"Mr. Shepherd, the plan came together while you were sleeping," Zirek explained. "Commander Zaweed was clear in his insistence that Asmin return. The YPJ brought her here instead."

"And where are they? You said there would be a dozen women," I asked, looking around at the otherwise empty house.

"They continued to Al-Malikiyah this morning," Asmin said. "It is just us."

"Why?" I asked.

"You said you wanted to help," Zirek answered.

"Hey don't throw this on me," I shot back. "You two came up with this plan while I was sleeping."

Zirek nodded. "We did. Asmin and I have much in common, including al-Amani."

"I am confused," I said, scratching my head. "What about the convoy? Was that a lie too?"

Zirek shook his head. "We will strike tomorrow before it goes into Turkey."

"With just the five of us?"

"If you fight as well as Zirek has told me, then we should have more than enough," Asmin said.

"Ok, but first, no more secrets," I said, still stuck on why Zirek would want to join Asmin's cause. "What is the connection you two have with this Amani guy?"

Zirek frowned. He finished his food and downed the last of his tea as I waited patiently for him to fill me in. As he pushed the bowl aside, he cleared his throat and sat back in his chair.

"Do you remember what I told you the night we had dinner?" Zirek asked. "About my family?"

I nodded. Thinking back to Zirek's story of his family being brutally murdered by Al Qaeda in Iraq brought back a flood of memories of my own family's death. I had done a good job of pushing that to the back of my mind, but I couldn't stop the images of Chelsea's little hand against the windows of the burning bus from rushing back. I closed my eyes.

"At the time, Mosef al-Amani was nothing more than a foot soldier with Al Qaeda, but he was there. He was one of the men that crucified my son and burned my wife alive after raping her again and again. As Daesh grew in strength and number, al-Amani moved up in the ranks, becoming a brutal executioner of Christians and Muslims alike. It is said that the crucifixion of the children was his idea," Zirek said softly.

I opened my eyes and looked at Zirek. Tears rolled down his scarred cheeks as he stared at the table in front of him. It was clear to me that we all had skin in this game.

"Zirek told me about your pain," Asmin said, her green eyes seemed to penetrate my soul. "The man you seek, Ayman Awad al-Baghdadi, is very powerful within the Islamic State. He is known to be the Minister for Foreign Operations. If it is revenge you seek, al-Amani will know the path to al-Baghdadi."

"I really don't know what I seek anymore," I said, breaking eye contact. "But I'll help you. No more secrets."

"We should start planning, then," Zirek said, apparently shaking off the memories of his own family. "The convoy will be on its way to Turkey in less than twelve hours."

"Just show me where to shoot, boss," I said with a wry smile.

CHAPTER THIRTY FIVE

That evening, after gathering food, supplies, and water, we left Sihel under cover of darkness. We had briefed the plan in the old woman's kitchen before we all tried to get some sleep. I wasn't convinced that we could pull off such a complicated plan with just the five of us, but Asmin and Zirek seemed confident that we could easily disable the convoy and destroy the oil.

We had picked out an ambush point along the convoy's route. We would spend the night there and be ready for them as they headed north toward Turkey the next morning. Our route across the dirt roads and farmlands would take us just under four hours, leaving us plenty of time to prepare before the estimated arrival of the convoy at just after 10 a.m.

The wind was howling as Zirek drove us down winding dirt roads toward our objective. The visibility was terrible. I could barely see more than a few feet in front of us. It was worse than the dense morning fogs I had grown used to living in south Louisiana. And although the windows were up, it felt like the dirt had entered the cab of our four-door pickup. I could feel the grit in my teeth as I sipped water to keep my mouth from getting too dry.

The terrain changed from flat farmlands to rolling hills as we headed west toward the main highway running to Qamishli, the border city near Nusaybin in Turkey. The wind calmed and visibility improved as the terrain grew more rugged.

Several hours later, as we neared the target highway, the terrain once again turned to flat farmland. We found the observation position from the map, high ground just over 500 meters from the highway, nestled between a cluster of villages on either side. It was a large hill near a dried out river that gave us the optimum view of the approaching convoy. The dried riverbed also gave us concealment since it snaked toward the road and then paralleled it to the south.

We parked the Hilux truck at the base of the hill on the opposite side from the highway and hiked the rest of the way, setting up just over two-thirds the way up the western slope. I set up a shooting position with Zirek and then found a place to take a nap. I checked my watch as I positioned my backpack as a pillow. It was just after 5 a.m. By my calculations, we had arrived with nearly five hours to spare until the convoy rolled through.

I was jolted awake by someone grabbing my arm. As my eyes fluttered open, I saw a woman kneeling over me.

"Sweetheart?" I asked as I came to. I was certain it was Lindsey. *Was I still dreaming? Had I died?*

"Shepherd, you must wake up," the woman said. As the neurons continued firing, I realized that it was Asmin. It was eerie how similar the two women were. I tried to shake it off.

"What is it?" I asked as I sat up and looked at my watch. I had slept through the sunrise, but it was only 7 a.m., we still had plenty of time to prepare.

"Look!" she said impatiently, pointing toward the highway.

I looked up to see a convoy of four trucks with bed-mounted machine guns racing south toward our position. The lead and trail vehicles flew black Islamic State flags from the bed. I grabbed my rifle as I saw them peel off the main road and turn onto the dirt road leading toward our position.

"Zirek," I whispered. I crouched as I moved toward him. He had already taken up his position at his spotter's scope. To our left and right were Ajwan and Terlan covering our flanks as always.

"Daesh death squad," Zirek said as he watched them through the scope.

I lowered myself to my rifle and flipped open the dust covers. The convoy sped past us and turned into the nearest village. I watched through my scope as a dozen men dismounted and stormed the village. A few men of the village attempted to fight, but the gunner of the lead vehicle mowed them down using the bed-mounted fifty caliber machine gun.

"We have to help them!" Asmin cried. I looked back over my shoulder. She had grabbed binoculars from her bag and was watching the carnage unfold with us.

"No, we cannot," Zirek said.

The gunfire stopped as the ISIS fighters took over the village. They were all wearing desert fatigues, their faces covered in black. In less than twenty minutes, they had established complete control.

"They're going to kill them!" Asmin said. I turned back again to see her drop the binoculars and go for her own rifle, a Russian-made SVD sniper rifle. Zirek dropped his scope and stopped her.

"What are you doing?" he growled.

"I will not sit here and watch them kill more innocent people," Asmin said, wrestling away from his grip as she moved toward me to get a better shooting position.

"If you shoot, you will give away our position, and our mission will fail," Zirek warned. "We cannot help these people."

"I don't care about your mission!" Asmin protested. "Those people are going to be executed."

While Asmin and Zirek continued their debate, I turned my attention back to the scene below. The camouflaged fighters rounded up four men and dragged them to the makeshift market at the center of the village. A man dressed in all black exited the lead vehicle and strolled casually toward them. I estimated that it was about a five-hundred meter shot, but the winds were still unpredictable. It wouldn't be a cakewalk by any means.

Four men of the death squad stood behind their hostages as the man in all black approached. A fifth fighter ran out from the same truck carrying a tripod and camera. He hastily set it up in front of the hostages.

"They're going to film an execution," I said.

"No!" Asmin cried. She cleared Zirek and dropped to a knee, steadying her aim, presumably at the man dressed in black.

I flicked off the safety and stretched my finger, aiming for the fighter next to the man in black. The four camouflaged men drew their knives as the man in black appeared to be making a speech to the camera. The man I focused on held his blade to the terrified villager's throat.

"Don't do it!" Zirek barked.

The man in black appeared to give the order. I exhaled slowly as the man I had trained my sights on bent down to go to work. As my finger settled on the trigger, I saw the man in black suddenly drop as brain matter sprayed on the face of the hostage positioned in front of him.

I hadn't heard a sound, but I looked up to see if Asmin had shot. She was still fighting with Zirek, who had escalated his resistance by trying to move her from her shooting position.

"What the fuck?" I said softly as I looked back at the hostage takers below. Two more men lay on the ground with brain matter splattered on the ground. The two remaining Daesh cowards released their grips on the hostages and ran for cover.

"Did you see that?" I said, turning back to see Asmin and Zirek facing off. "Someone took them out."

"What?" Asmin said as she pushed away from Zirek and used the scope on her rifle to survey the situation.

When I looked back at the village below, the rest of the death squad fighters were running toward the vehicles. They shot wildly in all directions, not sure where the shots had come from. They all ran past the vehicles, scattering as they abandoned their unit and ran toward the next village.

One by one, the mysterious, silent sniper picked them off, until one of the fighters managed to turn back, get into a vehicle and speed off to the south. I wondered if the ghost sniper had intentionally allowed him to escape.

Putting down my rifle, I grabbed Zirek's spotter scope, using my counter-sniper SWAT training to attempt to locate the ghost sniper. We were arguably in the best shooting position, but there was no one anywhere around us. I searched other places I thought might be good locations for the shots the ghost sniper had taken, hoping to catch a glimpse of what I thought were Special Ops guys doing good work.

"What is going on?" Zirek asked.

I handed him the spotter scope and pointed to the village. "Someone put an end to this death squad," I said.

"I should have done it myself," Asmin said.

"And you would have given away our position," Zirek said angrily. "You must learn to control yourself."

"I will not stand by and watch innocent people die," Asmin shot back.

"If you do not use restraint, *you* will die," Zirek replied.

I didn't really want to get in between two pissed off, battle-hardened warriors, but as I checked my watch, I realized we had less than an hour to get set up for our mission.

"I know I'm just the American here, but we might want to consider getting ready for the convoy," I said as I stood.

"Are you able to follow orders?" Zirek asked, refusing to take his focus off of Asmin.

"I will do what is necessary," she said defiantly.

She grabbed her bag and started down the hill toward the ambush location. As much as her appearance reminded me of Lindsey, her demeanor was a polar opposite of the love of my life. Lindsey was always quiet, reserved, *soft*. Asmin was pure energy – a blazing fireball of energy. I could see how she had earned the *Lioness* moniker.

She was truly a warrior – queen of the desert.

CHAPTER THIRTY SIX

The convoy sped down the empty highway toward us. I watched through my rifle scope as it came into view. I had been expecting pickup trucks similar to the ones that had raided the village. Instead, what I found were up-armored Humvees with roof-mounted machine guns. It wasn't going to be as easy as Zirek and Asmin seemed to think.

A half mile north of the approaching convoy, I scanned ahead to see the roadblock set up by Ajwan, Terlan, and Zirek. It had been a last minute change of plans. Upon seeing the abandoned ISIS vehicles, Zirek had called a tactical audible.

The convoy of two oil tankers sandwiched between the two up-armored Humvees slowed as it approached the roadblock. Ajwan and Terlan, dressed in ISIS fatigues, stood in front of the two trucks that were parked nose to nose. Terlan held his hand up as the lead Humvee slowed to a stop.

I watched as the passenger hastily exited the lead Humvee and stormed toward Terlan, arms flailing as he appeared to be ordering them to let the convoy pass. We had no radios between us, a flaw in the plan I really hated. Beyond body language, there was no way for me to know if the plan went sideways.

I took aim at the gunner manning the lead Humvee's machine gun. He seemed ready to mow down Terlan and Ajwan as they talked to the angry fighter.

As the man seemed to berate Terlan, Zirek appeared from the passenger seat of the truck. He was wearing all black, having stolen the executioner's attire. There was a noticeable change in the angry fighter's demeanor as Zirek calmly talked to him. I imagined Zirek telling the man exactly what we had briefed – the road ahead was not safe. It had been taken by a YPG unit, and the shipment would be destroyed if they did not detour.

Zirek pointed to his left toward me. They had blocked the road beneath my position on the hill, just past the dirt road that led to the village with dead ISIS fighters. The man seemed to nod in agreement and walked back to the Humvee.

The convoy followed as the lead Humvee turned right and headed toward me. I kept my sights on the roof machine-gunner of the lead Humvee. When the last Humvee turned onto the road, Zirek and company hurried into the ISIS trucks and gave chase.

The convoy approached my position slowly down the narrow dirt road. I aimed center of mass, just above where I thought the man's body armor might be, near his throat. I exhaled slowly as I squeezed the trigger. The round struck the man in the throat, dropping him into the cab of the Humvee. Seconds later, the convoy came to a screeching halt and armed fighters dismounted.

The men fired blindly in my direction, hitting well short of my position as dust flew from the dusty hillside. As they tried to return fire in vain, the first tanker suddenly erupted in an earth-shattering explosion triggered by the explosive Asmin had successfully placed while the leader had argued with Zirek.

Zirek and company blocked in the rear Humvee, letting loose with the fifty-caliber bed-mounted machine guns on both trucks. The dismounted fighters seemed confused and disoriented as they scrambled for cover. They attempted to return fire. I picked them off one by one, causing a crossfire that created even more confusion.

I dropped a fighter as he tried to get back into the lead Humvee to escape, but I wasn't able to reset my aim in time to stop the trail Humvee. It was apparent someone had finally taken command amidst the confusion and ordered a tactical retreat out of the line of fire.

The trail Humvee reversed, slamming into the truck with Terlan as he attempted to shoot back in vain. The hit knocked him out of the bed of the truck and nearly pushed the truck on top of him.

The Humvee pulled forward and then reversed again, this time pushing Terlan's truck out of the way as he just managed to escape. With no way to stop the Humvee, I continued focusing my fire on the dismounted fighters.

The tanker truck driver attempted to turn around but jackknifed the trailer on the small road as it slid into the ditch. As I continued to move from fighter to fighter, I saw Asmin run in from the left, AK-47 blazing. I covered her as best I could while she ran toward the tanker.

As she neared it, she pulled out the rest of the C4, attaching it to the side of the trailer. She moved quickly with grace and efficiency. It was mesmerizing, but as I watched Asmin work, I missed an approaching fighter.

Asmin ducked out of the way just as the man fired and hit the side of the tanker. I tried to cover her, but the two danced in and out of my line of fire, making a clean shot impossible. Asmin drew a blade from her survival vest and dispatched the fighter with a flurry of thrusts to his neck.

I shook off the distraction and covered her escape. As she jumped into the dry riverbed for cover, she detonated the truck, sending another fireball skyward.

Turning my attention back to the Humvee, I saw Zirek's truck ram it in a makeshift PIT maneuver. The Humvee slid into the dry riverbed a dozen or so yards from where Asmin had taken cover. The driver attempted to maneuver out of it, but Ajwan tossed a grenade into the cab through the gunner's port in the roof. There was a muffled *THUMP* and it slowly rolled to a stop.

I scanned the area for additional threats with my scope and then picked up Zirek's spotter's scope and checked again. There were bodies everywhere, but no sign of movement. We had taken out a dozen or more fighters and destroyed the two tankers. *Mission success*, I thought.

I gathered my gear, stuffing the optics in my bag and rolling up my shooter's mat before I shouldered my sniper rifle and picked up my M4. I headed down the hillside to rendezvous with my team.

I jogged down the dirt road toward the wreckage and bodies, carefully scanning each to ensure none were still alive. As I cleared the second tanker, I saw Asmin and Ajwan standing near Terlan's truck. As I got closer, I found Zirek kneeling next to Terlan who was lying in a pool of blood.

Pulling the first aid kid from my backpack, I rushed to Zirek's side to render aid. Zirek shook his head as I dropped to my knees to help. Getting a closer look, I realized that Terlan had been shot in the chest and abdomen several times and his legs were broken.

"He's dead," Zirek said as I checked for a pulse and airway.

Ignoring him, I started CPR. Zirek immediately pulled me away. "It's no use," he said.

"Fuck!" I yelled.

The seemingly successful mission had just become a failure.

CHAPTER THIRTY SEVEN

When the dust settled and the smoke from the burning tankers started to clear, the villagers that had been saved by the ghost sniper came out to help us. They were all sure that we had been the ones that had saved the four men from execution and treated us like heroes as a result.

They helped us bury Terlan. We had an informal ceremony that evening. Zirek spoke as a few of the villagers gathered with us to pay respects.

Zirek didn't say much after the burial service. He had met Terlan in an earlier battle. He knew him to be a brave and noble man. He felt personally responsible for Terlan's death.

We spent the night with the villagers. I found out that it was another Christian village. The ghost sniper had taken out a notorious ISIS death squad known for its brutal propaganda videos. We heard rumors about other ISIS leaders being taken out in similar fashion. Despite Zirek assuring them that we had nothing to do with it, some of the villagers remained convinced that it had been our work.

The small village hosted us for two days after the tanker ambush while we regrouped. Zirek and Asmin debated for hours whether to push forward and find al-Amani or return to Al-Malikiyah and face the propaganda machine.

Losing Terlan had hit Zirek hard. I could tell that his already tepid commitment to finding al-Amani was fading as a result. It seemed Zirek had trouble handling the loss of men under his command. I thought that might have been why he had left the battlefield in the first place and focused his efforts on training and recruitment. I didn't blame him.

For my part, I had grown indifferent. The fighting was an adrenaline rush, and a release of the rage I felt for the death of Chelsea and Lindsey, but I really had no personal stake in killing al-Amani. He was just another faceless terrorist, one of the many heads of the hydra known as ISIS. For each leader we killed, another would instantly take his place. With nowhere else to be and no one who cared back home, I was just along for the ride.

On the third day, Zirek decided that we should go to Al Hasakah. Asmin had convinced him that the only way to honor Terlan properly would be to finish what we started. Going back to Al-Malikiyah would end our team and leave al-Amani for the Americans or Russians to deal with - something we all agreed was unlikely.

Zirek still had friends in Al Hasakah. He had been a commander during that battle. He thought one of his men could help us pin down al-Amani's location in Raqqa. I still held out hope that it would also lead us to al-Baghdadi, the man who had planned and propagandized the attack that killed my family.

We drove the up-armored Humvee we had taken from the convoy and arrived late that evening. To my surprise, Zirek's friend was actually an American CIA Case Officer named Dwight Lincoln.

He was a middle-aged man with dark hair and a patchy beard. I couldn't pick up an accent, but he said he was from Oklahoma originally and had been with the CIA for nearly fifteen years. After meeting with him in the market, he took us to his safe-house.

"You're Alex Shepherd," Lincoln said as he escorted me to my room.

"How did you know?" I asked.

"We don't get many Americans around here," Lincoln said with a shrug. "Besides, it's hard to miss you. You're pretty famous, Mr. *Wolf.*"

"I don't follow," I said.

"You're a cop, right? Family killed in the Louisiana attacks?" Lincoln asked with raised eyebrow.

"What's your point?" I snapped.

"My point is you need to be careful around here," he said. "The American news media just started running a story about you a few days ago. There was an embedded BBC reporter with a YPG unit in Ma'shūq who wrote a story about you. The American cop on a quest for vengeance against ISIS."

"Whatever," I said.

"Just be careful," Lincoln said as he shrugged and started to walk out. "When ISIS connects the dots, they're going to put a pretty big bounty on your head. They *love* high visibility executions."

"Didn't work so well for them with Asmin, did it?" I said.

As Lincoln spun around, I immediately regretted opening my big mouth. It was clear that he hadn't recognized her until that point.

"The girl! She's *The Lioness?* Holy shit! Are you serious?" Lincoln shouted excitedly.

"Nevermind," I said, trying to deflect.

"This is awesome!" Lincoln said as he walked out.

My room was a bedroom in a four-bedroom apartment in downtown Al Hasakah. Austere for American living conditions, but it was the best I had experienced since landing in Iraq. For the first time in months, I slept in an actual bed with sheets.

We all slept well that night. The next morning over breakfast, Lincoln seemed obsessed with Asmin. He referred to her as *Lioness* and wanted to know everything about her. He confessed that he had been somewhat skeptical of her accomplishments. He had heard that she had killed a dozen men in the Battle of Kahtanieh with nothing more than a handgun and a field knife.

"My unit lost many good men and women that day," Asmin deflected as we sipped our coffee on the couches in the living area. "That battle was very fierce."

"But you are from Turkey aren't you?" Lincoln asked.

"You know much more about me than I know of you," Asmin replied as she shifted uneasily on the sofa.

"It's my job, ma'am," Lincoln said. "Besides, you are very famous in Western culture. The Lioness who kills ISIS. It's a great story, given the way ISIS treats women."

"My father was from Mosul," she continued. "He moved to Turkey after the first war with the Americans, where he met my mother. When the Americans left Iraq, he went back to help my uncle move to Turkey. But when he got there, Al Qaeda executed him along with my family there."

"AQI," Lincoln said. "What later became the Islamic State."

Asmin nodded. "I was only eighteen years old at the time, but I after I saw the videos they posted of the execution, I decided to fight. I left Turkey five years ago, and I haven't been back since."

"You're only twenty-three?" I asked incredulously. She had the beauty of a woman in her young twenties but carried herself like a much older, more mature woman.

"I will be twenty-four next month," Asmin replied.

"So you joined the Kurdish Army?" Lincoln asked.

"I wanted to join the YPG, but they told me that they did not allow women to go into Iraq and fight with them. They made me join the YPJ, where I trained for nearly two years. When the Syrian civil war began, the Kurdish government allowed us to fight," she said.

"You are a very strong woman," Lincoln said. "And you have been inspirational to many women. When the reports of your death came out, the whole world mourned. Why haven't you let anyone know you survived?"

"I do not care about fame," Asmin said. "Al-Amani killed my sisters – my best friends, in Hasud. He has raped many women and kills for sport. He must die, and if I had gone back to Al-Malikiyah, it would never happen."

"This is why I contacted you," Zirek said. "I thought you might be able to help us find him in Raqqa."

"Well, for starters, he's not in Raqqa," Lincoln replied.

"Where is he?" I asked.

"I did some digging last night. The last info we had was that he had gone to Aleppo," Lincoln said.

"Where is that?" I asked.

"Nearly four hundred kilometers from here in rebel-controlled territory," Zirek replied. "Do you know what he is doing there?"

"That part is not clear," Lincoln said. "It is rumored that he and several other cabinet members have gone to broker a deal with the rebels."

"What kind of deal?" I asked.

"Support against the Asad regime," Lincoln said. "The Russians recently withdrew most of their ground forces. But there is another theory."

"What is that?" Zirek asked.

"There is a theory floating around that the rebels took control of sarin gas canisters in Aleppo. He may be attempting to acquire them for other purposes," Lincoln said with a pained expression.

"A terrorist attack?" I asked apprehensively.

Lincoln shrugged. "It's just a theory. There's no evidence that the rebels even have the sarin gas canisters. But the fear is, that if they do, al-Amani may try to acquire them. They could use them either here or in their European operations," he replied casually.

"What is the American government going to do about it?" I asked angrily.

"There isn't much we can do," Lincoln said. "We have Special Operations Forces teams working in southern and eastern Syria and Iraq, but Aleppo is rebel territory sandwiched between ISIS and government territory. We can't get there right now."

"Why the fuck not? Send fighters and bomb them to hell!" I shouted.

"It's not that easy," Lincoln said. "The Russians installed an advanced Air Defense System for the Syrians, and we're still supporting the rebels against Assad. We just can't do that right now, especially not on what amounts to a rumor."

My indifference to al-Amani was suddenly gone. If he was planning an attack on innocents with chemical weapons, we had to stop him or die trying. I would not let another family suffer as mine had.

"Then we will go there and kill him before he can," Asmin said.

Lincoln shook his head. "You'll never make it there alive," he said. "Everything between here and there is ISIS, rebel, or government controlled. You will be captured, tortured, and killed before you even make it halfway there."

"And you," Lincoln said, pointing at Asmin. "When they discover that you're still alive, they're going to make an even bigger spectacle of your death."

I looked at Zirek. He appeared to be deep in thought next to the stoic Ajwan. I could tell he was calculating the risk of such a suicide mission.

"We can't just ignore the threat!" I said. "That's exactly how they were able to massacre a school bus full of kids."

"That wasn't our fault," Lincoln said. "The FBI had data on the group nearly a year before it happened, but politics got in the way."

"I don't care!" I yelled. "I'm not going to let it happen again. Zirek?"

Zirek looked up at me and nodded before looking to Lincoln. "My old friend, you have been a great help and a gracious host. Tomorrow, we will leave for Aleppo."

CHAPTER THIRTY EIGHT

L incoln gave us supplies and more weapons and traded our Humvee for an armored Toyota Landcruiser before sending us on our way the next morning. We detoured north through Kurdish-controlled territory to avoid confrontation with ISIS fighters. It added two hours to the five-hour journey, but we couldn't afford the added risk of running into an ISIS checkpoint.

Skirting the Turkey-Syrian border, we managed to make it into the rebel territory without incident. There was a collective sigh of relief as we drove through the first village proudly displaying the rebel flag. Although they weren't our ally, they were far less interested in us than ISIS fighters would have been.

We stopped that night in the rebel-controlled city of Marea to meet with a man Lincoln had said could give us an exact location of al-Amani and the rumored chemical weapons. The city showed signs of heavy bombing. We drove around craters and burned out vehicles while passing crumbling buildings. It looked to have been the scene of heavy fighting between the government and rebels.

The streets were mostly empty. The city looked like a ghost town. I guessed that most of the people still there were fighters or people who refused to leave. The rest had fled to Turkey and other border countries as refugees from the ongoing war.

Our contact, Ahmed Uthman, was standing on the street in front of the address we had been given. He waved to us, recognizing the Landcruiser as we drove up. He matched the description Lincoln had given us to the letter – short, fat, and bald with a neatly trimmed beard. Zirek parked the Landcruiser in front of the shoddy building, and we exited, carrying our gear.

"You are right on time!" Uthman said. "Mr. Lincoln said many good things about you."

He helped us with our gear and escorted us inside. His apartment was on the top floor, a small flat with minimal accommodations. It was nothing like the suite Lincoln had been using.

Lincoln had told us very little about Uthman. He was a rebel fighter with the Aleppo resistance that the CIA had trained and supported. Lincoln trusted him but warned us that allegiances in the Syrian civil war shifted with the wind. We needed to keep our guard up at all times.

"I trust your journey was uneventful?" Uthman asked as he closed the door behind Ajwan.

"We were fortunate," Zirek responded. "Mr. Lincoln tells me that you can help us find al-Amani?"

Uthman smiled. "You waste no time," he said. "Please, at least have a seat."

He ushered us to a small table in the corner of the room. There were only four chairs. Asmin and Zirek sat across from Uthman. I looked at Ajwan who nodded for me to take the last chair as he walked away and stood near the door, keeping watch with his AK-47 at the ready.

"I apologize for my impatience, but time is not on our side," Zirek said.

"You're *her*," Uthman said, studying Asmin. "*The Lioness!*"

Asmin smiled sheepishly. "My name is Asmin," she said.

"You died in Ma'shūq!" Uthman yelped. "You should not be here."

"Can you help us?" Zirek asked, trying to refocus Uthman.

Uthman nodded. "Al-Amani is meeting with Colonel Abu Hammam of the Jaysh al-Islam at the Carlton Citadel Hotel," he said.

"Does he have chemical weapons?" I asked. "Is that rumor true?"

Uthman frowned. "I do not know."

"You don't know?" I pressed. "Aren't those your people?"

"Ah, another American," Uthman said. "No, I am not with the Jaysh al-Islam. I am part of the Army of Mujahedeen, a group your CIA has supported up until recently."

"Why up until recently?" I asked.

"You must ask Mr. Lincoln that question," Uthman replied. "I only know that they withdrew support when the Russians arrived and began bombing us."

"How long will al-Amani be in Aleppo?" Asmin asked, interrupting Uthman's lesson on the Syrian Civil War factions.

"No one knows for sure, but I'd guess a few days," Uthman said, eyeing Asmin. "You are much more beautiful in person. Do you know what will happen if they find out that you are still alive?"

"That is not of your concern," Asmin snapped.

"It should be of yours," Uthman said, turning to Zirek while pointing at Asmin. "This girl isn't even attempting to hide her identity. If she is discovered, you will all die."

"I appreciate your concern," the ever diplomatic Zirek said. "We will make every attempt to prevent that. What else can you tell us about al-Amani?"

"He is in Aleppo to broker a deal between the Army of Islam and the Islamic State. I am not sure of the nature of the deal, but I have been told that they intend to carry out the transaction at the Aleppo Airport. It's quite baffling really."

"Why is that?" I asked.

"Because the airport was returned to the Syrian government's control nearly two years ago. It is exceedingly risky to conduct business there, unless..."

"Unless what?" I asked.

Uthman cleared his throat. "Well, it has been said that the Syrian government in Aleppo has members sympathetic to the rebel cause. You see, the Free Syrian Army consists of many former Syrian military officers. It is possible that Colonel Hammam is using those sympathizers to broker the deal for chemical weapons."

"Do you know when that transaction will take place?" Zirek asked.

"I could find out, but truthfully, that is not of my concern," Uthman said.

"It's not?" I asked. "So if ISIS uses chemical weapons against your group - against your family, then that's ok?"

"My family was killed by a Russian airstrike last year," Uthman said solemnly.

"We have all lost a great deal in this war," Zirek replied softly. "But we must prevent more innocent people from dying. Will you please help us?"

Uthman considered it for a moment. The all-too-familiar-look on his face told me everything I needed to know about what was going through his mind. I had seen it in Zirek and Asmin, and had felt it firsthand. It was the feeling of loss and sorrow, a feeling that never quite went away. And just when you thought it had, something minor triggered it to come rushing back.

"You are friends of Mr. Lincoln," Uthman said, breaking the silence. "He has done much for me and my people. I will go with you to Aleppo and introduce you to a man that will know exactly where they will be."

"Who is he?" I asked.

"Colonel Hammam's top lieutenant," Uthman replied.

CHAPTER THIRTY NINE

A t daybreak, we headed toward Aleppo with Uthman. He did his best to maneuver us around rebel checkpoints and conflict areas, but as we neared the city, we found ourselves staring at a road blocked by tanks.

"That flag is Asa'ib Ahl al-Haq," Uthman said from the back seat. "Haidar al-Karar Brigades."

Haidar al-Karar Brigades? The kaleidoscope of various factions was dizzying. How anyone could keep track of all the different players in this region was beyond me. It was a mess.

Zirek slammed his fist against the steering wheel and looked for a way to turn around without drawing attention to us.

"Bad guys?" I asked.

"They are backed by Hezbollah and the Iranians. Shia Muslims here to assist the Assad regime," Uthman explained.

As Zirek turned around, I looked back to see the sudden streak of a rocket-propelled grenade racing toward one of the tanks. It exploded in a brilliant flash of light and sparks as gunfire erupted behind us.

"Jesus fuck!" I yelled as I watched the fighting unfold. "Friends of yours?"

"Get out of here Zirek!" Uthman yelled as Zirek mashed the accelerator to the floor, causing the Landcruiser to fishtail as we sped away from the fighting.

Zirek took us back north. We had tried the western approach to the city, but as we escaped the battle behind us, we realized that the best bet was to double-back and try the Industrial District on the eastern side. There was a heavier concentration of rebel fighters, but less fighting and fewer pro-government factions.

At least, that's what Uthman told us. I didn't know how much I actually trusted the short bald man. Part of that distrust was fueled by my lack of understanding of the battlefield. I had no idea who was friend and who was foe. There were just too many different factions – some fighting together one day and at war with each other the next.

After two hours of detouring, we finally made it to the Industrial District. I heard the faint sound of what I thought was a fighter jet overhead as we drove past the bombed out buildings.

"Do you hear that?" I asked, straining to hear the jet noise over the idle chatter between Zirek and Uthman. "Are we near an airport?"

"No, the airport is nearly ten miles due south," Uthman said.

The noise grew louder, seemingly directly overhead. Zirek kept driving as I strained to look through the bullet-resistant glass at the sky above. As the noise became deafening, I suddenly saw a fighter fly right over us, pulling straight up and disappearing.

I strained to find the jet as it sounded like it had turned back around. Seconds later, a nearby building exploded. The ground shook as Zirek nearly lost control of our vehicle.

"Syrian Air Force!" Uthman yelled. "Go! Go!"

Zirek once again slammed the accelerator pedal to the floor. The Landcruiser engine screamed as we fled the scene. I lowered the window and found the fighter as it turned back around. The tiny dot grew larger as it approached.

As it made a second bombing run, I saw another sudden streak flash across the sky. Someone had launched a shoulder-fired missile in the fighter jet's direction. The missile impacted just as I saw a dark speck fall from the bottom of the jet. There were two flashes followed by parachutes as the pilots ejected, just as another building exploded from the second bomb. The jet broke apart in a fireball and fell toward the city.

"Holy shit!" I yelled as Zirek continued racing toward the city. "Are you kidding me!"

"Welcome to Aleppo," Uthman said.

* * *

Lieutenant Turkmani met us near an abandoned café a few blocks from the Citadel Hotel. We left Ajwan and Asmin behind with the Landcruiser, careful not to let Asmin be seen in public.

Turkmani appeared to be older than Zirek. His hair and beard were both very gray. He greeted Uthman and then Zirek, ignoring me as I stood behind them. Uthman and Turkmani spoke for several minutes in a language I neither recognized nor understood, before transitioning to English as they sat down at a table with Zirek.

"I can confirm that al-Amani is here with us," Turkmani said.

"Since when does Jaysh al-Islam ally itself with Daesh?" Zirek asked.

"It is a maneuver that I do not understand," Turkmani said, shaking his head. "But Colonel Hammam believes that this will bring about the downfall of Daesh."

"What is he planning?" Zirek asked.

"We have captured sarin gas canisters from the Syrian Army. Colonel Hammam has brokered a deal with al-Amani to hand over three canisters in exchange for the release of Abu al Alloush," Turkmani said.

"How does this bring about Daesh's downfall?" Zirek asked.

"They're hoping ISIS uses the canisters against Western targets, which would force the U.S. military to intervene," I interjected. It was a clever scheme, but I didn't see how it could work. Thousands of people would just die horrible deaths.

"Colonel Hammam believes that al-Amani will attempt to smuggle the canisters into Europe," Turkmani said. "The West will have no choice but to finally destroy the Islamic State."

"When is the exchange?" Zirek asked.

"Tonight at 8 p.m. They will meet in Hangar 17 at the Aleppo International Airport to make the exchange," Turkmani said.

Zirek slid an envelope full of crisp U.S. hundred dollar bills that Lincoln had given him across the table to Turkmani. "Thank you for your trouble," he said.

Turkmani peeked inside the envelope and smiled before stuffing it into his pocket. "Will that be all?" he asked.

"Can you get us a layout of the airport and hangar before this evening?" Zirek asked.

"I will see what I can do," Turkmani replied.

CHAPTER FORTY

Hangar 17 was located on the western end of the Aleppo airport, isolated from the commercial terminal and military hangars. Under cover of darkness, we made our way in through a hole in the dilapidated perimeter fence, sneaking toward our observation position on the south side of the airport.

After the meeting with Hammam's lieutenant, Uthman returned to Marea in another vehicle, leaving the four of us to execute the night's mission. He had held up his end of the bargain, providing us with schematics, meeting times, and other intel on the exchange between al-Amani and Jaysh al-Islam.

We maneuvered toward the observation position we had picked out during our planning. It was a communications shack five hundred meters from the hangar on the southwest corner of the airfield, just past the runway.

Ajwan and I helped Asmin and Zirek climb on top of the shack and set up. Unlike previous missions, I picked up perimeter security. It was Asmin's mission, and Asmin's shot to take. I was happy to step aside for her.

We took different sides of the shack as Zirek set up his spotter scope and Asmin lay prone against the shack's tin roof. I used the Trijicon 4 x 32 ACOG scope on the top of my M4 to check out the hangar.

The large hangar doors were open, revealing a troop transport of some sort with several armed men in what appeared to be Syrian Army uniforms standing around both inside and outside the hangar.

I looked back up at Asmin. She appeared calm and focused as she dialed in the range and elevation on the scope of her SVD sniper rifle. I still couldn't get over how young she was. She was far too young to be in this war. Her youth had been stolen from her.

I went back to scanning for threats in the immediate area. There was a densely-packed borough behind us. The sounds of the city were drowned out by an aircraft taxiing for takeoff nearby. Surprisingly, the airport was still open despite the rebel threat.

I turned back to see three SUVs approaching from the eastern side of the airfield. I shouldered my M4 and grabbed my M40 sniper rifle, flipping open the scope's dust covers as I took a better look.

I watched as a group of armed men got out of the lead SUV and quickly opened the door to the middle SUV. The trail SUV's fighters disembarked and set up a perimeter facing us.

Out of the middle SUV emerged al-Amani. He looked exactly like the photos I had seen of him, with a thick dark beard, dressed in all black. He was followed by another man with his hands bound in front of him and a hood over his head. Al-Amani grabbed the prisoner roughly and forced him toward the hangar.

I looked back up at Asmin. I could see her shift slightly as she tracked al-Amani. Zirek whispered something to her – I assumed he had sensed her anxiety and was trying to calm her. She needed to stick to the plan.

Al-Amani held on to the hostage's arm as they entered the hangar and stopped a few feet from the transport truck. He exchanged a greeting with one of the Syrian Army soldiers, and then another soldier brought out a rugged case from the back of the truck. He put it down and opened it.

I couldn't tell what was in it, but I assumed it was the chemical weapons Lincoln had talked about – sarin gas canisters. Al-Amani nodded and then pushed the hostage toward the Syrian soldiers.

The aircraft that had been taxiing took the runway. Its engines were deafening as it throttled up and began its takeoff roll. I looked up from my scope to take a look – a Russian cargo aircraft.

As I turned back to watch the rest of the exchange, the man next to al-Amani suddenly flinched as blood splattered over him. I shifted left to see al-Amani crumple to the ground. *Shit.*

I looked up and saw Asmin cycle the bolt on her rifle. She had used the jet noise of the departing aircraft to mask her shot, but she had still taken the shot way too early. The plan was starting to fall apart.

Asmin and Zirek scrambled to pack up and climb down from the communications shack. I watched as the Syrian soldiers took up defensive positions around the hangar. A few fired blindly in our direction, but only managed to hit dirt a few hundred yards in front of us.

"What are you doing?" I yelled as I helped Asmin down.

"I could not wait any longer!" Asmin replied.

"What about the chemical weapons?" I asked as I turned to help Zirek.

"It won't matter without Amani!" Asmin said.

We didn't have time to debate the point. The decision had been made, and we needed to get out of there. The return fire grew more intense, although it was still not yet aimed at us.

We ran through the field, past the perimeter road, and to the fence. Ajwan held the peeled back fence for us as we scurried through, sprinting toward the nearby Landcruiser.

As we reached the Landcruiser, bullets started peppering the bulletproof panels. Syrian Army soldiers on the nearby street had spotted us and were giving chase. We piled in, ducking as the shots cracked the bullet-resistant glass.

Zirek took his place in the driver's seat. When everyone was safely in the vehicle, he sped off. I looked behind us to see one of the pickup trucks with bed-mounted machine guns giving chase.

"We've got company!" I yelled as more bullets hit the armored panels in the rear.

Zirek weaved back and forth through the narrow roads as we tried to escape. The truck behind us gave chase, following us out of town as we cleared the airport area. I considered shooting back but thought better of it. It was safer in the armored SUV than hanging out the windows. Our escape rested solely on the shoulders of Zirek as we slalomed through the light traffic on our way out of the city.

As we reached the outskirts of the city, I heard the sounds of a helicopter off in the distance. There were now two trucks hot on our tail, giving chase as they shot at us. Zirek did his best to remain unpredictable, dodging car after car as he sped down the two-lane highway.

The *THUMP THUMP THUMP* sound of rotor blades grew louder. As I looked out the window from the front passenger seat, I found the source. It looked like the attack helicopter from *Rambo*

III. It had two tandem bubble canopies and an array of rockets on small wings to either side.

It banked hard in front of us, rolling out on a collision course. Zirek swerved hard left as it fired rockets at us. The Landcruiser's tires squealed as they struggled to maintain grip with the pavement. The explosion hit in front of us, narrowly missing as Zirek overcorrected the opposite direction.

As he swerved back to the right, the back end of the Landcruiser fishtailed around. The top-heavy SUV suddenly went airborne, rolling as the world seemed to spin. I flopped around, bouncing off the windshield and ceiling. I struggled to hold on as we rolled around and around.

The Landcruiser came to a rest on its roof. It felt like every bone in my body had been broken. I faded in and out as I looked up to see Zirek still strapped into his seat. I heard screaming outside.

I tried to look back. The backseat was empty. The doors were open. I saw darkness and then Chelsea, holding her stuffed police bear. She stood yelling for me to pick her up. I reached out, finding Lindsey standing next to her. I tried to speak but couldn't. They faded to a blur. I could still hear yelling outside.

I felt someone grab my arm as the darkness took over and the sounds faded away.

CHAPTER FORTY ONE

I awoke face down with my hands bound behind me and my feet in shackles. As I came to, I heard the drone of a diesel engine as we bounced along a rough road. There was a bench in front of me and an olive-green canvas roof covering above me. I realized I was in a military transport of some type. It reminded me of the back of the military surplus five-ton vehicles we used for high-water rescues with the sheriff's office.

I tried to move, but my restraints were too tight. It was hard to breathe. My chest and ribs hurt. I had probably broken at least one. I was sore and my head was throbbing.

"Zirek," I called out softly. Someone immediately kicked me in the stomach, knocking out what little air I had left in my lungs. I choked and gasped for air. He yelled something at me in Arabic.

As I recovered, I rolled to my side to face my attacker. He was carrying an AK-47 and looked very angry. I saw another body lying on the floor. I hoped the rest of the team had managed to escape.

The last thing I remembered was the helicopter. Everything beyond that was a blur. It was as disorienting and confusing as the day I had awoken in the hospital after the attacks in Louisiana.

I didn't recognize my captor. The man wore no uniform. I knew it really didn't matter though. They would kill me and use me for their sick propaganda campaign. I wished I had died in the SUV. I was a dead man either way.

I had no sense of time as we bounced along the road. After what seemed like hours, the transport pulled to a stop. The captor put a burlap sack over my head and forced me to my feet. My knees felt weak. I barely had the strength to stand as I fell in line behind the other hostage.

I could see through the worn spots in the sack that the person was roughly as tall as me. It ruled out the possibility of Asmin. I had lost my religion after the attacks in Louisiana, but I prayed that she was OK. I couldn't stomach the idea of another beautiful woman dead at the hands of these monsters.

The tailgate dropped and they guided us out. It was still dark. The wind was howling, blowing dirt and sand under the sack over my head. I tried to cough, but my chest hurt and my lungs burned. All I could muster was a wheeze.

One of the guards jammed a rifle butt into my back to push us along. I rear ended the prisoner in front of me. They walked us into a building.

Staring at the ground through the opening in the hood, I watched it change from dirt to dusty wooden floors. They pushed us into a dark room. I heard the door slam shut and a lock click.

"Zirek?" I whispered in the darkness. "Ajwan?"

There was no reply. As I lay on the floor, I drifted in and out of sleep. I dreamed about Lindsey, but she turned into Asmin. *The passion. The fire.* She was a special woman. Their souls seemed so similar. In another life, I might have even pursued Asmin romantically.

The guards came in some time later. With the light on, I could see that the other prisoner was Zirek. He had been gagged. The guards entered and also gagged me before forcing us to change into orange jumpsuits.

I had seen the ISIS hostage videos before. If that's who held us, we were on a one-way trip to execution. The guards chained us to the wall and threw a few good punches before leaving. It was even harder to breathe with the gag stuffed in my mouth and my hands chained above me.

I didn't sleep any more that night. I couldn't. I knew what lay ahead. I found myself wishing for it. I just wanted it to be over with – to go see Lindsey and Chelsea. The time had finally come.

The next morning, the door was flung open, and new guards entered. Their faces were covered. I could only see their dark, evil eyes. They unchained us from the walls and bound our hands behind us. I felt a needle stick into my neck. A warm sensation rushed through my body.

They dragged us out of the small building and into the blinding sun. I saw a camera set up in front of an ISIS flag. The guards walked us to the camera and forced us to our knees.

Whatever they had injected into me started to take effect. I felt like I was in a lucid dream. My body tingled. There was an overwhelming sense of euphoria.

Each guard took a side, holding their AK-47s loosely pointed at us as we waited. I saw a man dressed in all black emerge from a nearby building. His face was also covered, and he had a leather shoulder holster for his sidearm. He walked behind us as a man whose face was clearly visible took his place behind the camera.

The man behind the camera fiddled with the camera and then pointed to the masked man in all black. A red light on the camera illuminated.

"Allahu Akbar," the man said. He spoke in English with a slight British accent. "The Great Satan of America has sent its emissary of death to kill our women and children. The American named Alex Shepherd, and known as 'The Wolf,' has personally killed over a hundred women and children in his brutal crusade against Islam."

I could barely feel anything, but his words were very clear. Lincoln had been right. The man behind me knew who I was and had exaggerated the rumors of my efforts on the battlefield. They were going to use me as propaganda. I wanted to speak but couldn't. I couldn't move at all, nearly paralyzed by whatever they had injected me with.

"This man is the embodiment of the atrocities that Americans come to our country to commit every day. They bomb us from the sky and send their assassins to kill our families," the man continued.

"But Allah is on the side of the Islamic State, and it is through Allah's will that we have captured *The Wolf* and his handler, Commander Zirek of the Rojava militia," he said. I could see him waving a knife at us as he spoke.

"These men are responsible for heinous war crimes against the Islamic people," the man said. "But their freedom can be purchased."

He paused before stepping behind me. "If the American government should wish to have its cowardly American soldier back, his freedom can be purchased for two hundred million dollars. The government must promise to never allow him back on these holy lands again," he said.

The man sidestepped to Zirek. "The Kurdish people may have their Commander Zirek back for the price of one hundred and fifty million dollars," he said.

"These prices are not negotiable, and our gracious offer expires in seventy-two hours. Should either government fail to purchase their freedom, then we will be forced to punish them for the transgressions of their governments in accordance with our own laws," the man said.

He stepped back between us and stood for a moment before the cameraman raised his hand and the red light extinguished on the camera. When the filming was finished, the man said something in Arabic to the cameraman and then pulled the black mask down from his face.

He waved for the guard to take Zirek away as he squatted down next to me. "The famous *Wolf* from America. It will be a pleasure to kill you," he said. His English was flawless. I was convinced he was a British citizen that had come to Syria to fight.

"Who are you?" I asked weakly. I could still barely speak.

The man laughed. "My name is Mohammed al-Kuwaiti. You should have stayed in America."

"Where...Asmin," I managed.

The man's laugh turned even more sinister. *"The Lioness!* Yes! You gift-wrapped such a wonderful package for us in Aleppo. Commander Zirek, the Lioness, and the Wolf. How nice of you!"

"Where?" I mumbled.

"There are much bigger plans for her. The world will hear her scream for mercy and know that the Islamic State offers no such comfort to the enemies of Allah," he said before nodding to the guard to take me away.

"No!" I managed.

"You Americans," he said as he stood in front of me. "You think the world bends to your will – that you are the leaders of the world. But I have news for you. The world bends only to the will of Allah. The caliphate is that will. You cannot stop it."

"Fuck y-"

He punched me in the gut, knocking the wind out of me before I could get the words out.

"I will send for you when we are ready," he said ominously. "You will see the consequences of your arrogance."

CHAPTER FORTY TWO

They brought me to a holding area separate from Zirek. They kept my hands bound behind my back but didn't bother chaining me to the wall. The drug they had given me had started to wear off, leaving me with the worst hangover I had ever experienced.

I tried to figure out an escape plan but came up with nothing. The thought of being used as propaganda for those demons infuriated me, but at the same time, I wasn't afraid of death. My drive to survive was fueled only by wanting to save Zirek and Asmin.

I had no idea what had happened to Ajwan. I hoped he had gotten away, but I had a feeling he had either died in the crash or during capture. It was likely more merciful than what he would have experienced with Zirek and me – at least that's what I told myself.

My anxiety was fueled by my urge to save Asmin. My stomach was empty, but the thought of her being executed by one of these animals made me want to throw up. The mental image made me relive Lindsey's horrible murder. *I had to save her.*

After what seemed like hours since I had been locked in my new cell, the guards returned. They gagged me and walked me back out into the desert. Based on the sun, I guessed it was early afternoon.

This time they didn't inject anything into my neck as they walked me to their filming area. I turned to see them escorting Zirek out of wherever they had been holding him. He was bloodier and more bruised than before. They had beaten him, either for interrogation or just the fun of it.

They escorted him to what looked like a large pole. They forced him to strip naked and then made him lie down on the pole. The camera man walked with them, filming ever move.

Once he was made to lie down, they appeared to wrap metal wire around his wrists and the pole and then drove spikes into his hands. I realized what the pole was. It was hard to see from my vantage point, but they were crucifying Zirek.

I tried to scream out but couldn't. Zirek didn't scream or cry. He seemed resigned to his fate as they drove the last spike into his feet. Five men helped to stand the crucifix up. Blood dripped from his hands and feet.

Al-Kuwaiti returned with his face covered once again. He began to speak in front of the camera with Zirek in the background.

"The Kurdish people must know that this is what happens to its fighters. Your government has abandoned this man, refusing to pay for his freedom. The Quran calls for crucifixion to punish those who pervert the will of Allah. This man is no different."

A man standing off camera handed al-Kuwaiti a torch. He held it up for the camera to see and then dropped it. A wall of fire sped toward Zirek. It reached the base, engulfing Zirek and the entire cross in flames. Everything had been soaked in an accelerant.

For the first time, Zirek screamed out in pain. I tried to stand, but the guard next to me drove the butt of his rifle into my neck, causing me to fall face first into the sand. The pain was excruciating, but I forced myself back up to my knees. I looked back up to see al-Kuwaiti talking into the camera, but this time I heard nothing but Zirek's screams.

I tried to stand once more. The guard started to strike me again with his rifle, but I dodged this attack and drove my bare foot into the back of his knee, causing him to buckle.

I stood. My arms were bound behind me, but it didn't matter. I ran toward Zirek. There was nothing I could do, but I ran toward him anyway. I was tackled by another guard before I could make it to him.

His screams stopped as the flames engulfed the crucifix. More guards arrived, punching and kicking me. They beat me mercilessly.

I tried to wrestle away, but it was no use. I rolled over onto my back as they continued kicking me. The fire eventually slowed to a smolder. I saw Zirek's charred body, still hanging from the metal wire and spikes they had driven into him.

The guards eventually stepped away from me. As I lay beaten in the sand, al-Kuwaiti appeared over me with his mask removed. He smiled as he stood over me.

"Don't worry, Mr. Wolf Shepherd," he said mockingly. "Tomorrow, you will have your fifteen minutes of fame, as they say."

The guards dragged me to my feet as I started to lose consciousness again.

"And I have something much better in mind for you," he said with a sinister smile.

CHAPTER FORTY THREE

I assure you, you will tell me what I want to know," al-Kuwaiti said angrily as he stood over me.

They had left me alone for several hours after watching Zirek's death, but sometime late that night, one of the guards had brought me to an interrogation room. The guard strapped me to the chair and proceeded to beat me mercilessly.

When he was satisfied that I had lost the will to resist, the guard left, and al-Kuwaiti entered. He wanted to know everything about my involvement with the YPG – how I found them, where they trained me, how they assigned missions, and what they had planned.

I was vague in my answers. Some of it was due to not wanting to betray my newfound brothers in arms, but most of it was because I just didn't remember. All the events of the last six months had started blending together. I couldn't have answered even if I had wanted to cooperate.

"Why did you seek out al-Amani?" al-Kuwaiti asked again.

"Asmin," I slurred. My lips were swollen, and my eyes were starting to follow suit. I could barely see the angry jihadi.

"You will beg for your own death if you do not cooperate with me," he said. "Why did this woman want to kill him? How did she find him?"

"He…killed…her unit," I said, struggling to get the words out.

"Who told you he would be in Aleppo?" al-Kuwaiti demanded.

I started drifting in and out of consciousness. I could barely think. I wanted to answer his question, but I couldn't remember. Everything was a blur.

"Turk…Turkman…Turkey," I mumbled.

Al-Kuwaiti backhanded me. "Do not test me!"

"Kill me," I groaned.

"You will die tomorrow," al-Kuwaiti said as he pulled out a blade. "But you can still die a quick death if you cooperate and answer my questions. If not, I will ensure that you experience the *Khazouk*. Do you know what that is, Mr. Wolf?"

I didn't look up at him. I couldn't. I didn't have the strength to do anything anymore. I shook my head slowly.

Al-Kuwaiti let out an evil cackle. "It is very gruesome, you see. We will mount a stake in the ground and then place you on it by driving it through your rectum so that you can just barely tip-toe to stand up. You won't die immediately, you see. Our people are very skilled at missing vital organs. It can take up to forty-eight hours. It is a punishment reserved for the most deviant of infidels, and it will be a slow, painful death. Is that what you want?"

I didn't care. I couldn't feel anything anymore anyway. I was already dead. I gave him the best shrug I could muster.

"As you wish," al-Kuwaiti said angrily. "Tomorrow, you will find the fires of hell that you so desperately seek. You will join your friend Zirek in the pits of hell."

As he turned to walk out, he suddenly turned back to me and laughed. "What, you thought we were really going to wait seventy-two hours for a ransom? Ha!"

Al-Kuwaiti nodded to the guard and then turned toward the door once more. The lone bulb hanging from the ceiling suddenly extinguished, and the room went dark.

Al-Kuwaiti yelled something in Arabic to the guard, and then I heard boots on the wood floors as the guard ran out of the room. I could hear movement in the rooms next to us, but I couldn't make sense of what I was hearing.

"Americans!" al-Kuwaiti hissed.

The light of the full moon shining through the window behind me cast just enough light that I could barely make out al-Kuwaiti's silhouette as he paced nervously back and forth.

I heard a momentary burst of gunfire. I waited for follow-up shots but heard none.

Al-Kuwaiti ran to me and started to free me from my chair, presumably to use me as a human shield. As he struggled to cut the restraints with his knife in the dark, there was a loud bang with a brilliant flash of light.

As my eyes adjusted, I saw the silhouette of al-Kuwaiti turn with his knife up. He charged a man entering the room but was quickly taken to the ground as I heard screaming and the cracking of bones.

"Clear," a male voice said. I could see only silhouettes from the moonlight entering the window. There were at least four men; their eyes reflected the green from what appeared to be night vision goggles. The goggles had more tubes than the typical monocular we usually used back home with SWAT.

One of the men slung his rifle across his back and rushed to me. He finished the work of cutting my restraints. "Can you walk?" he asked.

I grunted and tried to stand, but my knees buckled.

"I'll take that as a no," the man said casually. They didn't appear nervous or rushed. They all seemed to project a cool confidence in their voices.

"Alright, let's move," the other man said. "Punisher Six One, Millertime."

They all spoke with recognizable American accents. I felt a sense of relief rush over me as the man hoisted me into a fireman's carry on his shoulders. The American government had sent a special ops team to rescue me. I knew I was in good hands.

I heard al-Kuwaiti groan as they forced him to his feet and brought him with us. I was carried out into the moonlit desert. As the light from the full moon shone on the four men, I noticed they all had beards and were dressed in black tactical gear. There was a smoothness about their movements as they covered our escape. I noticed it because it was something we had always trained to achieve with SWAT, but these guys seemed to have nailed it. They were just very fluid as a team.

I heard a helicopter rapidly approaching as the man carrying me took off at a jog. There was more gunfire from the direction of the building we had just left, but it was immediately silenced as the rest had been. The helicopter swooped in, kicking up sand. I closed my eyes.

"You cannot defy the will of Allah! You will all die a coward's death!" al-Kuwaiti yelled defiantly as we boarded the helicopter.

"Not tonight, bub," one of the men growled before I heard the satisfying crack of a rifle butt hitting the jihadi's face.

CHAPTER FORTY FOUR

The helicopter landed at what I thought was a U.S. air base. I was met by doctors and nurses in military uniforms who hoisted me onto a stretcher and rushed me inside. I heard the helicopter's engines spool up and depart as I was wheeled into the hospital.

I was poked and prodded as the doctors went to work checking me. They gave me IV fluids and pain meds. It was hard to keep track of all the people scrambling around me.

"Where am I?" I asked weakly as a nurse took my vitals.

"Incirlik Air Base in Turkey," she said. "Don't worry; you're safe now."

I saw men with body armor and rifles as the nurses moved me to another room. The men took up positions outside the room as the medical staff went through more tests. They took blood and x-rayed my ribs. The medicine they had given me started to kick in. I felt euphoric as I drifted in and out of sleep. It reminded me a little of whatever the guards at al-Kuwaiti's Jihad Headquarters had given me.

They moved me to a room at some point. I slept through most of it. I was exhausted. The lack of sleep, beatings, and mental strain of watching Zirek die had all taken a heavy toll on me. I was completely disoriented.

At some point the next morning, I was awakened by a nurse checking my vitals. As she left, a man wearing green scrubs and a surgical mask hanging loosely around his neck entered.

"Mr. Shepherd, I'm Lieutenant Colonel Andre Dyson. I'm the attending physician here at the Incirlik Medical Center on base," he said.

"Hey doc," I mumbled, still drunk from the medication.

"Can you tell me your name?" Dyson asked as he picked up my chart and flipped through it.

"Alex Shepherd," I replied. I tried to watch him, but everything was still blurry. I could feel the swelling had gone down in my eyes, but it was still hard to see anything.

"Very good," Dyson replied. He put the chart back in its container at the foot of my bed and walked to my left side. He gingerly picked up my left arm and checked my pulse, counting off the beats as he stared at his watch.

"You've been through quite a lot," he said as he gently put my arm down. "How do you feel?"

"I'm hurting," I said. Even with the pain meds, I felt as if I had been run over by an 18-wheeler.

"I'll adjust your pain medication, but some pain is to be expected. You have a mild concussion, a broken rib, and a bruised lung. You're very lucky, given the circumstances," he said.

I let out an exasperated groan. *Lucky.* I still didn't feel lucky. Nothing that I had been through in the last six months made me feel lucky. Luck simply wasn't a part of my life anymore. In my mind, luck would have been dying with my family in the movie theater parking lot, not barely surviving torture at the hands of a sadistic madman.

"I need to save her," I said, thinking back to Asmin. We were running out of time. I couldn't stomach the thought of her dying. I wanted to save her or die trying.

"Who?" the doctor asked.

"Asmin," I said softly.

The doctor frowned. "Is that who was in captivity with you?" he asked.

I nodded weakly.

"You can tell all of that to the Special Ops guys. They're the ones that brought you in," he said.

"Who?" I asked.

"I don't know," he shrugged. "SEALs, Delta...whoever pulled you out of Syria. No one ever tells us who they are. It's *classified*, they always say. Above my paygrade I guess. I'm just here to get you healthy so you can go back to the states."

"I can't go back," I said.

"Well, that's something you'll have to work out with the State Department. That's also above my paygrade," he said. "My responsibility is to get you out of here healthy. Your prognosis is good, as long as you rest and we can get some fluids back into you."

The doctor nodded and turned to walk out. "Please let the nurses know if you need anything. I've ordered a patient-controlled pain medicine pump for you. You should have that this morning."

Shortly after the doctor left, a nurse appeared as promised and set up what she called my "PCA." She showed me how to work the button, explaining that I could only press it once every four hours, but that I shouldn't hesitate if I felt pain. It was the same setup I had been given in the hospital in Slidell in the wake of the school bus attack.

As soon as it was connected to my IV, I pressed it, feeling the warm, tingling feeling rush through my arm. Within seconds, I was out, sleeping away the misery of the last few days.

I awoke a few hours later to a nurse again taking my vitals. As I came to, I saw a man with a red beard and tan baseball cap standing with his arms folded at the foot of my bed. He was wearing a tan shirt and tactical pants. When the nurse finished, he politely thanked her and then followed her to the door, locking it as she left the room.

"Who are you?" I asked weakly. He looked familiar, but I couldn't place it. He was like something out of a movie – the stereotypical special ops type with the long hair and operator beard. We had many guys on SWAT who tried to imitate the look during November when the Sheriff allowed us to grow beards, but the guy in front of me was the source material. There was no question in my mind that he was authentic.

"You can call me Kruger," he said gruffly.

Kruger? Was that a nickname or something? Like Freddie Kruger?

"Ok," I said. "Are you with the military?"

"Not quite," Kruger said. "But I was on the team that pulled you out of Al-Bab."

"Is that where we were?" I asked.

Kruger nodded. "But I'm sure you're tired, and I have things to do, so let's get to the point. I just have a few questions, and I'll be out of your hair."

"Wait! Please! You have to save Asmin!" I pleaded.

Kruger frowned. "I just have a few questions for you."

I struggled to sit up in the bed. "Let me help you find her," I said. "They're going to execute her if we don't do something now."

"You were a counter-sniper when you were with SWAT, right?" Kruger asked, ignoring my continued pleas.

"That was a different time," I said.

"Right, because you're *The Wolf* now?"

"I didn't come up with that," I replied.

"I didn't come up with *Kruger* either, but here we are. I'm aware of how you got your name," Kruger said.

"How?"

"There was a reporter from the BBC embedded with the Kurdish forces at the battle of Ma'shūq. He interviewed a man who spoke of an American sniper who saved him. The man said you fought like a wolf, and the reporter ran with it. You're all over the news back home, bub. Big celebrity," Kruger said.

"Great," I replied sarcastically.

"And of course, the news media being what it is, they traced your origin back to your career as a law enforcement officer in Louisiana and the death of your family in that attack. The story blew up quickly, especially with you being a wanted man and all," he said, shaking his head.

"Wanted?"

"Some hooker in Mississippi tried to make a deal after getting busted by a NARC unit for pushing coke. She claims you killed a fat little Imam up there," Kruger replied.

"Is that why you're here?"

"Do I look like I care about that shit, bub?" Kruger asked. "I know the man you *allegedly* killed. I say good riddance."

"Then why are you here?"

"Two reasons," Kruger said. "First, I need to know how you found al-Amani and where the chemical weapons went."

"Commander Zirek had all the contacts," I responded. "He knew a guy with the CIA who pointed us to rebels with intel."

"Lincoln," Kruger hissed. "That little weasel."

"And I don't know where the weapons went. We were captured after Asmin shot al-Amani. Please, we have to go find her. Al-Kuwaiti said they had her and were going to kill her."

Kruger grimaced and then looked away.

"What? What happened? You know something? Tell me!"

"Look, bub, I'm going to tell you something. You're not going to like it, but it is what it is at this point. All we can do is move forward," Kruger said softly.

"What? God! No! Please no!" I yelled, realizing what he was about to tell me. My eyes welled up. I suddenly felt very claustrophobic and wanted to break out of the bed.

"I'm sorry," Kruger said. "They took her straight to Raqqa. We couldn't find her before they made the video."

"God! No! No! Please!"

"I know it's hard, but all we can do now is kill the son of a bitch that did it and stop him before he kills more people with these sarin canisters," Kruger said.

Tears streamed down my face as I thought of what those animals had done to Asmin. It was as if all the pain from the loss of my family was suddenly rushing back. I wanted to curl up and die.

"God…" I said between sobs.

"God had nothing to do with this," Kruger said gruffly.

Kruger grabbed the PCA dangling from my bed rail and pressed the button. It beeped as I felt the warm sensation once again. It did nothing to numb the pain I was feeling deep within my chest. I could barely breathe.

"You need to get better," Kruger said. "And when you do, we will talk again."

"What is there to talk about?" I sobbed. "Lindsey is dead! Chelsea is dead! Asmin is dead! Zirek is dead! I want to be dead! Why don't you just kill me now? Put me out of my misery!"

"Maybe Alex Shepherd is already dead," Kruger said. "But I'm offering *The Wolf* a chance to live again. I'm offering you a chance at *vengeance*."

"I don't care!" I shrieked.

Kruger left my bedside and headed toward the door. "Think it over, bub. I'll be back in a couple of days."

He unlocked the door and walked out, but as the pain medicine started to take effect, his words still hung in the air.

Alex Shepherd is dead.

CHAPTER FORTY FIVE

I spent two days in the hospital. By the end of my stay, my body had started to feel better, but my soul was still crushed. I was devastated by the loss of my friends, and the memories of my family haunted me even more. The temporary relief I had found while fighting with the YPG was gone. I had reached new lows of depression.

Zirek, Asmin – my entire team – it was just so hard to process. In some ways, it hurt just as much as losing my family. They had become my new family, and just like Lindsey and Chelsea, the women in my life I would've given anything to protect, I had let them down. I had failed Zirek and watched him die at the hands of a madman.

And Asmin. *Beautiful Asmin.* She was so young and vibrant. She didn't deserve to die, much less at the hands of those monsters. I blamed myself. I knew I should never have pushed to help her. If I had just let her go back with the YPG and not pushed to help her, she might've survived.

I was wheeled through the front door by an orderly where a black Mercedes SUV waited. The driver exited and approached me. He was bearded and looked as much the operator-type as Kruger had, but his beard was dark brown, and he looked a little younger than the red-bearded man that had broken the news about Asmin.

"Kruger couldn't get away, mate, so I'll be driving you to him," the man said with a heavy British accent. *British? Who were these people?*

"Who are you?" I asked suspiciously.

"The name's Sullivan Winchester," he replied. "I work for Kruger."

Finally. A real name.

"They call me Cowboy," he added.

"Of course they do," I replied. *A British guy named Cowboy? Kruger? Seriously, who the hell were these people?*

"Well, alright then Wolf, let's get to it," he said as he grabbed my arm to help me stand from the wheelchair. *Wolf? Seriously?*

"Where are we going?" I asked as I stood gingerly. I had walked a bit with the nurses, but I still felt fairly weak, especially after standing. The doctor said that it would take another day or two for me to fully regain my balance.

Cowboy held a finger up to his mouth. "That's classified, mate. Can't talk about it in public. C'mon."

After helping me into the back seat, Cowboy drove me across the base to what appeared to be an abandoned hangar. As we pulled up next to it, I realized it was anything but abandoned — there were men inside working on a Blackhawk helicopter like the one that had picked me up, plus two more AH-6 "Little Bird" helicopters. Aside from the misplaced British guy, I was convinced that I had stepped into a scene from the *Blackhawk Down* movie based on the Battle of Mogadishu. *Definitely Delta.*

"So what are you? British SAS?" I asked as Cowboy opened the door for me.

Cowboy smiled. "That's a really good guess, mate. But not anymore," he said.

"What do you do now then?" I asked.

"You'll see," Cowboy replied.

He led me through the hangar to a set of downstairs offices. We passed a room filled with computer servers and laptops. A young kid – probably mid-twenties – sat typing away at a laptop. He had spiky jet black hair and hipster-looking black-framed glasses. He looked up briefly as we passed and then took a swig from an energy drink before going back to work.

Cowboy led me to a flight of stairs. It was tough climbing them – I was still very sore, but my curiosity was now piqued. I wanted to find out who was behind this operation.

He brought me into a room that looked like an office. "Have a seat anywhere you like," he said as he walked off. "Kruger will be with you in a minute."

There weren't many seating options. The desk was barely more than a folding table, and the chairs were of the folding variety. I took one of the folding chairs and flipped it around to face the door as I waited for the mysterious Kruger to arrive.

Moments after I was settled, Kruger walked in. He entered quickly with an air of authority. It was slightly intimidating.

I stood slowly as he walked in. He extended his hand and said, "Glad you could make it. Sorry I wasn't there. Something came up at the last minute. I hope Cowboy wasn't too much of an asshole."

As I shook his hand, I just had to ask. "What's with all these nicknames? Why was that guy calling me Wolf?"

"I am sorry about that. It may be a bit premature," he replied as he took his seat at the desk across from me. "But we don't use real names here. Field operators get callsigns. It's safer that way."

I spun the folding chair around and gingerly sat back down.

"What kind of unit is this? Special Ops?" I asked.

Kruger stared at me for a moment. I could tell he was debating whether he wanted to spill the beans or keep me in the dark. He seemed to be studying me.

"Mr. Shepherd, I owe you an apology," he said finally.

"An apology?"

"The reason you are here is that we...I...fucked up, and for that, I am truly sorry," he said. He had a look of genuine concern.

"Fucked up how? You mean I shouldn't be seeing all of this?" I asked.

Kruger stood, walked to the front of the desk and leaned against it as he held his head low.

"Your family is dead because of me," he said, his voice suddenly wavering.

"What?" I asked. The flood of emotions came rushing back, and my hands started to shake. The mere mention of my family's death sent me into a frenzy. I was angry, sad, and even a little scared.

"A little over a year ago, my team and I were tracking a man named Tariq Qafir. He worked with ISIS, and we found out he was planning to use portable surface to air missiles in an attack. We tracked him to America and found his base of operations in Mississippi," Kruger said in a low voice.

"Utica," I said, remembering the terrorist training camp I had visited.

Kruger nodded and continued, "When we got there, we found that Qafir had planned a horrific series of attacks. They wanted to strike soft targets in America and were using school bus mock-ups to practice."

School bus mock-ups. I closed my eyes, seeing the burning school bus and that animal throwing my wife's severed head at me. I heard the screaming children. My body started to shake.

"Qafir killed himself before we could find out what he had planned, but we knew some of his men had escaped. Because we were working on another incident with national security implications at the time, we handed it off to the FBI. I was uncomfortable with it, but I sincerely thought that with Qafir and most of his men dead, the immediate threat was over," Kruger said.

I sat silently staring at Kruger. I relived the attacks in my mind as I processed what he was saying.

"We got wind of an attack and tried to stop it, and we did. We stopped the attack in Texas. I thought the Mississippi cell was no longer a factor, so we focused on the one from El Paso because that was the credible threat we had at the time," Kruger said, shaking his head.

"My wife was beheaded. My daughter was burned alive," I growled.

"I know," Kruger replied. "And for that, I am truly sorry. I fucked up."

I closed my eyes as I felt my chest tightening. It was hard to believe what I was hearing. I felt like I was having another panic attack. Everything had been taken from me. I wanted to die.

But as I opened my eyes and looked up at Kruger, I noticed the pain in the red-bearded operator's eyes as well. There I sat with an elite operator sitting in front of me, nearly in tears as he took responsibility for one of the most horrific terror attacks in American history.

As easy as it would have been to blame him for ruining my life, I just couldn't. I was still both sad and incredibly angry, but I realized he was no more responsible for the death of my family than a deputy who couldn't stop a crime in time. People always wanted to blame the police for not getting there fast enough, but the reality was that it was really the criminal's fault.

The death of my family, the death of Asmin and Zirek, the horrific war crimes I had witnessed in Iraq and Syria, they weren't Kruger's fault or even my fault. They were done by savage animals. The only people to blame for the overwhelming loss I had felt were the vile terrorists in the Islamic State. They were the true wolves that preyed on innocent sheep. Kruger and I just happened to be the sheepdogs that hadn't been able to stop the attack in time.

"But how is this your fault?" I asked as I looked Kruger in the eyes. "What did you do?"

Kruger had a pained expression. "I didn't stop it. I *couldn't* stop it."

"Did you really do everything you could when you found out?" I asked.

"Yes," he replied.

"Then there was nothing more you could have done. You can't blame yourself for these monsters," I said.

"But we didn't stop them, and that is a failure I will take with me to my grave," Kruger said. "I am so sorry."

"When I got to Utica, the compound was a crime scene. Someone had killed Kamal, the guy that helped plan the attack. Was that you?"

Kruger nodded. "After the attack, we knew where to look. We took out what was left of the cell and found another cell in New Orleans that was planning something even bigger."

"Is that why you rescued me and brought me here? Because you feel responsible?"

"We were in country because we learned that ISIS intends to use sarin gas in an attack in Europe. We were operating in western Iraq and Syria on a series of kill or capture missions of top ISIS leaders when we learned that al-Amani had been killed by your team during an exchange with defectors from the Syrian Army.

When the video demanding your ransom was released, I made it a priority for us to find and recover you – yes, because I felt responsible," Kruger said.

"What about Asmin?" I asked.

Kruger let out a soft sigh. "We didn't know she was taken to Raqqa. When we intercepted the chatter that she was captive in the same incident, we thought she was with you. The video came out after we dropped you off at the hospital. I am sorry."

"I want to see it," I said. I didn't really know why, but I wanted to see the video of Asmin's execution. I *needed* to see it.

"That's probably not a good idea," Kruger said.

"I don't give a fuck what you think is a good idea," I snapped. The sadness had suddenly morphed into rage.

"It's graphic," Kruger warned.

"I don't care," I said angrily. "I want to see it."

Kruger held up his hands defensively. "Fair enough. I'll make it happen."

* * *

Kruger brought me back downstairs to where the guy with the hipster glasses was working on his computer.

"Coolio, please pull up the Lioness video," Kruger said.

"Are you sure, boss?" Coolio said as he spun around. *Coolio?* The name actually distracted me from my building rage. The kid looked nothing like the famous rapper. There seemed to be no rhyme or reason for his nickname.

Kruger nodded. Coolio shrugged as he spun back around and pulled up the video, maximizing it on the screen as he hit play and wheeled himself out of the way.

I stood with my arms folded as the ISIS flag appeared and sitar music with an Islamic chant began playing. The screen cut to another masked man.

"That's Ayman Awad al-Baghdadi," Kruger said as the man on the screen began speaking.

I was almost seeing red as I clenched my fists. I didn't blame Kruger for anything, but al-Baghdadi made my blood boil. *He* was the man that had ruined my life. *He* was responsible for the death of my family.

Al-Baghdadi went through the same nonsensical rant as al-Kuwaiti and the other videos. He spoke of the higher purpose of the Islamic State and the caliphate and the call to rid the world of the non-believers.

The camera cut to Asmin. She was on her knees, her head held low and her hands bound behind her. I wondered if they had given her the same injection they had given me to prevent her from resisting or seeming defiant.

"And this…this is proof of Allah's will. Through great deceit, the infidels claimed that this woman killed nearly a hundred Holy Warriors. They spoke of the shame brought upon a warrior that is killed by a woman, and championed her like the false prophets that they are. The cowardly infidels even sent an imposter to take her place in combat and in death. But as you can see, we have found the one they claim to be The Lioness," al-Baghdadi said.

He walked over to her, grabbing her by her hair and picking her head up. The camera zoomed in on her face.

"But a Lioness she is not. She is merely a sorcerer," al-Baghdadi continued as he dropped her head. "She has served as an adequate sex slave, but she is neither pure nor worthy of being the wife of anyone here. She serves only as a lesson from Allah that false prophets will not be tolerated. And as the Quran instructs, she must die. She must serve as an example to all who would try to create false prophets. This behavior is insulting to the very nature of Islam and shall not be tolerated. Allahu Akbar."

Al-Baghdadi pulled a hunting knife from its sheath on his belt. "Let every person who sees this know the glory of Allah!"

He walked behind her and picked up her head. Asmin closed her eyes, making no protest as he went to work, hacking at her neck in a sawing motion. It was horrific, but I could not turn away. The blade didn't seem very sharp. He continued sawing as blood poured from her neck.

I saw my wife in that video. It was exactly what I had imagined them doing to Lindsey on that school bus. Asmin's lifeless face was indistinguishable from Lindsey's.

Asmin's body fell limp as al-Baghdadi pushed it forward with his boot and finished severing her head. He held it up proudly. The camera panned as he walked to his right where a stake had been driven into the ground. He put her head on it, her lifeless face toward the camera.

"Let this be a lesson to all who would test the will of Allah," he said triumphantly. The video faded to black as the ISIS flag and chanting music returned.

"Is it over?" I heard the computer analyst say from the back.

I wanted to kill al-Baghdadi. All of the pain and soreness I felt was muted by the rage inside me. I had never been so angry in my entire life.

"Are you ok?" Kruger asked. I jerked away as he tried to put a hand on my shoulder.

"I'm going to kill that motherfucker!" I screamed.

CHAPTER FORTY SIX

Y ou don't scare me," al-Kuwaiti said defiantly. "I have
been trained in your tactics."
I watched the interrogation on an LCD monitor in
Kruger's office. Al-Kuwaiti was bound to a chair in the middle of
the room and wearing an orange jumpsuit. Kruger wasn't in the
picture yet, but I knew he was standing just behind the camera.

Kruger had escorted me out of the computer analyst's
workspace after the video. I was so mad that my blood pressure
had spiked. I could feel the veins in my head and neck throbbing.
I couldn't see straight as tears streamed down my face. Kruger
had to physically restrain me to keep me from destroying the
place.

He brought me back to his office and told me to sit behind his desk. He turned on the monitor and told me to enjoy the show before walking out. As I watched them bring al-Kuwaiti into the room, I lost any hope of calming down.

"You haven't been trained in my tactics, bub," Kruger growled from behind the camera.

"You cannot torture me, you cannot touch me," al-Kuwaiti replied with a nervous laugh. "The music you have played to annoy me has not worked. I am used to not sleeping for many days. I am a soldier of Allah! I cannot be broken!"

Kruger appeared from behind the camera, lunging toward al-Kuwaiti as he connected with a right cross. Blood sprayed everywhere, and al-Kuwaiti yelped. Kruger reset and stepped behind al-Kuwaiti as the jihadi spat blood and tried to recover.

"You cannot do this!" al-Kuwaiti screamed. "I have rights! Your government forbids it! You will be punished!"

"Punished?" Kruger asked. He leaned over al-Kuwaiti's shoulder. "I don't work for any government, bub."

Al-Kuwaiti shook his head. "I don't believe you!"

Kruger pulled out something from his pocket. It looked like a Velcro patch, but I couldn't see through the monitor. He tossed it on al-Kuwaiti's lap. The jihadi's eyes widened, and he gasped in horror.

"I don't believe you!" al-Kuwaiti shrieked.

"What do you think?" Kruger asked as he stepped between al-Kuwaiti and the camera.

"Shaytan!" al-Kuwaiti yelped.

"My Arabic is a little rusty. Satan? The Devil? No, that's not me," Kruger said as he leaned in. "I'm *much* worse."

The defiant façade suddenly melted away. Al-Kuwaiti was fidgeting. His eyes darted around the room. He was sweating. Kruger had somehow gotten to him with only one punch and a few words. It was riveting to watch.

"So here's how this is going to go," Kruger continued as he started to pace around the room. "If you answer my questions truthfully, that will be the end of it. I won't hurt you. You might even be treated as a human tonight."

"I know nothing!" al-Kuwaiti said, somehow managing a fleeting burst of defiance.

Kruger was instantly on him, his hand wrapped around the jihadi's neck. "But if you don't – if you lie to me or refuse to answer – I will make you talk. You see, everyone breaks eventually, even people trained in interrogation resistance. The only question is how much you can endure before you are begging me to let you tell me everything. A man like yourself? I won't even break a sweat."

"Allah will protect me! Allahu Akbar!"

"Keep thinking that, bub," Kruger said. He walked away from al-Kuwaiti to what looked like a table in the back of the room. He picked up what looked like a Taser X26 and pulled the trigger. It made a loud crackle. I saw al-Kuwaiti jump and his facial expression change to pure horror.

"Fully charged," he said. "Plenty of time for you to change your mind."

Kruger picked something else up from the table and put it in his cargo pants pocket on his left leg. He walked back to al-Kuwaiti and squeezed the trigger in front of his face. The Taser once again let out a loud crackle.

"Ever used one of these?" Kruger asked.

Al-Kuwaiti nervously stared at the Taser, saying nothing as Kruger held it up in front of him.

"It's pretty basic, you see. Right now, with no cartridge, it's just a localized pain. Like this."

Kruger pressed the Taser down into al-Kuwaiti's thigh and squeezed the trigger. Al-Kuwaiti yelped and futilely tried to jerk away as Kruger let the Taser go through its five-second countdown before removing it.

"See? That's not so bad, right?" Kruger asked. "I mean it would probably be worse on your junk, like this."

Kruger drove the Taser into al-Kuwaiti's crotch and squeezed the trigger. Al-Kuwaiti screamed in pain. Kruger removed it well short of the five-second timer as al-Kuwaiti continued to scream.

"Oh come on," Kruger said. "It's not so bad. It only gets worse from here."

Kruger pulled out the object from his pocket. With a closer view, I realized it was a Taser cartridge with the wires wrapped around it. He held the ends and let the cartridge unwind toward the floor. The cartridge looked a bit different than the normal ones we used in the field. Instead of probes, the ends were alligator clips used to connect to skin or clothing. It was the same setup I had seen in training when we had to "ride the lightning" in order to be certified to use the Taser.

"You see, the Taser is most effective when there is a circuit to complete. What you just felt was nothing more than a bad static shock, but this…this is what incapacitates people. And I'm sure it'll feel even worse clipped to the places I have in mind," Kruger said, pointing to al-Kuwaiti's genitals.

"You can't," al-Kuwaiti said weakly.

"Sure I can," Kruger replied. "Even in the military, this sort of thing was allowed in extreme cases of imminent chemical, nuclear, or biological threats. And although those rules don't apply to me anymore, we're still looking at an imminent threat. Don't worry, bub, no matter what happens, I'll sleep soundly tonight."

Al-Kuwaiti stared at Kruger, who was still holding the cartridge up by the alligator clips. "Choose your next words carefully, bub. I have always wanted to get creative and try this while waterboarding," Kruger warned. "You know what waterboarding is, right?"

"Please..." al-Kuwaiti said. It was almost a whisper. He had seemingly lost his will, or ability, to fight.

Kruger bent down over al-Kuwaiti. I couldn't tell, but it looked like he was attaching the clips to al-Kuwaiti's crotch. When he stood, he held up the cartridge in an exaggerated movement and attached it to the end of the Taser.

"Do you remember the rules?" Kruger asked.

Al-Kuwaiti nodded nervously. I wanted nothing more than for him to pull the trigger. The terrorist monster had brutally murdered Zirek and so many others. He deserved more than just being tased in the balls. He deserved a brutal death.

"How did al-Baghdadi get the sarin canisters?" Kruger asked.

"A captain with the Syrian Army!" al-Kuwaiti shouted. "They had an exchange at the Aleppo Airport, but al-Amani was killed. His lieutenant brought the Lioness and the canisters to al-Baghdadi in al-Raqqa."

"Where in Raqqa?" Kruger barked.

"They are gone now!" al-Kuwaiti screamed. "They were to leave after he executed the girl."

"Where were they going?" Kruger asked.

"Ramadi!" al-Kuwaiti replied.

"Why?"

"I don't know," al-Kuwaiti said.

"Wrong answer," Kruger replied. He squeezed the trigger. The Taser made less noise than before as the surge of electricity traveled through al-Kuwaiti's genitals. The jihadi screamed as his whole body tensed. Kruger stopped it after two seconds, not giving him the full five-second ride.

"Please!" al-Kuwaiti pleaded.

"What were the rules?" Kruger asked. "Repeat them to me!"

"Don't lie or refuse to talk," al-Kuwaiti said weakly.

"Now, let's try again," Kruger said. "Why did al-Baghdadi bring the canisters to Ramadi?"

"To smuggle them into Spain and Germany with the refugees leaving from there in three days," al-Kuwaiti replied, still trying to catch his breath.

"Where?"

Al-Kuwaiti's eyes widened. "Where what? Please! I don't understand the question! Don't do it again!"

"Where in Ramadi? Where is al-Baghdadi staying?" Kruger asked.

"There's an abandoned factory – I think it used to be for ceramics and glass, it's near the Euphrates. Please! That's all I know! I swear!" al-Kuwaiti replied.

"I believe you," Kruger said. He pulled the trigger once more, letting al-Kuwaiti take the full five-second ride as Kruger dropped the Taser and walked out.

Two men appeared and disconnected the Taser from al-Kuwaiti's genitals before dragging him out of the room. Shortly after, the camera feed turned to static.

I sat alone in the office for twenty minutes. The sight of al-Kuwaiti infuriated me, but seeing Kruger deal with him was strangely satisfying. I wanted to kill al-Kuwaiti in the worst imaginable way. The man deserved a slow, painful death for what he had done.

Kruger walked in and sat down in the folding chair across from me.

"Whatever you're planning, I want in," I said.

"You're in no condition to go on an OP, and there's no way we could train you to work with us that quickly," Kruger said, shaking his head.

"You still never told me who you work for," I said. "What was the patch you threw at al-Kuwaiti? He seemed to recognize it."

Kruger pulled the patch out of his pocket and tossed it on the desk in front of me. It was black with a white skull and three triangles on the skull.

"Holy shit," I mumbled. It was the same logo I had seen in the village in Iraq above the dead ISIS fighter.

"You've seen it?" Kruger asked.

"We stand against evil," I said, repeating the translation from the words I had seen written under the skull with the interlocking triangles in Iraq. "Abu al-Nasef."

"He wasn't exactly cooperative, but if you had seen what he had done," Kruger replied.

"Oh, I did," I said. "I saw the mass graves. Wait; there was an ISIS death squad in eastern Syria, on a road going to Qamishli. Someone – a sniper – took out them out during an attempted mass beheading in a village. Was that you as well?" I asked.

Kruger shook his head. "No, but you've met him. That was Cowboy. He used to be a British Special Air Service sniper. And the man in black you saw was Abu Darda – known as *The Executioner* for ISIS in eastern Syria."

"Wait, how do you know I saw him?" I asked.

"We had a drone overhead," Kruger said. "Although we didn't realize it was you until after Lincoln told us you were in Aleppo."

"You said he was a weasel – why?"

"Lincoln was in it for Lincoln. He was always about career. He helped arm al-Nusra and some of the rebel groups that turned out to be not so friendly to us. He's part of the reason the rebels were able to get the gas canisters. It's all about money and power to him," Kruger said.

"Did he warn them about us?" I asked.

Kruger shrugged. "I wouldn't put it past him. Asmin had a huge bounty on her head before it was first reported that she had died. It's entirely possible. But don't worry, he's no longer a factor."

"Should I even ask?"

"No," Kruger replied flatly.

"You still haven't told me who you work for," I said.

"I'm a private contractor," Kruger replied. "Our group is called Odin, named after the Norse god of war. Odin's origin story is best told by the boss himself, so that'll have to wait for another day, but Odin has been around for over a hundred years. We go where no one else will because we are above political agendas."

It was mysterious, but I liked it. I had grown tired of the bullshit red tape back home, and I could see that our own military was hamstrung by the same red tape. It was exciting to know that a group like this existed.

"You're going to kill al-Baghdadi, aren't you?" I asked.

"If he doesn't give up when I ask nicely, then yes," Kruger said with a nod.

"Please," I said. "You have to let me be a part of this. That man is directly responsible for the death of my family. He was the mastermind. You're not the reason I'm here. *He is*. He killed Asmin. *He* took everything from me."

"I don't—"

"I know you don't owe me anything, but if you really feel like you failed me and want to make up for it, please. Please do this for me," I pleaded.

Kruger sat with arms folded, staring at me. He appeared to study me as he considered my request.

"Please," I said softly. "I have nothing left."

"Well, this was a conversation I had intended to have stateside when we got you home, but I suppose now is as good a time as any. Welcome to Odin," Kruger said as he extended his hand.

"Thank you," I said as I shook his hand.

"Let's go meet the rest of the team."

CHAPTER FORTY SEVEN

O din consists of operators from all over the world," Kruger explained as he gave me a tour of the hangar. "We've hand-selected some of the best from the British SAS to Russian Spetznaz to American SOF operators. Everyone you meet here is highly experienced."

He led me downstairs past the cyber analyst and his computers. "That's Coolio. He's an MIT graduate and computer genius. He's our computer guy on this team. There are other teams operating in other spots around the world. Once we get back to our headquarters in Virginia, you may be assigned to one of them, or you may stay with us."

"Virginia?" I asked. "What about that whole 'wanted' thing?"

Kruger smiled through his thick, red beard. "As I said earlier. Alex Shepherd is dead. He, unfortunately, died as a result of his injuries in the base hospital. Very tragic. Case closed."

It was a weird concept to me, but it made sense. I felt like I had died with my family. Now it was just official. Alex Shepherd is dead. I doubted anyone cared. There was no one left to mourn for me.

"Anyway," Kruger continued as we stepped into the hangar, "we have a fleet of various aircraft, piloted by some of the best pilots in the world. That tall guy over there is 'Shorty.' He used to be with the 160th Special Operations Aviation Regiment – the Nightstalkers. He can get you in and out of any hotspot in the world."

The Nightstalkers. I remembered reading about them before – first in the book and later the film *Blackhawk Down,* and then in reading about special operations missions in Iraq and Afghanistan. They were considered one of the most elite aviation units in the world.

"Besides our own fleet, we also get support missions from some of the countries we support. Of course, it's always off the books. Nothing we do is ever acknowledged – that's kind of the point," Kruger said.

He led me across the hangar to another set of doors and offices. There was a break room with a large table and four other operator-looking types sitting around shooting the shit.

"Wolf, I'd like you to meet Beast, Cuda, Tuna, and you already know Cowboy," he said. They each gave me a nod and went back to their conversations or reading their books. I still couldn't get over the nicknames. And now, even I had one. *Wolf. Was this real life?*

"Beast is a commie bastard from Russia – former Spetznaz. He's the breacher on this team," Kruger said, pointing at the big guy in the back. His name made sense at least.

"The little fella is Cuda – former Filipino Commando and an explosives expert. He's also a pretty good cook, if you like dog that is," Kruger said.

"Fuck you, and that's not even a Filipino thing asshole," Cuda shot back.

"Tuna here was an Army Ranger, so you might not get anything more than a few grunts from him every now and then," Kruger said.

"That's all the pillow talk your mom needed last night, dick," Tuna replied without looking up from the book he was reading.

"Every now and then, he'll try to insult your mom, but don't worry, the jokes never make any sense," Kruger said. "Just humor him. He's a damned good medic when you need it."

"Fuck you!" Tuna shot back.

"What about you?" I asked Kruger. "What's your background?"

"Pretty boy Delta!" Tuna interjected.

"Army SFOD-D. I served as a sniper and then interrogator before I got out. I did a little time as a Sheriff's Deputy in Florida between jobs," Kruger said.

After seeing the interrogation with al-Kuwaiti, I couldn't imagine the angry redhead as a cop. His internal affairs file had to be at least six inches thick.

"Fellas, I've asked Wolf to join the team. He was a sniper on his SWAT team and spent some time killing Daesh fuckers with the YPG in Syria. He's good people, treat him accordingly," Kruger said.

"Welcome to the party, mate," Cowboy said. "I guess I'm not the newest bloke anymore."

"Don't think you're getting out of doing my laundry, rookie," Tuna said, turning to Cowboy.

"Does a thong really count as laundry?" Cowboy asked.

"I'll let you two figure that one out," Kruger said. "Let's go, Wolf."

He led me out of the break room and into the room next door. The walls were lined with tactical gear hanging from pegs. Above each peg was a strip of duct tape and a nickname written in black sharpie.

"We'll get you gear. We usually roll with the H&K 416 as our primary rifle, and if you're the sniper type, we have the SCAR Sniper Support Rifle or, my personal favorite, the M110 SASS. If you have a special request, we can usually get it. We're usually pretty well funded for whatever gear you need," Kruger said.

He walked over to a large Pelican Case and opened it. "Have you used Panoramic Night Vision Goggles?" he asked, pulling up the weird NVGs I had seen during the rescue with the four tubes.

I shook my head as he handed them to me.

"Operation is the same as normal NODs, just a little heavier, but your field of view is much better. We use these for night ops, which is pretty much all the time in this theater," Kruger explained.

"And this is the body armor we use," Kruger said, handing me what appeared to be a plate carrier with short sleeves.

I braced as he let go, expecting it to be heavy, but as he stepped away, I realized it was very light – almost like a jacket.

"Are the plates missing?" I asked.

"Carbon nanotubes," Kruger replied. "A hundred times stronger than steel, but extremely lightweight and durable. Produced by MIT. It's still experimental, but we've already had a guy on another team get shot while wearing it and live to tell about it. It's also stab resistant."

I lifted it up and down a few times. I couldn't believe how light it was.

"They're still working on the pants to make a full suit. I've heard sometime next month we should be able to get fitted for them," Kruger said.

Kruger put the body armor back in the case and escorted me out. He showed me the meager sleeping accommodations – cots in the middle of an empty room with foot lockers sitting at the foot of each. It was still better than what I had experienced in captivity.

"Alright, so that's the tour. One last thing," Kruger said.

"What's that?"

"There are three basic rules for being a part of Odin: First, never kill or harm an innocent or civilian. Second, do not steal or pillage from noncombatants. And finally, always cover and fight for the man next to you," Kruger said. "The rules are non-negotiable. Failure to comply is unacceptable, copy?"

"I got it," I said. It seemed like common sense, but the fact that Kruger had to spell it out for me gave me the impression that somewhere down the line someone had taken things a bit too far.

"Good," Kruger said. "I told Tuna to find you in the hangar at 1400. That should give you enough time to get some food, shower, and a quick nap."

I had no idea what time it was, but I figured that was plenty of time. I was starving, and a nap sounded like a good idea.

"Tuna is going to get you up to speed on how we do business. I know you want to be on this OP, but if you feel like you're not ready, don't hesitate to speak up. We have it covered – I am just doing this for you because I know you need this," Kruger said.

"I'll be fine," I said.

"I'm also not going to let you put the team in jeopardy, so Tuna will have the final say on that," Kruger said. "Any questions?"

"Thank you for doing this for me," I replied.

"Don't thank me yet," Kruger said. "You've got work to do."

It all felt so familiar. The tests and the looming OP reminded me of Zirek. My fists clenched as I remembered the heinous execution Zirek had suffered at the hands of al-Kuwaiti.

"Kruger," I said. "One more thing."

"Send it," Kruger said.

"What's going to happen to al-Kuwaiti?" I asked.

Kruger smiled. "You want to put a bullet in his head, don't you?"

I considered it for a moment. I honestly didn't. He wasn't worthy of such a quick death. It was a waste of a bullet.

"No," I said after a long pause.

"Are you sure?" Kruger asked.

"I'm sure," I said, growing more confident in the closure I was starting to feel.

"Good," Kruger said. "You're making progress. As for al-Kuwaiti, it seems he killed a pretty high-ranking Jordanian officer last year – a nephew of the King or some such. They've been looking for him for a while, and they're willing to pay."

"Odin takes money from foreign governments?"

"When it aligns with our objectives, sure. And in this case, our objective is to give al-Kuwaiti the worst fate imaginable. You saw what I did in there. The Jordanians will be twice as ruthless before they put that miserable cockroach out of his misery," Kruger said.

"Good," I said. "Fuck him."

CHAPTER FORTY EIGHT

If someone had told me a year ago that I would one day be speeding down the Euphrates River in Iraq in a Rigid-Hulled Inflatable Boat (RHIB), I would have told them they were smoking dope. But here I was, lying prone while holding on to one of the mooring ropes as we sped south in the pitch black night.

I was running on adrenaline. I hadn't felt this much nervous energy since my first SWAT roll. Tuna had given me his blessing after a crash course in team tactics and maneuvers. Kruger's team wasn't all that different from the way we had trained in SWAT – except they did everything twice as fast and three times as smoothly. From there, we went straight into briefing the mission.

At 0300, the helicopter took us to a point just north of Ramadi along the Euphrates. The RHIB was already waiting along the eastern bank. I had no idea how it had gotten there. I still had a lot to learn about Odin and how it operated. We pushed it into the river and headed south for the target.

The Panoramic Night Vision Goggles took some getting used to. With every bump, it felt like my head was being jerked forward. I tightened the nape strap on the helmet as Tuna had instructed me, but they were definitely heavier than what I was used to. They nearly turned the dark night into day, however. The field of view was amazing, and the image was exceptionally clear compared to the older equipment I had used.

The rest of the equipment was just awesome. It was nice not having to carry thirty pounds worth of gear and armor. I felt naked carrying the suppressed H&K 416 with such light body armor. Except for a slight mobility restriction, it was almost like wearing no armor at all. I just hoped it worked as good as it felt.

I carried eight extra magazines for the H&K and four extra magazines for the P228 in my drop leg holster. Even with all that extra ammo, I still felt lighter than I did on SWAT. It made the soreness in my chest from my ribs slightly more bearable. However, breathing was still a difficult task, especially with exertion.

We snaked around the Euphrates, entering the city of Ramadi. It was dark for such a large city. The power grid was hit or miss, a byproduct of years of war and the recent capture by ISIS. There were a few sporadic lights along the river banks. We passed under a bridge that was completely dark. It had no lights – no passing cars. The curfew ISIS had enacted was in full effect.

We landed the RHIB at the preplanned spot roughly six hundred meters north of the ceramic and glass factory. After dismounting, Beast and Tuna dragged it farther inland, although I suspect Beast did most of the dragging.

While Beast and Tuna secured the boat, Cuda dropped to a knee and removed his backpack. He retrieved and assembled a small micro-UAV drone and launched it by hand. Its motor buzzed to life as it took off toward the factory.

"Good handshake," I heard the computer analyst 'Coolio' say over the in-ear secure satellite communications piece.

We regrouped as a fire team. As we had briefed, I joined Kruger and Beast while Tuna led the sub-team consisting of Cuda and Cowboy. We used bounding movements between the two fireteams, moving quickly in the open as we moved from the landing zone to the perimeter fence. I pushed through the pain to keep up, feeling like a fat kid trying to run with pro athletes.

Beast removed bolt cutters from his pack and cut a hole in the perimeter fence, holding it open as we sprinted through while the others covered. The factory was quiet. There was no movement anywhere around.

"Punisher One One, *CORVETTE*," Kruger said over the tactical frequency, using the code word to let Coolio know that we had infiltrated the outer perimeter.

"Oracle copies," Coolio replied. "Checking for heat signatures now."

We moved to a position of cover behind a series of chemical storage tanks. Kruger pulled out a tablet from his backpack and connected to the drone feed as Coolio piloted it around the facility. It picked up the heat signatures of two men in a roving patrol on the west side of the facility and several more inside.

Kruger held up his hand and motioned for us to keep moving. We moved in two columns, I followed close behind Kruger, covering to his left. Cowboy and Beast alternated covering the rear as we moved between the storage containers toward the roving patrol.

Without slowing, Kruger fired his suppressed rifle, hitting the first ISIS guard. Tuna followed up and dropped the second as we spread out into a V-formation moving toward the front of the factory. I did my best to keep up. They moved much more efficiently than anything I had ever experienced with SWAT.

We stacked up on the door. It opened outward. Beast checked it and gave a thumbs up, indicating that it was unlocked. He stood to the right side of the door as the rest of us stacked up on the left. When I felt Cuda squeeze my shoulder, I squeezed Tuna's. In turn, he squeezed Kruger who nodded at Beast.

Beast violently pulled the door open, and Kruger bolted inside. As Kruger moved left, Tuna entered and turned right. Just as I had been trained, I went straight ahead, clearing in front of me. Cuda nearly ran over me – I was much slower than he had expected. The door opened into an open area. There were a dozen vehicles lining the factory floor in various states of repair.

I heard Tuna fire three times, dropping an ISIS fighter before I heard, "Clear."

"Oracle, Punisher is *VIPER*," Kruger said, using the code word for established in the target building.

"Or…copies…in…min…" There was static as Coolio tried to reply.

"Oracle, say again," Kruger said.

Static. Our comms were down inside the building. We could hear each other, but for whatever reason, we had lost our link to Coolio.

We split up into our fireteams to clear the bottom floor of the factory. I followed Kruger as we went room to room. I heard the faint register of suppressed weapons from the other team, but so far, our team had come up empty – no sign of al-Baghdadi.

We regrouped with Tuna and moved toward the stairs. Cuda and Beast stayed to cover the bottom floor while Kruger, Tuna, Cowboy, and I went upstairs. As we reached the top, Kruger dropped a man that had stirred to investigate the noise downstairs. He kicked the man's rifle aside as we continued past him.

There was more static over the radio as Coolio tried to say something else. Judging by the timing, I guessed that it was related to the helicopter extract that was supposed to happen fifteen minutes after Kruger called *VIPER*.

We stacked up on a nearby office. I covered as the other three cleared it. I heard more suppressed gunshots as they took out more fighters. With the room clear, they emerged, and we continued down the hall to the last office.

Kruger removed a flashbang from his bag. It was the only remaining room – if al-Baghdadi was in there, we were going to take him alive. At least, that was the plan. I was still itching to put a bullet in the man's temple.

Cowboy kicked open the door, and Kruger tossed in the flashbang. It exploded with a brilliant white flash of light and deafening noise. Kruger moved in with Cowboy and Tuna in trail. I covered the hall, peeking in only to see Kruger and Tuna flex-cuffing two men in the room. As I looked closer, I recognized al-Baghdadi. It took every ounce of restraint not to put a bullet in his head, but I had a feeling Kruger had come up with a fate that would be much worse for him.

"Cuda, place charges on those vehicle-borne IEDs and let's move to extract on the roof," Kruger said over the tactical frequency. Our radios seemed to work fine within line of sight, but we were still unable to hear anything Coolio said.

I grabbed al-Baghdadi's right arm and helped Cowboy force him up to the roof. Beast showed up behind us and helped Tuna with the other prisoner, nearly lifting the man from his feet as they hauled him up the stairwell. I could hear the thump of rotor blades as the Blackhawk approached to take us to safety.

As we reached the top of the stairs, Kruger pushed the door open. I suddenly heard the sound of AK-47 gunfire followed by return fire from the Blackhawk's minigun. I was barely up the stairs when I heard an explosion outside.

The sound of the minigun stopped. I could hear the turbine engines spooling up and down. We stopped midway up the stairs.

"Get down!" Kruger yelled as he reentered the doorway and pushed me back into al-Baghdadi. I lost my balance as I fell into him, causing a chain reaction as the Blackhawk impacted the roof. We rolled down the stairs to the next level as the roof partially collapsed above us.

There was dust and debris everywhere as part of the stairwell collapsed and the cockpit of the Blackhawk penetrated the roof.

As the dust settled, I heard more gunfire. It sounded like it was coming from multiple directions, shattering the windows. We all started to pick ourselves back up, assessing injuries of ourselves and each other. I breathed a sigh of relief as I saw Kruger emerge from a pile of rubble and toss his helmet and broken PNVGs to the side.

"Fuck!" Kruger yelled.

Fuck was right. We had just lost our ride home in the middle of ISIS territory.

CHAPTER FORTY NINE

I helped Cowboy secure the prisoners in one of the nearby rooms, and then Tuna and I went to help Kruger. After picking himself up from the rubble, he had rushed to the Blackhawk wreckage. The pilot had managed to shut down the engine – or it had shut down on its own - I couldn't tell which. The helicopter, from the cockpit all the way back to the minigun, had crashed through the roof and was resting on what was left of the metal stairs we had just dived from.

"Help me get Shorty out of here," Kruger said as he tried to maneuver around the wreckage. I saw the two pilots still strapped into their seats. The one in the right seat was moving around but appeared to be in a great deal of pain. The left seat pilot didn't appear to be moving at all as he sat slumped over in his seat. His arms hung loosely by his sides. I assumed the worst.

Kruger climbed carefully to Shorty's side. The wreckage seemed unstable. I knew that it was in danger of collapsing the rest of the way through the roof at any moment. He used one of the rails from the metal stairs as a step as he unstrapped the big pilot.

Tuna and I maneuvered as best we could to help Kruger. I heard Cuda yell "Contact" as a volley of rounds shattered more glass downstairs. They returned fire, ducking beneath the windows for cover as they did their best to hold off the onslaught of attackers.

"His leg is broken, and he might have a spinal injury," Kruger said as we eased Shorty out of the cockpit. He groaned in pain as the three of us carried him down the remaining stairs to the second floor and put him down outside the office where the two prisoners had been stashed.

"I think Alf and Rocko are dead," Shorty said as Tuna started first aid on his open wounds.

I went back to the helicopter with Kruger. He climbed into the helicopter and over Shorty's seat toward the other pilot. After checking the pilot's pulse, Kruger shook his head angrily. He tried unstrapping the pilot, but the harness was stuck. He pulled out a knife and cut the pilot free.

"Help me get him out," Kruger said. "We don't leave anyone behind."

The Blackhawk seem to teeter precariously against the stairs as I slowly climbed into the cockpit. I had done similar extrications with Fire and Rescue while working traffic accidents, but nothing involving a platform that was at risk of falling two stories into an explosives factory below. Every shift the helicopter made felt like it might be the one that sent it plummeting into the bomb-laden cars.

As we pulled the second pilot out of his seat, Tuna arrived to help lower him onto the stairs.

"Shorty has lost a lot of blood," Tuna reported. "We're going to need a MEDEVAC ASAP."

We moved the body to the solid second level, away from the stairs and went back for the gunner.

"Cuda, SITREP," Kruger said as we returned to the helicopter.

"Standard Hadji tactics," Cuda replied over the radio. "Onesy-twosy pot shots, but no full on assault yet."

"Keep me updated," Kruger replied. "Let me know if you need me to send Cowboy down to you."

"Wilco," Cuda replied. "But I think we've got it for now."

As we reached the Blackhawk, it appeared to be slowly rocking back and forth. "I don't see Rocko," Tuna said, as he stuck his head in the cockpit, trying to look into the main cabin for the gunner.

"He's in there," Kruger said, pushing Tuna out of the way.

"This thing looks pretty unstable man, if you move too far aft, the whole thing could come crashing down with you in it," Tuna warned.

"I'll take my chances, bub," Kruger said.

Tuna grabbed Kruger's arm. "Yeah, but think about the risk. If that thing comes crashing down, it could set off whatever concoction of IEDs they set up in those cars, and it'll take out the second floor as well. I'm tracking with what you're saying, but it's a mission failure if we all die."

"Wolf," Kruger said, turning to me.

"Sir?" I asked.

"Go downstairs and relieve Cuda," Kruger said before activating his transmitter. "Cuda, I'm sending the new guy down to take your spot. I need your services up here."

"Copy that!" Cuda yelled.

"Move!" Kruger ordered as he pointed for me to head to the second set of stairs toward Cuda's position.

"Bloody hell, we've got company on the south side!" Cowboy announced over the tactical frequency.

"Change of plans," Kruger said over the radio. "Wolf and Cowboy, take the south side from the second level. Tuna, you go with Beast and cover the north end. Cuda, get your ass up here and let's get Rocko out of this chopper."

CHAPTER FIFTY

Cowboy was already busy picking off ISIS fighters as I joined him in the office. He had opened one of the windows and was using his suppressed H&K 416 to stop the advance of the fighters from the south.

"You cannot defeat them," I heard from one of the prisoners. "Allah guides their bullets."

It was al-Baghdadi. Despite the hood over his face, he was well aware of what was going on. We were surrounded, facing an advancing army of fighters, and he knew it.

I ignored him and set up in a window on the opposite side of the room from Cowboy. The sun had just started its upward trek, giving me enough light to see through the scope without the night vision attachment. For the first time, I saw what we were up against.

There were at least fifty armed fighters carrying AK-47s and using the smaller buildings surrounding the factory as cover. They took potshots from behind cover. Judging by the bodies out in the open, it appeared that Cowboy had been picking them off as they tried to advance on the factory.

From our mission brief, I knew that the factory had only three entrances – two on the north side and one on the south side. It made our tactical problem a little easier when it came to defending the factory, but it didn't help us with an escape route. There would be no way out to the south without going straight through the fighters, and I had no idea what we were facing on the north side.

I opened the window and took aim. I found the nearest fighter. He was using a Conex container as cover and would step out into the open to shoot. I regretted not bringing one of the sniper rifles Kruger had shown me. I had completely underestimated this mission.

When the fighter popped out to shoot, I fired three rounds center of mass. He stumbled backward before falling. I moved on to the next one. I had no idea how long we could keep this up, but I knew ammo conservation would be important. Every shot had to count.

"How do we get out of here?" I asked as Cowboy continued with shot after shot.

Cowboy kept shooting without looking up at me. "Outside comms are jammed. I think they set up a jammer to keep the car bombs from detonating downstairs. Our only way out is to make it back to the boat. Way too hot for another helo even if we could talk to Oracle."

"They will dance on your bodies in the streets," al-Baghdadi added.

Ignoring the terrorist behind me, I went back to shooting. The rising sun and pending daylight did little to slow the advance of the attackers. They didn't seem to care about the cover of darkness. Instead, the fighting grew more intense. They started taking more chances.

"How many magazines do you have left, mate?" Cowboy asked.

I took a quick inventory. I was on my second magazine change, leaving me with six rifle magazines and four handgun mags left.

"Six!" I replied.

"Give me two of them," Cowboy said.

Cowboy continued firing as I pulled the two magazines out of the pouches and tossed them to him. When he felt them hit his feet, he stopped momentarily to do a mag change and then went back to shooting.

As I changed my own magazine, I heard Kruger enter the office. I looked back to see him carrying the tablet.

"I still have a drone feed. Looks like a convoy of technicals and a tank are approaching from the old armory," he announced. *Technical* was the term they used for the pickup trucks with bed-mounted machine guns.

"Any word from Oracle?" Cowboy asked.

"Negative – we're comm-out still," Kruger replied.

"Wolf, how many mags do you have left?" Kruger asked.

"Counting what's in my rifle – four, plus my handgun mags," I replied.

Kruger tossed an extra mag to me. "You stay up here and keep popping them. Cowboy, come with me downstairs. They're getting close on the north side, and we are going to work on disarming two of those cars and getting the fuck out of here."

"Copy that," Cowboy said.

"Can you handle these two alone?" Kruger asked me, pointing to the prisoners.

"I'll manage," I said, going back to work outside.

"We're going to get out of here, bub," Kruger said confidently before he and Cowboy left.

"You will die a coward's death," al-Baghdadi said when Kruger was safely out of earshot. "You will beg me to let you live, just like your *Lioness*."

"Fuck you," I said as I went back to work in the window.

Al-Baghdadi let out a sinister laugh. "You don't think I know who you are? She told me about you before I killed her. The kafir thought you were going to save her. I told her that you were a coward, and of course, I was right."

I wanted nothing more than to put a bullet in the jihadi's head. He was the embodiment of evil. He had taken everything from me, but I knew that the only way to defeat him was to get the team out of there alive to kill more of his kind later. And the only way to do that was to focus on keeping the remaining fighters at bay until Kruger and the team could figure out an exit strategy.

I moved from window to window, staying low as I did to avoid return fire. The fighters outside seemed unfamiliar with the proper front sight alignment. Most of their shots hit above or below me. I still wasn't a huge fan of getting shot at, but their lack of proficiency was a tactical advantage.

The fighters seemed to be coming from all directions, converging on our position. What was once fifty or more had turned into well over a hundred by the time the sun had come up. A few of them had Rocket-Propelled Grenades (RPGs). I prioritized my shots accordingly. The walls were doing a good job of providing cover from the rifle rounds, but an RPG hit would be devastating.

"Wolf, how are you doing up there?" Kruger asked over the tactical frequency. We were lucky that it at least worked between us.

"Three mags left," I said. I had just under a hundred rounds left between the three mags and what was left in my current magazine.

"We should be out of here in about ten mikes," Kruger replied. "We're prepping two of these cars."

Two cars sounded like a tight fit for two bodies, an injured giant pilot, two prisoners, and six operators. I trusted Kruger though. He seemed to have his shit together. I knew his plan would work. *It had to.*

I kept shooting. Each fighter got two center of mass shots. Headshots were too risky with moving targets, and I needed to conserve ammo and make every bullet count. I was worried that I would run out of ammo before we even had a chance to get out of the factory.

"You came here for the sarin canisters," al-Baghdadi said, continuing his taunts. "But you are far too late. They are on their way to Jordan as we speak. You Americans are so naïve. You will believe anything."

"Kruger, this asshole says the canisters aren't here," I relayed over the tactical frequency.

"That checks." Kruger said calmly. "Get ready for extract. Five mikes."

Five minutes. It seemed like an eternity. I focused on shooting and controlling my breathing. My adrenaline was surging, and my heart felt like it was going to burst out of my chest.

I swapped to my last magazine. *Thirty rounds.* I still had my handgun left, but it wouldn't be nearly as effective from this position. I hoped the guys downstairs had done a better job of conserving ammo.

Just as I thought there was a chance of getting out alive, I heard someone yell, "RPG!" There was a loud explosion that seemed to rock the building. The floor rumbled beneath me. There was a brief pause, and then I heard the gut-wrenching sound of metal bending.

I looked back out the door just as the cockpit of the Blackhawk separated and went crashing down on the vehicles below. It sent up a cloud of smoke and debris that filled the factory.

My heart sank as I ran to the door. "Kruger!" I yelled over the tactical frequency.

Silence.

I froze as I looked down at the scene below. The cars had been destroyed as the helicopter wreckage and the last flight of the stairs had landed on top of them. I saw no movement. I yelled out for anyone but heard nothing. *Fuck!*

I ran back to the window, not sure of what to do. I needed to get downstairs and check for survivors, but if the fighters made it into the building, it was all over anyway.

As I stopped at the window, I saw a wall of fighters approaching the building. The lack of return fire and the explosion from the RPG had emboldened them. I flipped the select fire switch to AUTO and sprayed bullets until the bolt locked. I had taken as many of them out as I could, but I was out of bullets.

I slung my rifle around my back and ran back to the wreckage. I yelled out once more, hoping anyone would respond. *Nothing.*

"Kruger, Wolf, radio check," I said over the tactical frequency.

Silence.

I ran to Shorty who was still leaning against the wall near the office.

"Shorty!" I yelled. His eyes were closed. I wasn't sure if he was even still conscious.

"Don't let them take you alive," Shorty said weakly.

"We're gonna get out of here," I said defiantly.

"We're fucked," Shorty replied. He held his Kimber Ultra TLE 1911 loosely in his hand. I knew what he was thinking. I was thinking the same thing.

"Sit tight for a minute," I said.

I ran and looked over the edge of the railing. "Kruger!" I yelled down toward the factory floor.

Still nothing.

I heard al-Baghdadi laughing in the office behind me. I drew my Sig P228 and turned toward him. I pulled the hoods off both men.

"If you surrender now, I will make your execution a quick one," al-Baghdadi said.

I put the barrel of the gun up to his forehead.

"You won't kill me," he said with a laugh. "You Americans are all the same."

I closed my eyes. I saw Chelsea and Lindsey and Asmin. They had all been victims of this man's brutality. If we died in this factory, and he escaped, he would kill even more innocent people.

"Do you hear that?" al-Baghdadi said, still laughing. "They're here."

I could hear chants and cheers as the fighters approached. It sounded like they had made it downstairs.

"Fuck you," I said.

I pulled the trigger, sending brain matter into the wall behind him. As I watched him slump over, I turned toward the other prisoner. I had no idea who he was, but as far as I was concerned, it was guilt by association. He stared blankly at me as I turned the weapon to him.

"Allahu Akbar," he said. I pulled the trigger, hitting him just above his right eye as he slumped over onto al-Baghdadi.

I ran out to get Shorty. As I reached him, my stomach turned. I hadn't heard the gunshot, but Shorty had put his 1911 in his mouth and pulled the trigger. We all knew what ISIS would do if they captured us. I didn't blame him.

I ran back down the stairs. The bottom was blocked with debris. I yelled out once more, hoping to find any survivors. When there was no reply, I dropped to my knees.

I still had three-and-a-half eighteen-round magazines left, but against the approaching army of fighters, I knew it would be useless. Like Shorty, I had reached the end of the road.

The most elite group of operators I had ever witnessed had just been taken out. I was alone, facing an insurmountable threat with just a few handgun magazines. I knew my fight was over. All that was left was to prevent these monsters from another public execution for propaganda. It was time to go home to my girls.

Putting the gun up to my chin, I closed my eyes. I was scared at first, but as I saw visions of Lindsey holding Chelsea, I suddenly felt at peace. I said a small prayer for forgiveness. I knew I was probably going to hell, but I asked God to give me just one more chance to see my girls.

A tear rolled down my cheek as I flicked off the safety.

CHAPTER FIFTY ONE

BRRRRRRRRRRRRRT

I had started to squeeze the trigger as I heard it. The chanting and yelling suddenly went silent outside. There was sporadic gunfire, but it didn't sound like it was hitting the building anymore.

I opened my eyes. I heard more yelling – still in Arabic – but it didn't sound like jubilant chanting anymore. Something had changed outside.

BRRRRRRT BRRRRRRRRRT

I heard it again. There were multiple explosions off in the distance. The metal stairwell shook. And then I heard the sound of a jet flying over. *Friendlies!*

I made my way down the stairs. Two fighters attempted to climb in through the window. I dispatched them with my Sig P228 and continued forward. The wreckage of the helicopter and roof stairs covered the entire factory floor, crushing the cars and scattering debris everywhere. There was no chance anyone had survived it.

As I moved toward the door, I saw a leg underneath the debris. Pushing it out of the way, I saw Beast. His lifeless eyes stared back up at me. I looked up in time to see the south door kicked in and two fighters enter. I shot, hitting both of them center of mass before taking cover behind a helicopter panel.

There were more explosions followed by jet noise outside. I could tell that there were at least two jets orbiting overhead. I at least had some chance of survival.

As I continued walking toward the south door, I heard banging and muffled yelling. It sounded like English. I wandered around the wreckage, trying to find the source.

BRRRRRRRT

There were more explosions outside. I shot another ISIS fighter trying to enter. It seemed like the number of fighters was decreasing.

I walked to where a scaffolding had crushed a car. The banging grew louder. There was so much debris on the floor it was hard to tell where the bottom was. I started to make out voices. They were yelling in English. "Help!"

Kruger?

My adrenaline surged. I hastily moved away pieces of helicopter, car, and building debris. As I moved some of the pieces out of the way, I noticed a door. *A basement!* It was blocked by a large piece of concrete.

There was another series of explosions outside as I started to try to move the blockage. It barely budged as I pushed it with my arms. It had to have been at least two hundred pounds of solid concrete.

As I started to turn my back against it to push it out of the way with my legs, another fighter entered through the window. I fired, missing the first shot. As he made it into the room, he raised his rifle at me. I fired two more times, hitting him in the chest and neck before he stumbled forward into a piece of debris, impaling himself as he fell.

I went back to work on the piece of concrete. My feet slid along the dusty floor as I pushed. I strained as hard as I could, but I was still weak from the days prior. The banging continued.

BRRRRRRRRT

The yelling outside turned to screams. I heard a loud crackle in the air as whatever the jets were shooting seemed to explode right outside. I knew we had to get out of there.

I coiled up against the concrete and pushed as hard as I could. The concrete moved just enough to clear the door. It was partially broken and jammed, but I was able to pull it open.

As I got it open, I saw Kruger, Tuna, and Cowboy staring up at me.

"About bloody time!" Cowboy yelled.

I helped them out one by one. Tuna and Cowboy seemed to be in good shape, but Kruger limped as I helped him out. "You alright?" I asked.

"Broke my fucking ankle!" Kruger growled. "How's Shorty?"

I shook my head. I didn't have the heart to tell him what had happened.

"Fuck!" Kruger yelled. "And al-Baghdadi?"

"KIA," I said.

Kruger shrugged. "We need to get the fuck out of here. Have you seen Beast or Cuda?"

"Haven't seen Cuda," I said. "Beast is…gone."

Kruger slammed his fist on the nearby car. "Goddammit!"

"I'm glad to see you guys," I said.

"We barely made it," Tuna said. "Found this basement when we pushed the car out of the way. Jumped in right after the RPG hit."

BRRRRRT BRRRRRRRT

"Sound of fucking freedom!" Tuna said after hearing the jets outside. "A-10s! Fuck yeah!"

"What's the plan, boss?" Cowboy asked, turning to Kruger. Kruger was still shaking his head, pissed that he had lost so many on his team.

"We need to get to a place where we can get comms to Coolio and get a MEDEVAC mission," Kruger said. "No fucking way can we carry everyone out through that shit."

Cowboy raised his rifle and pushed Kruger out the way, taking out another fighter trying to enter the building. "I'm almost out of ammo, mate."

"I am out of rifle mags," I said, holding up my handgun. "Just a few mags left on this."

"There's an office building about a hundred meters south of here," Kruger said, shaking off the anger of losing so many men. "We hump it to there, hole up, and re-establish comms."

Kruger pulled out his tablet. The drone still orbited overhead. I looked over his shoulder as he connected. The picture looked dramatically different than before. There were far fewer heat signatures looming outside. As the camera panned, I saw several fleeing in technicals. There were two or three trucks on fire and a tank smoldering at the edge of the screen. The A-10s had been doing good work out there.

"Good," Kruger said. "They're on the run. We just need to get to that office and call it in."

"Can you walk?" Tuna asked Kruger.

"No choice," Kruger said. "Let's get a weps check. What are we working with?"

"One mag left," Cowboy said.

"Two mags," Tuna said.

"And I have three," Kruger replied.

I shrugged.

Kruger handed Cowboy a magazine. "Wolf, pick up that AK over there," he said, pointing to the dead guy I had shot earlier. "See if he has any spare mags on him."

As I ran over to the dead fighter, I passed one of the cars. I don't know why, but I looked under the vehicle as I passed. I froze as I saw a boot underneath. Dropping to my knees, I moved pieces of rotor blade out of the way and found Cuda lying underneath the car. He wasn't moving.

I checked his pulse. It was weak, but there. "I found Cuda!" I yelled.

Tuna and Cowboy rushed over to me. They helped me pull him out from under the car. He was alive, but barely. The MEDEVAC mission had just become even more important.

"I'll stay here with Cuda," Kruger said. "You three get to that office and establish comms."

"I'm not leaving you by yourself," Tuna said. "We've already lost too many."

"I'm no good to you out there anyway," Kruger said. "I'll stay here and hold this place down."

"I don't fucking care. Remember Axe? I'm not going through that shit again," Tuna replied.

"Don't worry, I don't have a family to talk to," Kruger said.

"Bullshit!" Tuna yelled.

"It's not a request; now fucking get moving, bub," Kruger barked.

I picked up the AK-47 and found two more magazines on the dead guy.

Cowboy pulled two magazines out of Cuda's carrier and offered them to Kruger.

"Give me the AK," Kruger ordered. "I've got my Sig, and it'll all be close range. Wolf needs those mags more than I do."

I handed him the AK-47 and two magazines. Cowboy handed me Cuda's old magazines.

With the doors blocked, we headed for the broken windows the ISIS fighters had tried to enter through. I heard more explosions and jet noise outside. As long as the A-10s were overhead, I felt like we had a chance.

I nodded to Tuna and Cowboy. Tuna took point as we each climbed through the window and took off toward the building. It was a hundred meters away. I struggled to keep up with the other two. My lungs burned and my body ached. The adrenaline had started to wear off. My legs felt like jello.

"Contact left!" Cowboy called before dropping a fighter. I focused on the right side, searching for any fighters. The sporadic gunfire from the AK-47s had stopped. The only noise was from the A-10s.

I looked up to see the big, twin-engine fighter swoop down over the retreating trucks. This time I saw the explosion before hearing the *BRRRRRRT* of the A-10's 30MM gun. The jet recovered and then climbed off to the right, dispensing flares as it did.

Less than a minute later, a second A-10 rolled in with similar results. They were keeping the fighters at bay. ISIS had started to retreat.

"Oracle, Punisher Six-Two," Tuna said, keying up his radio as we ran toward the building.

"Thank God!" came the reply over the radio. "I've been worried about you guys!"

"Oracle, we need a MEDEVAC mission, we have four KIA and two wounded, how copy?" Tuna said as we neared the building.

"Oracle copies, I have an Air Force search and rescue helicopter already on its way. They just wanted confirmation of survivors," Coolio replied.

"Tell them to get their asses here!" Tuna yelled.

"Oracle," Coolio replied. "I've got you on the drone, running south toward the offices. Is that right?"

"Affirm," Tuna said.

"Roger," Coolio said. "I'll see if I can get them to land in the courtyard in between the two buildings."

"Good copy," Tuna replied. "Punisher Six-Two out."

As we made it to the office, Cowboy kicked in the door. We quickly cleared the building and then set up near the window facing the factory. It offered us a good vantage point to take down any fighters trying to infiltrate the factory.

"Punisher Six-One, Six-Two, how copy?" Tuna asked, trying to get Kruger.

"Pun....Cop," came the static-filled reply.

"Shit," Tuna said. "So we can't talk to him."

"Sounds like he can hear us, mate," Cowboy corrected him. "We just can't hear him."

"Oracle, what's the ETA on that rescue bird?" Tuna asked.

"Ten minutes," Coolio replied over the radio.

"Get them to hurry," Tuna said.

The A-10s continued to do work just outside. I had a front row seat as they dropped bombs, shot rockets, and continued strafing with the 30MM gun. It was an awesome sight. I couldn't help but cheer for them as they made attack after attack, staving off the ISIS fighters trying to get to us.

We picked off the random fighter that made it through, but for the most part, we just sat watching the factory and waiting for the rescue helo.

"I'm patching the Air Force into this frequency, standby," Coolio announced over the radio.

"Punisher Six-Two, this is Pedro Five-One, how copy?" the voice said over the radio.

"Punisher copies, confirm you have the 9-line?" Tuna asked. I had no idea what he was talking about.

"Punisher, that's affirm," Pedro Five-One replied. "Confirm still a hot LZ?"

"Possible troops in the open, recommend overwatch," Tuna replied.

"Pedro copies," Pedro Five-One replied.

I saw two helicopters approaching from the west. One of the helicopters came in low and fast as the other broke off and orbited, laying down cover fire with the side-mounted mini-gun.

As the helicopter landed, we took off toward it. We were met by three men in traditional body armor and helmets with Air Force patches on their shoulder.

Cowboy and I helped set up a defensive perimeter around the helicopter as Tuna led the medics into the factory. A few minutes later, they returned with a litter carrying Cuda with Kruger limping behind them.

They were loaded into the helicopter, and the medics disappeared back into the factory with Tuna. We waited for what seemed like an eternity before they reemerged with Shorty and Beast's bodies on litters.

With the four loaded, the first helicopter lifted off and picked up a cover orbit. The second helicopter landed, and Tuna once again led them into the factory. Fifteen minutes later, they emerged with the bodies of the other helicopter pilot and gunner. Once they were all safely aboard, Cowboy and I fell back to the helo.

I stepped onto the helicopter, breathing a sigh of relief as it lifted off. I could see one of the A-10s orbiting above us. They had stopped their attack runs as the second helicopter had landed. The threats had been neutralized by their incredible firepower.

We took off and headed south over the Euphrates River, escorted by the A-10. I couldn't believe it, but I had somehow survived. I closed my eyes as I leaned my head back against the bulkhead. I saw Lindsey and Chelsea once again, but instead of sadness, I felt a calming presence. It was as if they had somehow been watching over me.

I felt like I had just been given a second chance at life – not as Alex Shepherd, but as *The Wolf*.

CHAPTER FIFTY TWO

The Air Force rescue helicopter took us to Baghdad International Airport where we were shuffled through their field hospital. Cowboy, Tuna, and I were given IV fluids due to dehydration and sent on our way, while Cuda and Kruger were held for further treatment.

We stayed in tents that they called their "Temporary Lodging Facility" for two days until Cuda was stable enough to transport. He had a concussion and massive cranial swelling, as well as several broken bones and some internal injuries. By every account, he was lucky to be alive.

We were all lucky to be alive. How the A-10 pilots had known to come find us was a mystery to me, but they had saved our lives.

Had I not heard the heavenly sound of their 30MM guns firing, I would've shared the same fate as Shorty.

That was still a subject I didn't know how to broach with Kruger. Shorty had done what any of us would have done while facing imminent capture. It had even been part of the brief – if you find yourself out of options and facing capture, it's your choice, but know that death by your own bullet is infinitely preferable to death at the hands of the jihadis.

Shorty had no way of knowing that the A-10s would show up or that Kruger and company had been trapped in the basement. He did what he had to do with the facts at hand. I knew Kruger would understand, but I just didn't want to be the one to tell him. The angry redhead still scared the shit out of me.

We waited outside the passenger terminal at Baghdad International as a C-130 landed and taxied in. It was all white and completely unmarked. It didn't look like any of the Air Force C-130s parked on the ramp.

It taxied up to us and shut down the two inboard engines as the Air Force line attendants chocked the wheels. The back ramp lowered, and a woman wearing a green flight suit emerged with a short, stocky bald guy also wearing the same green coveralls.

As they approached, I couldn't help but stare at the bald guy. He looked really familiar. I couldn't put my finger on where I had seen him before, but I was sure I had. He walked to the stretcher carrying Cuda and grabbed Cuda's hand, squeezing it before turning to Kruger.

Kruger shifted on his crutches and stretched out his hand. The man shook it. He had a concerned look on his face as he looked over the rest of the team. I couldn't hear what he said to Kruger due to the noise from the C-130 engines still running, but he seemed upset by the results of the mission.

The woman walked up behind him and went straight to Kruger. They exchanged a few words, and she pointed to the C-130. She rejoined the bald guy as he walked over to me.

"I'm Jeffrey Lyons," the man said, holding out his hand.

As I accepted the handshake, it suddenly hit me. *Jeffrey Lyons. Of course!* He was the mega-billionaire that did gun videos on YouTube. I had been a subscriber of his channel. He was always reviewing guns and gear and making videos about tactics while featuring hot girls. *But what the hell was he doing in Iraq? In a flight suit?*

"Alex Shepherd," I replied.

"Welcome aboard, Wolf," he said. "We'll have to have a beer when we get back to Virginia."

He moved on to Cowboy and Tuna without further explanation. *Wolf? How did he know?* The woman following him stopped in front of me.

"I'm Jenny," she said. "I'll be flying you guys back to Incirlik."

Finally! A real name and a real woman. She wasn't too bad looking either.

"Nice to meet you, Jenny," I said.

When Jenny and Lyons finished their meet and greet, they gave the go ahead to the medical staff to load Cuda and Kruger. We followed behind them, walking up the ramp and taking our seats in the webbed seating near the front of the aircraft.

"So what the hell is a guy like Jeffrey Lyons doing here?" I asked Tuna as he sat next to me.

Tuna laughed. "You mean you don't know?"

"Know what?"

"Dude, that's the boss!" Tuna yelled.

With the patients secured, Jenny and Lyons returned to the cockpit and started the two inboard engines. A few minutes later, we were taxiing for takeoff.

"The boss?"

Tuna nodded. "His grandfather started this group with a couple of other rich guys during World War I after the sinking of the *Lusitania*. They've been involved in every major conflict ever since. Now Mr. Lyons runs it with three other billionaires."

"Have you met the others?"

"Nah," Tuna said. "We stay pretty isolated in Virginia. That's above my paygrade."

"Lyons mentioned something about Virginia," I said. "What's there?"

"Our headquarters," he replied. "Don't worry; Coolio will get you hooked up with a new identity if that's what you're worried about. We stay gone most of the time anyway."

"Great," I said. *What the fuck was I getting myself into?*

I fell asleep as the plane took off. I was still exhausted. My body ached, and I was mentally and emotionally drained. The webbed seats were uncomfortable, but the droning of the turboprops outside lulled me into a sleep.

I awoke just as the plane touched down in Turkey. The pilots taxied to the remote hangar where we had done our mission planning. As the plane came to a halt, the big cargo door lowered. I saw the computer analyst with the slicked hair and hipster glasses waiting for us near the hangar entrance.

An ambulance sat on the ramp waiting to take Kruger and Cuda to the base hospital. Kruger waved them off, instead, hobbling toward Coolio using his crutches. Cowboy, Tuna, and I followed. I couldn't hear what Coolio and Kruger were talking about, but we followed them into the mission planning room that we had used to plan the mission in Ramadi.

We walked in and sat down around the table. There were maps and charts on the walls, a table, and a corkboard in the corner of the room with a picture of al-Baghdadi and the canisters.

Kruger sat at the head of the table and put his crutches down before rubbing his temples. He let out a long sigh before beginning.

"Before we start this debrief," Kruger began, "let's take a moment of silence for our brothers we lost a few days ago. To

Rocko, Shorty, Beast, and Alf, rest in peace brothers. To Valhalla!"

In unison, the others echoed *To Valhalla.*

"Alright, first things first. As far as I'm concerned, we failed," Kruger continued. "Unacceptable losses and the objective was killed. What was the bird's eye perspective, Coolio?"

Coolio cleared his throat and shifted uneasily in his chair. "Well, boss, we had a communications issue. The SATCOM frequencies seemed to be jammed. I could hear you, but you couldn't hear me. I think they were using barrage noise jamming on cellular frequencies to keep a stray signal from detonating an IED. Within close line of sight, your comms were fine, but anything outside of about fifty meters was one-way only. I was unable to relay that enemy fighters were approaching from the nearby ISF military compound that ISIS had taken."

"We've dealt with comm jamming before," Kruger said. "I take responsibility for not coming up with a secondary plan or keeping better tabs on approaching fighters. What else?"

"When I heard that the target was secured, I made the call to…" Coolio said before pausing. I could tell the loss was hitting him hard. "I'm sorry."

"Keep going," Kruger prodded.

"To Shorty," Coolio continued. "Who then pushed in from the hold point to make the roof extract. As they approached, they were hit with a shoulder-fired missile and reported that they had lost the tail rotor. They tried to put it down on the roof, but were already going too fast."

"Right," Kruger said. "We were unable to locate the canisters and were moving to the roof at that time and saw it unfold. We were able to get out of the way before impact, but the helicopter cockpit partially penetrated the roof. At that time, we switched to a rescue posture to extract Shorty and the bodies of Alf and Rocko."

"Again, due to comm-jamming, I was unable to relay that there were ISIS fighters approaching in all directions. I could see your heat signatures but couldn't communicate, so I hacked into CENTCOM and sent out an emergency Combat Search and Rescue alert with a CASEVAC mission request," Coolio continued.

The military stuff was Greek to me, but I got the feeling that this computer analyst was a huge asset for the team. He had saved our lives.

"The closest available air assets were a flight of A-10s out of Al Jaber in Kuwait sitting thirty-minute alert. It took a while for me to get all of the authentication done and get the messages out to convince people that a combined Special Operations mission needed air support," Coolio said. "I coded the mission under Joint Special Operations Command, so a lot of people are going to be confused in the coming days."

"Inside the factory, we set up north and south defensive positions," Kruger said. "I was confident at the time that we could hold the factory until we figured out an exfil plan downstairs. Once we completed the helo extract, Cuda thought he could get the cars disarmed and prepped for an exfil back to the boat on the river."

"We were ammo limited," Tuna interjected. "That's something we'll need to look into. We need a way to carry more supplies, even if the mission is only expected to last a few hours."

Kruger nodded. I saw him scribbling notes on a piece of paper in front of him.

"I left only one man upstairs to cover the south approach," Kruger said. "What I saw on the drone showed limited resistance, and I wanted more firepower where the tangos were attempting entry while we worked. Any issues with that, Wolf?"

I shook my head. "Only limitation was ammo."

"Noted," Kruger said before continuing. "We moved the vehicle out of the way and found a basement door. I sent Tuna down to clear it while we continued. What did you find?"

"Nothing significant," Tuna replied. "Just a few bomb-making supplies and car parts."

Kruger nodded as he wrote. "It was around this time that Beast called out an RPG. It actually went through one of the second-floor windows and hit what was left of the stairs to the roof that the chopper was resting on. I called for everyone to take cover."

"Thanks on that again, mate," Cowboy said. "If you hadn't pushed me into that basement, I would've been crushed."

"I jumped into the basement last and broke my ankle. Sounds like Cuda was able to take cover under one of the cars. Beast was unable to locate cover," Kruger said. I could see him clench his jaw. As the leader of the team, he seemed to take every loss personally.

"The Blackhawk cockpit broke off and crashed into the factory floor," Kruger continued. "The debris slammed the basement door shut and trapped us inside. Wolf, what happened upstairs?"

I took a deep breath and exhaled slowly. The tone of Kruger's debrief was professional and direct. It didn't appear that he wanted to sugar coat anything. I realized that I owed him the truth.

"I continued shooting until I ran low on ammo. When I ran to the platform to see what had happened, I saw the debris and wreckage covering everything. Comms seemed to be down between us as well. I made several attempts to raise you on the radio to no avail," I said.

Kruger nodded, taking notes as he motioned for me to continue.

"With fighters approaching and no sign of life from you guys, I executed both prisoners for fear that they might escape," I said.

Kruger said nothing, still taking notes.

"When I went back out, I saw that Shorty had taken his own life," I said softly.

Kruger looked up at me. He appeared angry. For a second, I thought he might reach across the table and choke me. Instead, he just nodded. "Then what happened?"

"The fighters outside became braver and approached the building. I ran out of ammo trying to stop them," I said.

"And then?" Kruger asked.

"And then I turned my handgun on myself," I said slowly.

"Why didn't you?" Kruger asked. His tone was very matter-of-fact.

"I heard the sound of the aircraft outside, and I realized there might be hope," I said.

"Coolio?" Kruger asked.

"After the A-10s scrambled, I did some digging to find out who the pilots were and what their backgrounds might be. I was able to get a datalink message to the flight lead that Special Operations Forces operators were holed-up in the factory with no outside communications. I used the drone feed to send him a digital nine-line," Coolio said.

"Good work," Kruger said.

"The flight lead also happens to be a friend of ours, which helped," Coolio added.

Kruger looked up from his notepad. "No shit?"

"I verified it myself," Coolio said. "I sent your callsign in the message. I'm sure he recognized it."

"I guess we're even now," Kruger said nonchalantly. "Wolf, continue please."

I shook off the confusion about the A-10 pilot discussion and picked back up. "As I went downstairs to find a way out, I heard you guys and moved the debris off the basement door," I said.

"Right," Kruger said. "Thanks."

"Tuna, I assume you were able to establish comms once you got outside of the jammer?" Kruger asked.

"Correct," Tuna replied. "Coolio connected us to Pedro Five-One, and we talked them in. By the time they got here, the ground picture had changed significantly."

"The A-10s were using rockets, bombs, and their guns," Coolio interjected. "From what I understand, they had no weapons remaining by the time they returned. They were also able to destroy the factory with a precision-guided bomb before leaving."

"Hell of a job, Coolio," Kruger said. "Great work."

"Thank you, sir," Coolio said.

"Alright, so, big picture, we fucked up," Kruger said as he looked around the room. "I could have done a better job in the planning phase. We need to work on a secondary comm plan if we do encounter jamming. We also need to get better intel. We were not expecting such a high-threat mission, and the canisters weren't on station."

"Al-Baghdadi told me that they were never there," I added. "Al-Amani had given us intentionally flawed information. I think we were set up."

"Noted," Kruger said.

Kruger looked at his notes again before continuing. "The deaths of Alf, Rocko, and especially Shorty are on me. This was my OP, and I failed them. I don't blame Shorty for what he did. He was working with the information he had at the time. It is my fault for putting him in that situation."

"Boss, you can't-" Tuna tried interjecting but was cut off by Kruger.

"With that said, we did manage to bring everyone home, and we had no further losses. Cuda will make it. We're here to debrief it and fix it for next time. Anything else around the room?" Kruger asked. "Cowboy?"

Cowboy shook his head.

"Wolf?" Kruger asked as he looked at me.

"I'm sorry," I said. "I really am."

"Anything else?" Kruger asked.

"No, sir," I said.

"Tuna?"

"You can't blame yourself," Tuna replied. "This is war, and Murphy always wins. It wasn't pretty, but all we can do is honor the dead, learn from our mistakes, and move on."

"Coolio?" Kruger asked, turning to the analyst as he ignored Tuna's advice.

"I don't have anything, boss," Coolio replied.

"Alright then," Kruger said. "Let's start packing up and get ready to demobilize. Our ride back to Virginia leaves in two days."

"Wait what about the canisters?" I asked.

"There's always going to be another threat," Tuna answered. "We will hand off a lot of intel to the United States intelligence community and go home to lick our wounds. If they can't act on it, we'll be back."

"We always come back," Tuna added.

Tuna's words hit me like a ton of bricks. *We always come back.* Unlike what I had been used to as a deputy, there would be no clear justice. It was a war, and with war came victories and defeats.

As I reflected on the way these professional operators approached the problem, I realized that I had been given a second chance – a chance to operate with these men for that very reason – to fight the war. Like Tuna said, it wouldn't be perfect. We wouldn't win every battle and prevent every attack, but we had to at least try, and when we didn't, we had to own up to it.

It was in that moment that I vowed to fight that war, to do everything within my power to stand against evil with my new brothers and sisters in Odin – to prevent another family from being torn apart by the evil monsters of the world, or die trying.

I had officially embraced my new life. Alex Shepherd had died with his family and passed through the gates of hell and back on a quest for vengeance. *The Wolf* was now on a mission of redemption.

EPILOGUE

Al-Jagbhbub, Libya
Fifteen Miles West of the Libya – Egypt Border
Two Months Later

A re you sure this is where they are supposed to meet?" I asked as I scanned the empty desert highway through the scope on my M110 Sniper Rifle.

"Relax, mate, they'll be here," Cowboy said.

As I lay prone on the sand dune overlooking the highway, I found the straw of my Camelbak and took a long pull. It was hot – at least a hundred degrees and climbing. I couldn't wait to get this over with so we could get back to Kuwait and then home to Virginia.

We were on a mission that was the culmination of a month's worth of picking up high value targets in Iraq and Syria. The American and British intelligence communities had drawn a blank in finding the stolen sarin canisters. Every lead they could track down said that the canisters were still somewhere in Aleppo.

But what we found was that al-Amani's claim that al-Baghdadi had taken them to Ramadi to smuggle in with the refugees had been a diversion. What Daesh had planned was a much more methodical method of getting them to Europe. That plan involved moving them through ISIS-controlled territory in Iraq over the course of several weeks.

Once in Iraq, they had transported them to the Jordanian border where a group known as The Sons of the Call for Tawhid and Jihad had taken them to Ansar Beit al-Maqdis in the lawless Sinai Peninsula. From there, the canisters would be moved to Libya, where the Islamic Youth Shura Council would then transport them the rest of the way to Italy and then Rome, where an ISIS cell planned to use them against the Vatican.

We were waiting for the meeting between the al-Maqdis and the Youth Shura to take place on the highway beneath us. It was one of our last remaining opportunities to stop the weapons before they entered Europe. Once the Youth Shura moved them through their operating area in Durna, the canisters would be much harder to track into Italy.

"Overlord Five-One checking in, ready for Fighter to FAC," a voice over the secure radio said.

"Send it," Cowboy said.

"Mission number six-two-four-alpha, two by F-16s, ten miles south of the hold point in the ten to fourteen block, two by GBU-54 and two by GBU-12, 500 rounds a piece of twenty mike-mike, thirty minutes of playtime, Sniper and rover capable, abort in the clear," Overlord Five-One said.

"Wombat Four-One copies, abort in the clear, situation is as follows: we are a British SAS team doing overwatch on a high value target meeting six hundred meters north of our position, request armed overwatch," Cowboy replied.

"Overlord copies," came the reply.

Cowboy looked up from his spotter scope and said, "Our air support is here."

"Wombat, Overlord has a vehicle approaching from the west," the flight lead of the fighters said.

"Wombat copies," Cowboy replied.

I looked up from my scope and saw a truck approaching from the west. It kicked up a dust cloud as it sped down the road beneath us.

"See?" Cowboy said. "Patience."

"The canisters are late," I said, looking at my watch.

"*Patience,*" Cowboy replied.

I watched the truck approach from the west. It stopped at the meeting location. Two men emerged, both dressed in all black. I couldn't imagine how hot they were. I felt like I was roasting and I was wearing desert tan and light body armor.

After ten minutes of waiting, Overlord Five-One finally reported seeing a car approaching from the east. I picked it up in my scope as it raced toward the meeting location. There were two occupants sitting in the front seat and one in the back.

"Tally target," I said to Cowboy.

The vehicle reached the truck and pulled to a stop in front of it. Three men got out of the car and exchanged greetings with the two Libyans who had exited the truck. The al-Maqdis were dressed in desert fatigues, unlike the Libyans. I flicked off my safety and waited. We needed visual confirmation of the canisters before shooting.

"I see five military-aged males, one of them is Hassan al-Bann," Cowboy said after flipping through the book of pictures we had of the leaders of each group. Al-Bann was the leader of the al-Maqdis. It was a good sign, indicating that the mission was important enough that he personally escorted the canisters.

I kept my crosshairs on al-Bann. He walked back to the trunk of the car and opened it. He reached in, emerging with a hard case. He carried it to the hood and opened it, displaying it proudly to the men of the Youth Shura.

I zoomed in with my scope. I could see two canisters nestled in the foam of the open container. "I'm contact two canisters."

"Same," Cowboy said before keying up his radio. "Overlord, this is Wombat, advise when ready for first nine line."

"Send it," came the reply over the radio.

"Type two, bomb on target, lines one through three N/A, line four per sensors, line five two vehicles and personnel in the open, line six per talk on, none, six hundred meters south, egress overhead, how copy?" Cowboy said over the radio, giving the fighters a "9-Line" to authorize them to strike the high value target. In the two short months I had been with Odin, I had learned an incredible amount about military operations from the former operators. It was a steep learning curve.

The flight lead read back the coordinates he had from his system and then said, "Ready for remarks and restrictions."

"Request one GBU-12 on each vehicle simultaneously, do not overfly friendlies, when can you be in?" Cowboy asked.

"Overlord copies, do not overfly friendlies. Two by GBU-12s," the flight lead replied, indicating that they would each be dropping a five hundred pound laser-guided bomb. "We'll be inbound in thirty seconds," he added.

"Copy, expect clearance on final," Cowboy said, picking up his binoculars as he looked in the direction of the fighters.

I kept my scope trained on al-Bann. The men seemed to be congratulating each other, reveling in the devastation that the canisters would create.

"Overlord Five-One flight in, tally target, visual friendlies," the flight lead announced over the radio.

"Cleared hot!" Cowboy said.

Al-Bann closed the case and handed it to the Youth Shura fighter.

"Overlord Five-One, two away, thirty seconds," the fighters announced.

"Wombat," Cowboy replied.

Ordinarily, we would've taken cover, but our vantage point gave us sufficient cover from any stray fragments flying our way. I continued watching al-Bann as the Youth Shura walked the case to his truck.

"Ten seconds," the flight lead said.

I heard the faint sound of jet noise. Al-Bann looked up just as the bombs impacted the trucks, creating simultaneous explosions that rocked the ground beneath us. Al-Bann was thrown from the blasts.

"Good hits!" Cowboy announced.

I watched Al-Bann. Somehow he had managed to survive and tried to get up and run. I set the crosshairs on his chest.

"One squirter," I said calmly as I exhaled and flexed my finger.

I sent the round downrange with a smooth trigger pull. It hit al-Bann in the chest, just below his neck as he tried to limp away. He immediately fell.

I reset to look for any other survivors. Satisfied that everyone was dead and the vehicles were destroyed, I looked up from my scope and gave Cowboy a thumbs up.

"Overlord, this is Wombat," Cowboy said.

"Go ahead," the fighter replied.

"Confirm you don't see any squirters?" Cowboy said.

"Standby," the flight lead replied.

A few seconds later, he followed up with, "Negative, both vehicles destroyed, I count five KIA."

"Wombat copies, thanks for the good work. We're out," Cowboy said.

Cowboy sat up on his knees as he gathered his gear. "Now *that's* how it's done, mate!"

I looked up at the columns of billowing smoke rising from the two vehicles. The canisters had been destroyed and we had managed to take out the leader of Daesh in Egypt. It was a huge success.

"Goddamned right!" I replied as I packed up my equipment "Let's go home."

Thanks for reading! Stay tuned for Book 7 in the Spectre Series in 2017.

If you enjoyed this book, please leave a review!

VISIT WWW.CWLEMOINE.COM FOR MORE INFORMATION ON NEW BOOK RELEASE DATES, BOOK SIGNINGS, AND EXCLUSIVE SPECIAL OFFERS.

<u>ACKNOWLEDGMENTS</u>

As always, I'd like to first thank you, the reader. Without your support, none of this would be possible. I've enjoyed getting to know many of you through social media and e-mail. I appreciate the kind words and reviews. Keep the feedback coming!

I'd also like to thank the men and women of the St. Tammany Parish Sheriff's Office. As you may know, I'm a Reserve Deputy with the STPSO, and I consider them family. Although this book has the "it could happen tomorrow" feel, I hope it never does. But I know that these men and women are professional and capable of handling just about anything. Thank you for keeping me safe, and thank you for letting me tag along and teaching me along the way.

To Doug Narby, Beverly Foster, and Pat Byrnes – you guys are still awesome. Thank you for being there for me and listening to my pestering requests to "read the next one."

To all my family, friends, and coworkers who have supported me along the way, thank you. I couldn't do this without you. Thank you for understanding and keeping me honest.

And finally, a special thank you to the long time readers of the Spectre Series. It has been a fun ride. It's hard to believe this is my seventh book. Thank you for giving me a chance with **SPECTRE RISING** and then sticking it out with me as I have learned and grown as an author.

With that said, stay tuned for the next Spectre book (Featuring "Wolf" Shepherd) very soon!

Thanks for reading!

C.W. Lemoine is the author of *SPECTRE RISING,*
AVOID. NEGOTIATE. KILL., ARCHANGEL FALLEN,
EXECUTIVE REACTION, BRICK BY BRICK, and
STAND AGAINST EVIL. He graduated from the A.B.
Freeman School of Business at Tulane University in 2005 and Air
Force Officer Training School in 2006. He has flown the F-16 and
F/A-18 in the Air Force and Navy. He currently flies for a legacy
U.S. airline. He is also a certified Survival Krav Maga instructor
and sheriff's deputy.

www.cwlemoine.com

Facebook
http://www.facebook.com/cwlemoine/
Twitter:
@CWLemoine